Playing
with Fire

Also by Katie Price

Fiction

Angel

Crystal

Angel Uncovered

Sapphire

Paradise

The Comeback Girl

Santa Baby

In the Name of Love

He's the One

Make My Wish Come True

Non-Fiction

Being Jordan

Jordan: A Whole New World

Jordan: Pushed to the Limit

Standing Out

You Only Live Once

Love, Lipstick and Lies

Reborn

Katie Price x

Playing
with Fire

CANCELLED

CENTURY

1 3 5 7 9 10 8 6 4 2

Century
20 Vauxhall Bridge Road
London SW1V 2SA

Century is part of the Penguin Random House group of companies
whose addresses can be found at global.penguinrandomhouse.com.

First published in Great Britain 2017 by Century

www.penguin.co.uk

A CIP catalogue record for this book is available from the British Library.

9781780893495
9781780893501 (Trade Paperback)

Typeset in 12.25/16 pt Baskerville MT Std by Jouve (UK), Milton Keynes
Printed and bound in Great Britain by Clays Ltd, St Ives plc

Penguin Random House is committed to a sustainable future
for our business, our readers and our planet. This book is made from
Forest Stewardship Council® certified paper.

Praise for Katie Price's novels:

'A page turner . . . it is brilliant' *Evening Standard*

'The perfect post-modern fairy tale' *Glamour*

'Angel is the perfect sexy summer read' *New Woman*

'A perfect book for the beach' *Sun*

'Glam, glitz, gorgeous people' *Woman*

'A real insight into the celebrity world' *OK!*

'Brilliantly bitchy' *New!*

'Celebrity fans, want the perfect night in? Flick back those hair extensions, pull on the Juicy Couture trackie then join Angel on her rocky ride to WAG central' *Scottish Daily*

'Crystal is charming. Gloriously infectious' *Evening Standard*

'Passion-filled . . . an incredibly addictive read' *Heat*

'Peppered with cutting asides and a directness you can only imagine coming from Katie Price, it's a fun, blisteringly paced yet fluffy novel' *Cosmopolitan*

Chapter One

'INDI! We've run out of champagne, a journalist is badgering the bride-to-be, and two girls from *TOWIE* are having a row.' The words came tumbling out of Ben's mouth in one sentence. The lanky 23-year-old, with a mop of blond hair falling over his red face, was out of breath from running through Park Lane Club in Mayfair to find his boss at the VIP entrance.

Indigo Edwards smiled and placed a hand on his shoulder. Poor Ben, she thought. He'd only been working as an assistant at her company, Glamour To Go Events, for a month, and this was his first gig: an engagement party for a millionaire investor and his supermodel fiancée in the swankiest club in London, packed wall to wall with rich and famous faces. It was just after midnight and the party was in full swing; the top-floor bar was completely sealed off for VIP guests, boasting sumptuous blue velvet sofas and dim lighting. A huge circular bar stood in the middle of the room, in the centre of which waiters were mixing up delicious red cocktails (the bride's signature colour). A series of doors led out on to the rooftop, where waiters carried silver trays of drinks, and the guests – footballers, actors and models – partied under the stars, gazing out over the London skyline. Indigo (Indi to her friends) had organised a lavish firework display for the stroke of midnight and a world-class DJ had flown in from Las Vegas just for the night. A glossy magazine was covering the event with gossip columnists lurking in every corner trying to get a story.

But Indi never lost her cool. Now twenty-seven, she'd worked since she was sixteen. At her local hairdressers, Halo Hair, she'd gone from receptionist to unofficial PR guru, turning huge profits for her boss after putting on a series of events to boost business, before studying Business and Marketing at Sussex University. After graduating with a 2:1 degree, she had landed a PA job in a local events company and had quickly risen up the ranks. Three years ago she had set up on her own. Soon enough, she'd quickly secured beauty clients for Glamour To Go, who paid Indi to put on launch parties for products and press days for journalists and bloggers. She also organised the grand opening for a high-end restaurant in London's Soho, another in Brighton and a high-street fashion show for a hot new brand. This was where she had met Tasha Phelps, the gorgeous English model who had begged Indi to organise her high-profile engagement party to Nicolas de Souza. It had taken five months to plan.

Indi took a deep breath.

'There's a crate of Veuve Clicquot in the basement,' she

told Ben. 'Grab two waiters and tell them to start bringing the bottles up and make sure everyone's glass is full. Get the photographer over to the *TOWIE* girls; they'll start smiling and stop rowing as soon as the camera's on them.' She glanced at her watch. 'We finish at two a.m. so at one fifteen a.m. radio the security team downstairs to make sure they're all on alert and that the cars are waiting for our star couple. They can't be the last to leave.' Flicking her long wavy hair – naturally chocolate-brown – and adjusting her headpiece, Indi headed into the crowd.

'I'll handle the journalist,' she called back confidently. She fought her way through the rooftop crowd as hands waved in the air and cheers erupted to the latest Beyoncé track played by the DJ. She spotted Miles Horner, a showbiz writer for the hugely successful website News Hub, hanging around Tasha, waiting to pounce on her for an interview.

'Indigo Edwards, aren't you a sight for sore eyes?' Miles grinned. Indi sighed. Miles had fancied her since the two had become friends while studying at Sussex University. Most of the boys at uni had fancied Indi. With the huge, dark blue eyes that had inspired the name her parents had chosen, naturally olive skin and long thick, wavy hair, a slim figure and five feet six inches in height, she was stunning.

'A roomful of models and you're the best-looking in here,' he continued. 'When are you going to let me take you for dinner?'

Indi broke Miles's gaze and cleared her throat. At six foot, with messy brown hair, an unshaven face and wearing black skinny jeans, a white shirt and black leather jacket, he was certainly attractive. In fact, he looked like he should be in a band rather than working for a tabloid website. But, despite his flirting with her, Indi had always found him immature and, dared she say, a bit of a sleaze when it came to girls. He certainly wasn't the type she'd go for, though she was so focused on work, it had been a while since she'd had any 'type' at all.

'Come on, Miles, you know I'm too busy to date anyone. I can't keep my business *and* a relationship afloat.' Indi didn't know how any career girls did.

'Always the same with you,' sighed Miles, knocking back his champagne and scrolling through his phone as it buzzed with alerts and emails.

'Anyway, listen,' said Indi. 'I told you that you were only allowed in here if you behaved yourself. Why am I hearing that you're harassing guests?' Miles opened his mouth to object but Indi placed a palm in front of his face.

'Tell you what, you leave my guests alone now and I'll give you an exclusive tomorrow that Bella Hadid is flying over for the wedding. Tasha told me yesterday and said I could give the story to one journalist. She met her at the Victoria's Secret show in Paris last year and now they're friends. I'll give you source quotes too but you have to back off now, OK?'

Miles draped an arm around her and kissed the top of her head. '*That's* what I'm talking about. Thanks, Indi!' he exclaimed. 'I'm buying you a glass of champagne to show my gratitude.'

Indi noticed Ben across the room and, ever the

professional, mouthed, 'Everything OK?' at him. He grinned and gave her a thumbs up before gabbling into his headpiece.

Turning back to Miles, she said, 'The booze is free, Miles, and you know I never drink while I'm working at a big event like this.' Too late. He'd already grabbed her arm and was off in search of a waiter.

'I have to work!' she protested. Not listening, Miles charged into the crowd, dragging her along, weaving through the sea of people with such speed he didn't even notice the group they were about to barge into. It was Nicolas de Souza, the millionaire business investor, with three men huddled around him, deep in conversation. Miles crashed into them, Indi stumbling behind him. She tripped right into one of the men, who quickly caught her before she fell right on top of him.

'Miles!' she fumed, standing upright and straightening her black pencil dress. He sheepishly shuffled away as she glared at him. Typical, Indi thought furiously. The four men looked at her in disbelief. 'Nicolas, I'm so sorry.' She blushed. 'Miles there was getting a little overexcited at the sight of your fabulous fiancée.' She was mortified. Then, to her relief, the men erupted into laughter. The one who'd broken Indi's fall grinned, showing perfectly straight white teeth, and draped his arm around her. 'Don't worry, it's not the first time a girl's fallen into my arms,' he said with a wink.

She looked up at him and a pair of striking dark green-brown eyes gazed down on her appreciatively. He was tall, at least six foot, with short dark brown hair and a square face with a hint of stubble. Taking in his tailored grey suit, she clocked that the top buttons of his white shirt were undone, revealing a hint of very muscular brown chest. He was drop-dead gorgeous, resembling Tom Hardy with his cheeky grin, gorgeous face and masculine features. For the first time she could remember, Indi was momentarily speechless. 'Um, sorry,' she muttered, blushing a deep red and quickly turning to Nicolas. 'Again, I'm so sorry,' she said, with more confidence now. 'Let me find a waiter to bring you all a brandy before the party ends?'

'Ahh, don't worry, Indigo, you have put on a wonderful engagement party for us and my Tasha couldn't be more delighted.' Nicolas beamed, his speech slurring a little (from too much champagne, no doubt). 'Have you met my friend Connor?' he said, gesturing at the tall, green-eyed Hardy-lookalike.

'We hope to do business together very soon. Connor, this is the beautiful and very intelligent Indigo Edwards, who made tonight happen.'

'Nice to meet you, Indigo.' Connor stretched out a hand, his emerald eyes looking straight into her own. 'Events? In that case, I'd love to hear more about what you do.'

Shaking his hand, Indigo was about to reply when Ben waved to catch her attention from across the room, frantically pointing to his watch.

'Pleasure to meet you, Connor. I'm so sorry, Nicolas, but I've just noticed the time and there are dozens of paparazzi outside so I must make sure your car is ready for you and Tasha, and ask the DJ to make an announcement that the party is nearly over.' And with that, she smiled, turned on her heels and got back to work. She might have been imagining it, but she could have sworn Connor was staring at her as she walked away.

It was past two a.m. by the time Indi returned to her north London flat. It took twenty minutes for the guests to file out of the club, security leading the celebrities into blacked-out SUVs that Indi had made sure were booked well in advance. She stayed back to ensure everything was in order at the bar. She gave her event staff instructions on how to dismantle the equipment, and checked that the photographer had taken plenty of fabulous pictures before jumping into her own taxi. 'Manor House, please,' she told the driver, slumping into the seat. Indi was exhausted. She gazed out of the window at the neon shop fronts and twinkly streetlights as the car sped through central London. Indi loved London at night. Her home town was so beautiful all lit up, the views made her feel calm and reflective. She ran through the evening's highlights in her head – the celebrities, the DJ, photographers, a guest list so packed that many were turned away at the door. The night had been a complete triumph and Indi knew she should feel proud. Why, then, was she not feeling more elated? There was a tension inside that she couldn't escape, a nagging feeling that followed her everywhere and the growing unease that something was missing from her life. But the anxiety wasn't going anywhere. She curled a long strand of hair around her finger, deep in thought. Her best friend, Hollie, would tell her to, 'go out and find a hot man', but Indi baulked at the notion that she needed a man to complete her. She did flash back to meeting Connor, though, his intense eyes resting on hers for a second longer than they should . . .

Indi's thoughts were broken by her phone vibrating in her hand: dozens of Instagram and Twitter alerts. She scrolled through rapidly. All the *TOWIE* girls had tweeted selfies with Tasha, pouting their glossy lips to the camera. Before he'd got steaming drunk, Miles had tweeted a picture of himself looking proud as punch with four Arsenal football players. Indi laughed to herself and was about to put her phone back into her black Michael Kors clutch bag when another picture caught her eye. It was of Nicolas, Tasha and Connor on Glamour To Go's very own Instagram account. Ben must have posted it earlier in the night, as promoting the event on social media was one of the jobs Indi had assigned him. Connor had his arm around a very slim, very beautiful woman with long jet-black hair and dark eyes. Indi didn't recognise her. The woman rested her head on Connor's shoulder and the group smiled to the camera. Of course, Connor would have a girlfriend, Indi thought. He was too gorgeous not to. She felt silly for thinking he was staring after her and stuffed the phone into her bag.

Chapter Two

Indi's alarm buzzed at nine the next morning and she lazily shut it off. She always gave herself a lie-in after a big event. And it was Sunday, after all. Snoozing for another half-hour, she finally dragged herself from her bed and immediately flicked open her silver iMac laptop to check the coverage of the previous night. The party was the top showbiz story on the *Mail Online* and News Hub, the website Miles worked for. As Indi eagerly read the article it told of how splendid all the guests looked, how lavish the club was and that Nicolas and Tasha were the perfect couple. Not a scandal in sight! Indi sank back into her white, plump pillows.

I surely deserve another ten minutes in bed, Indi thought dreamily. She was about to drift off when keys turned in the door and she heard the jingle of bracelets.

'Rise and shine, happy camper!' came a cheery voice – far too cheery and loud for this time in the morning, Indi thought suspiciously. It was her best friend Hollie. 'You decent in there, Ind?' Hollie asked as she burst into the bedroom before waiting for an answer and threw her slouchy grey shoulder bag on the floor.

'What if I hadn't been?' asked Indi in mock horror as her friend flung opened the curtains.

'Pah, like it's nothing I haven't seen before.'

Indi flinched at the bright May sunlight. 'Remind me why I gave you a key to my flat again?' Hollie gave her best friend a kiss on the cheek and slumped at the end of her bed. 'Because I'm your oldest friend in the world and your favourite person. And you said you'd come to a yoga class with me before Sunday lunch at your dad's. But first I want to hear absolutely *everything* about last night – don't miss out *any* details.'

Indi looked at her friend and smiled. Hollie was the biggest celebrity fan she knew, devouring all the gossip magazines every week. If the Kardashians were her subject on *Mastermind*, Hollie would win easily. Indi sat up in bed and stretched. 'OK, but I need coffee before I do anything, so let's go into the living room and I'll tell you everything.'

Indi's flat was small but she loved every inch of it and had taken pride in decorating it herself when she'd moved in the year before. Her bedroom was in a minimalist style with white walls and a huge built-in wardrobe with mirrored doors. Her king-sized bed sat in the centre of one wall with a wooden table on one side and a matching chest of drawers on the other. Ivory candles were scattered over them and a huge purple velvet armchair in one corner provided the only flash of colour. Indi liked her bedroom to be tranquil and sparse, but the rest of the house was a cluttered contrast. She followed Hollie through to the open-plan kitchen and living room, separated by a breakfast bar. A purple sofa facing an ancient TV was covered with pink and blue cushions and piles of washing, and the dark wooden coffee table was littered with magazines, notepads, coffee cups and a takeaway pizza box.

Hollie sat on one of the bar stools as Indi filled the kettle and placed a generous spoonful of coffee into huge mugs with the words 'What would Beyoncé do?' emblazoned over them – a housewarming gift from Hollie.

'Sorry about the mess,' Indi said as she took a pint of milk from her fridge and sniffed it to check it was still drinkable. Actually, there was nothing in her fridge aside from half a bottle of white wine and some yoghurt she was sure had seen better days. 'I've just been so busy with the event.'

'Oh please, like I'm one to talk,' replied Hollie, clasping her hands round the steaming mug of coffee. 'If I ever actually move out of Mum and Dad's, can you even imagine how long I'd last on my own before all the mouldy plates attracted a rat infestation?'

Indi giggled. The first thing she'd done when she'd moved into her rented, one-bedroom flat was get Hollie a spare key cut. Hollie often crashed over and Indi loved having her around. They'd watch films from Indi's bed, falling asleep before the ending as they'd done since they were kids.

'I'm bad enough when I'm alone but when you're here we're definitely a health hazard,' she said drily. 'How's the saving going anyway?'

Hollie shrugged. 'You know my parents are awesome, and I barely pay any rent, but travelling from Potters Bar into central London costs a fortune and it's not like I'm making big bucks.'

'And half your wages go straight to Zara and Topshop,' pointed out Indi.

Hollie worked as a make-up artist for MAC cosmetics at the department store House of Fraser on Oxford Street. The only thing she loved more than celebrities was make-up and fashion, forever obsessing over the latest trend. It utterly suited her though. Where Indi favoured classic blazers, blouses, skinny jeans and pencil skirts, Hollie always looked far cooler and more hip. Her outfit today was faded blue jeans, gold Converse trainers and a blue crop top, with a chunky gold necklace. She was five feet four inches and curvy, but knew exactly how to flaunt her features. Her mixed-race skin glowed with a hint of shimmer and her eyes were outlined with expertly applied electric-blue eyeliner while her dark Afro hair, dyed ombre blonde, was scraped back in a headband. The two had been best friends and inseparable since they were at primary school together.

'Like I always tell you, you should try to go freelance,' said Indi. 'I bet you'd earn a fortune if you could get a few celebrity clients.'

Hollie sighed. 'I'd love to but I'm not experienced enough.'

Indi tutted. 'You do such amazing, creative make-up. I can totally see you creating make-up looks for magazine campaigns and adverts. You belong in the fashion world! When Tina and I get you to do our make-up before a night out, you genuinely love it!' Tina was Hollie's sister, younger by three years.

'Well, I am doing the models at Essex Fashion Week again and hopefully my first London Fashion Week in September, which would be incredible, but we'll see. Anyway, enough of me. Tell me about last night. Who snogged who and who got the drunkest? And, most importantly, what did Tasha wear?'

Indi laughed and proceeded to fill Hollie in on every detail of the event, omitting only her stumble into Nicolas and Connor. In all the excitement of the press attention, she'd forgotten all about them. She regaled Hollie with the row between the *TOWIE* girls, how two models had sneaked off with a Premiership footballer, and that a singer from Little Mix had even made a fleeting appearance. Of course, she described Tasha's floor-length red Valentino dress in head-to-toe detail.

'This is going to be great for you, Ind,' said Hollie when Indi had finished. 'Do you think you'll get booked to do her wedding?'

'I don't think so. I've never organised a wedding before so wouldn't know where to start, but Nicolas has so many restaurants I'd love to be his go-to events girl. In fact, he's having a summer party on Tuesday at The Square if you want to come? I don't really fancy it alone.' The Square was a boutique hotel on Hanover Square in Mayfair, just one of Nicolas's many investments. Its first summer party of the year was hotly anticipated. Despite organising parties for a living, Indi was perfectly happy watching Netflix from her sofa with Hollie and a bottle of wine, but she knew that networking was vital for her business. And that she should learn to let her hair down once in a while. Fortunately, her friend was the best date she could have, and loved chatting to new people. Hollie was the most self-assured person Indi knew. She worked in a job she only half-liked (and was nowhere near challenging enough for her talent, Indi thought), spent so much of her salary on funding a fashion addiction that she wouldn't be moving out of her parents' place any time soon, but was perpetually upbeat. 'Nothing's as bad as you think,' she'd always say when Indi was stressed about a client or event. Her motto was, 'don't worry, just be happy', and she lived by it. Indi wished she could be so relaxed. Hollie was also the life and soul of any party, another trait Indi envied. She didn't like to use the term 'control freak', but . . .

Hollie's eyes widened. 'The Square? I'd love to, yes! I love it there. Will Tasha be there? You have to introduce me. And you deserve to let your hair down, hun.'

The two chatted excitedly for the next two hours, planning what to wear and whipping out their phones to look at different make-up looks on Pinterest. They completely forgot about their yoga class.

'Shit, it's almost twelve, we need to be at my dad's by one and I have to pick up dessert on the way,' exclaimed Indi, dashing to the bathroom. 'I'll jump in the shower.'

'Chill, babe, I've got Mum's car outside so it will only

take a few minutes to drive us over to Alan's,' called back Hollie.

Twenty minutes later, Indi emerged dressed in a denim shirt dress and flat gold ballet shoes. Her long slender legs were golden brown from an unusually hot spring in London. Unless she was hosting a work event and had her hair professionally blow-dried, Indi didn't bother with much maintenance. Instead, she ran some L'Oréal mousse through her towel-dried hair and let it dry naturally into long tousled waves. For make-up she just put on some Benefit Lash Effect mascara, peach blusher and nude MAC Honeylove lipstick (a donation from Hollie's vast make-up collection) and she was good to go. Hollie stared at her friend enviously.

'God, Indi, I wish I looked that good in twenty minutes. It takes me forever to sort my massive Afro.'

It was customary for the girls to bat compliments back and forth. 'You have the best skin in the world, though,' protested Indi. 'Come on or we'll be late.'

It was just before one p.m. when Hollie parked her mum's blue Peugeot 206 outside Alan's house in Palmers Green, north London. He had bought the house when Indi was seventeen and her younger brother Kyle, was eleven. Their mother, Alan's beloved wife Lou, had died two years before that, after a short battle with cancer. Despite being just fifteen, Indi had quickly become a mother figure to Kyle – and even sometimes her dad. She had taken on the bulk of the cooking, cleaning the house and sorting out bills. Indi went to university, thanks to her saved wages from the salon and her inheritance from Lou. Though she loved living alone now, she could never move too far from her family. They were her world and she loved fussing over Alan and Kyle, though Alan constantly told her that they were perfectly fine and that she should go out and see the world, even get a boyfriend. Indi would simply roll her eyes, though she did wonder what it would be like if she ever moved out of her comfort zone. She had a long-held fantasy to travel around South America, but never entertained it as something that might actually happen. Truth be told, going out of her comfort zone made her feel very tense.

Lunch at her dad's was her favourite time of the week. She let herself and Hollie into the house, a delicious smell of garlic welcoming them. Alan was pottering about in the kitchen wearing jeans, a faded Hawaiian shirt and flip-flops, muttering cooking instructions to himself while a muffled football commentary came through the radio. He beamed when he saw the girls and gave them each a hug.

'Hello, sweethearts.' He gestured to the radio. 'West Brom versus Hull City. Coming towards the last game of the season. Doesn't look good for Arsenal tomorrow.' He shook his head and then gestured to the stairs. 'Kyle's watching upstairs and I can't prise him away from the telly when any sport is on, as you know.'

Alan saw Hollie and Tina as surrogate daughters. He was great friends with their parents, Cat and Tim, who had been a tower of support to the Edwards family when Lou died.

'Don't we know it,' Indi said, placing ice cream in the freezer. 'What's that smell, Dad? Delish!'

'I've done fish pie and new potatoes and a big salad. I thought we could sit in the garden if you're not too cold, girls? It's a lovely sunny day. Food won't be ready for half an hour but there's wine in the fridge.'

'Amazing, thanks, Alan!' Hollie said cheerily, busying herself by grabbing cutlery. 'I'll set up outside. I'm sure Kyle will come down when he smells food.'

'How's he doing at the moment, Dad?' Indi asked as she grabbed a knife and tomatoes from the fridge.

'Oh, you know, love. He has ups and downs. He's running a lot, which I think helps, but it's difficult when he locks himself in his room and doesn't talk to me.'

Kyle had been diagnosed with attention deficit hyperactivity disorder when he was eight. Then at the age of nine, after Lou's death, he started to lash out and become aggressive towards other children at school. Now twenty-one, if he refused to take medication he was manic and prone to picking fights. But, when he did take it, the heavy doses made him spaced out and sad.

Indi chopped vegetables quietly as she thought about her brother, then Alan broke the silence by asking how work was going.

'Nicolas is having a big party on Tuesday which could potentially give me loads of new business,' she explained. 'Corporate events are where the money is. They'll all want Christmas parties, which need organising months in advance, so it would be great to land a couple of new accounts over the summer.'

'That sounds really good, love,' said Alan, always impressed by his daughter's business savvy.

'How's work with you?' she replied. 'Do you need me to take a look at the books?' A builder and electrician by trade, Alan was self-employed and ran his own small business.

'It's all under control,' he assured her. 'I know you stepped in after Mum died but I don't want you worrying about me when you have your own big-shot company to run.'

Indi frowned at her dad. She wished he'd let her help out more, but he would only accuse her of being a control freak. At that moment, Kyle skulked downstairs for a beer.

'Hey!' said Indi warmly, giving her brother a hug. Then, quietly, 'You OK?'

Silence from Kyle.

Hollie came bounding in from outside. 'That wine chilled yet, Alan?'

Alan sensed that Kyle might open up to Indi in private. 'Indeed it is, love. Tell you what, let's you and me take a drink outside and leave these two to finish making the salad. You can tell me how Tina's teacher-training course is coming along.'

As soon as they were out of earshot, Indi sat down at the wooden kitchen table. 'How did the job interview at the leisure centre go? Don't worry, I haven't told Dad. I know he'd only make a thing of it.'

Kyle stared at the ground. 'Really well until they saw on my application form that I was on prescription meds. Then they thought I was mental and didn't want to employ an unstable lifeguard.'

Indi slammed her wine glass down. 'Discrimination. Fully illegal, they're not allowed to say that.'

'They didn't say it in so many words, but you could tell that's what they thought,' Kyle said meekly.

'They won't think that when I'm through with them. I'll phone them first thing tomorrow.'

'No, Ind, don't do anything,' Kyle objected. 'It's not worth it and it's not important. I'll carry on working with Dad, it's fine. The other lads are teaching me the ropes. It was just for some extra money.'

Bless him, Indi thought. Kyle was insecure enough about being on medication, he didn't need judgement from anyone else.

'I just think being outside in the lido would be so good for you,' she said. 'You sure you don't want me to have a word?'

Kyle shook his head. 'Dr Sutton is starting me on a new drug next week. Might have fewer harsh side effects, he says.'

'That's good, mate,' Indi said, standing up and putting an arm around her little brother. 'I bet he thinks all the exercise you do helps, too. And hopefully you'll get on that Sports Therapy course next spring, right?'

'Yeah, but, Indi, I still don't feel right letting you put me through college,' Kyle protested.

'Quiet, you,' she said firmly. 'It's decided, and if you keep working for Dad over the summer you'll have a nice bit of money saved for yourself.' She sat back down and took a gulp of wine.

'Screw Live Leisure, anyway. When we were little, Hollie

peed in that pool. You don't want to bloody work there, do you?'

At this, Kyle burst out laughing. 'She didn't,' he said.

'Yep, and if you tell her I told you I'll burn your Arsenal scarf! Come on, let's go outside.'

As they ventured into the garden Hollie ran past them.

'Just off to the loo, I'm desperate,' she said, which prompted Indi and Kyle to look at each other and fall into hysterics.

The four of them spent the afternoon eating, drinking and chatting. They came inside when it got colder and Alan made a fresh pot of coffee and they tucked into the ice cream. Kyle groaned when Hollie made him give his opinion on Pinterest outfits she'd whittled down for Nicolas's party at The Square on Tuesday, but Indi knew he secretly enjoyed it. Kyle had always fancied Hollie, though she'd never see him as anything other than a little-brother figure. Not that he wasn't a good-looking boy. He and Indi had both inherited Lou's stark blue eyes, and Kyle's hair was dark brown like hers, but he'd shaved it into a buzz cut. At six feet three he was tall and lean from running and weight training.

'Hey, Kyle, guess who was there last night?' Indi said. 'Harry Kane and Eden Hazard. One day you'll have to come out with me to meet some of the Premiership players.' Indi knew exactly how to work her little brother. He beamed.

'Aw, definitely, Ind! See if you can score me a date with one of those models you always hang around with, too, yeah?' And, with a rare glimmer of confidence: 'I bet they're just waiting for a special guy like me to sweep them off their feet.'

Hollie spluttered out her wine. 'Special *looking*, you mean, K!'

Kyle playfully punched Hollie in the arm, but remained in a good mood for the rest of the blissful, lazy afternoon.

Chapter Three

Saskia Taylor slammed down her phone in frustration. It was the fifth time she'd called Nicolas de Souza in the past week and he hadn't picked up, nor responded to any of the emails she'd sent him since the announcement. Six days ago he'd written a statement on his company's website, explaining that the Degree Hotel was undergoing a programme of renovation and expansion and that the latest addition to the premises was a new club. 'More news to follow when we issue an official press release,' read the statement. 'But I couldn't wait to share this exciting news about the next stage in my venture.'

Saskia glanced at her gold Chanel watch. Eight a.m. For most people, it would be perfectly reasonable for them not to answer their phone at this hour, but Saskia knew full well that Nicolas rarely stopped working. She'd been on conference calls with him in the past at six a.m. while he was on the treadmill. There was no way that, on a Monday morning a week after announcing that he was carrying out all these improvements to the Degree Hotel, he wouldn't be up and about already. She frowned to herself and tapped her shellac-manicured fingers on her kitchen table, thinking about what her next step should be.

Saskia had known Nicolas, a permanent fixture on the luxury nightlife scene, for a long time. A new club of his meant one hell of a launch party, and Saskia was desperate for the gig. At aged forty, her career in public relations spanned nearly two decades. After graduating from Cambridge University at twenty-two, her first job was as a junior PR in an interior design company, working her way up to PR manager. Eventually she set up her own company, Sass PR. In the noughties it had been hugely successful and she had landed campaigns for top fashion, beauty, lifestyle, travel and nightlife brands, even scooping an industry award for PR of the Year in 2006.

But work was drying up. In an age of social media, Saskia was lagging behind. Other than emailing and having a basic grasp of WhatsApp, she wasn't exactly digitally savvy. Even her fifteen-year-old daughter, Millie, who used to idolise her, now seemed to think Saskia was useless. Millie was far more interested in posting Snapchat videos than chatting to her mum. Sass PR was taking a hit and Saskia needed to move with the times. She'd already lost Nicolas's engagement party gig months earlier, to some new party girl on the block who she'd never even heard of. Sapphire someone? Topaz? Anyway, she couldn't afford to lose this one.

Saskia's daughter Millie sprang down the stairs, breaking Saskia's train of thought.

'Mum, can you give me a lift to school? I've got all my history textbooks and gym kit and they're sooooo heavy.'

'Of course, darling! I'm heading into the office now anyway. Get your things together and I'll grab my keys.' Saskia relished any opportunity to spend time with her daughter, who usually walked to school with her friends, or made Saskia park up the road so she wouldn't have to be seen with her.

'Wicked, thanks, Mum.'

For once, Millie seemed in a good mood, so Saskia decided to capitalise on it when they were in the car.

'How's the exam revision going, then, darling? Do you need me to help with anything?'

'Nah, it's cool. Just getting on with it, really.' Millie's eyes were glued to her phone as Saskia slugged through south London's rush-hour traffic.

'What's so interesting?' Saskia enquired.

'This party at the Park Lane Club over the weekend looked amazing. Why can't you do parties there, Mum?'

'Ha! Darling, I went to the opening of that club ten years ago. Trust me, it's had its day.'

'Doesn't look like it. It was Tasha Phelps's engagement party and *all* the celebrities were there. It's one of the top three showbiz stories on *Mail Online*, look.'

Saskia's heart sank. Of course, Nicolas's party had been *this* weekend. A few years ago, Saskia would have been the first person on the VIP list. Now she didn't even get an invitation. As a red light forced traffic to a standstill, Saskia snatched the phone out of Millie's hand and started reading. Her daughter was right: the homepage of the showbiz section was dominated by Saturday's lavish party. Models, fit sportsmen and their glamorous wives, actors, TV personalities. Many of them Saskia didn't even recognise, they were so young and cool, but she could spot a celebrity a mile off, and there was no doubt that this party had bagged plenty of them. Saskia scowled as she read through the story.

'The star-studded party was from the genius brain of Indigo Edwards, 27, whose Glamour To Go events company has caught the eye of every celebrity in town.'

'Mum! Green light, green light!' Saskia was concentrating so hard on the story she hadn't even noticed the cars beeping behind her.

'Sorry, darling!'

Saskia lurched into gear and sped off down the road, so deep in thought and bubbling with rage she didn't hear Millie grumble, 'God, you're *so* embarrassing.'

As always, Indi clicked straight back into work mode, her comfort zone, on Monday morning, writing pitches for new clients and starting to plan a press launch for a brand: a new, hip, online interiors shop that sold metallic cushions, neon signs and coffee tables from cool Scandinavian designers. Indi planned to get coverage in the top high-end magazines. She worked from home two days a week and three days a week in a rented office space with Ben.

Eating a box of sushi from itsu at her desk, she scrolled through Twitter and Instagram as she always did at lunchtime. There was the usual list of 'people you should follow' suggestions, and one of them was Connor Scott.

Curious, Indi clicked on his Twitter page. In his profile picture he wore a black suit jacket with a crisp white shirt; he was smiling to the camera and looking disarmingly handsome. She scrolled down. His bio simply read: 'Owner and manager, Print Room, Shoreditch.' She knew the name well. Print Room was one of the coolest restaurants in London, always packed with celebrity diners, famous for decadent after-parties at the bar. Indi shut down the page and went back to work.

At seven the next evening she was hastily applying make-up in the back of a black taxi on her way to The Square hotel in Mayfair, where Hollie was waiting for her. Indi's last meeting had run over and she hadn't had time to go home and change, so she'd made a last-minute dash to Mango and picked up a midnight-blue, sleeveless silk blouse. It went perfectly with the slinky grey pencil skirt she already had on, plus the hot pink Louboutin heels she'd stuffed in her bag that morning. Indi was always on the go, so her standard daytime wardrobe was a pencil skirt or printed cropped trousers worn with a loose shirt or smart t-shirt and blazer. She wore Kurt Geiger pumps to hop on and off the tube, but always changed into heels for client meetings. Her clothes were all bought on the high street, but she splurged on expensive shoes and the few pairs she owned she wore all the time.

Still a few minutes' drive away from The Square, she checked in on the *Mail Online* website to see what the latest showbiz headlines were. One of the stories on the website was about the happy announcement that an actor from the

TV show *Peaky Blinders* and his girlfriend were expecting a baby. She was five months pregnant. Indi knew the actor because he and his cast mates had all come to the Park Lane party on Saturday (partly to promote the new series of the show, which would be starting any day now). The story even featured a picture from the party. Indi herself appeared in one of the paparazzi shots, behind the group of sexy British actors from the show, who she'd escorted out and had led to a waiting SUV. Indi cringed slightly. She much preferred to stay behind the scenes, and hated the idea of being pictured in public, but reasoned that every reader would be focusing on the celebrities, not her. She scrolled down to the hundreds of reader comments that were at the bottom of the story. *Who's the fat slag in the background?* read one. *Her boob job needs redoing, it's all lopsided. Stupid fame-whore trying to get in the picture. Pathetic!*

Indi suppressed her fury. It was hardly as though she'd asked to be in the photo! It was really shocking how bitchy some reader comments could be, and particularly annoying since the only fake thing about her in that picture were her MAC eyelashes. She shook her head and shut off her phone as the taxi pulled up to The Square.

'You're late,' scolded an impatient Hollie as Indi paid the taxi driver at precisely 7.20 p.m. 'Cheryl Cole and Liam Payne just walked in with a guy who looks *exactly* like a young Tom Hardy!'

'Sorry, Hol, my meeting ran over and I was so rushed I had to do my make-up in the cab.'

Hollie peered at her friend's face. 'Smoky black eyeliner, check, lashings of mascara, check, nude lip and bronzer on the cheeks,' she said. 'You look gorgeous as always, babe, but I wish you'd let me play around with your make-up from time to time. A statement lip in bright pink or dark purple would look absolutely stunning on you.' A smoky eye and subtle lip had been Indi's signature party look for almost a decade. She stuck to what she knew.

Hollie looked sensational in a pale blue body-con dress, which clung to her every curve. Her sexy hair was out in full force and her bee-stung lips coated in bright red. 'Now let's get in there.'

The hotel's Square Mile Bar on the twelfth floor was ultra-sleek and modern, with clusters of white square sofas and glass tables with vases of white roses and rose-scented candles. Waiters carried trays of mojito cocktails and ice-cold champagne. Floor-to-ceiling windows boasted views of the dusky pink London skyline and guests poured on to the balcony to watch the sunset and pose for selfies.

'Ooh, let's get a picture,' said Hollie, scooping up two glasses of champagne.

No sooner had Indi taken her first delicious sip than she heard her name called and noticed Tasha Phelps sashaying towards her. The model looked immaculate in a figure-hugging black jumpsuit, bold red lipstick and her long blonde hair in a sleek ponytail. She hugged Indi warmly, as if they'd been friends for years. Indi loved how friendly she was, despite being one of the country's top models, and introduced her to Hollie.

'Lovely to meet you, Hollie, and love the outfit. Indi, so good to see you. Did you get the flowers I sent you yesterday?'

'Yes, Tasha, thank you so much. That was lovely of you. Ben couldn't wait to post a picture of them on Instagram, of course.'

'It was the least I could do after the engagement bash you threw us. Apparently there was some bullshit story on News Hub about Bella Hadid being my bridesmaid, though.' That was the tabloid website Miles worked for. Typical!

'Bloody hell, Tasha, I'm sorry. I told one of my contacts she was coming to your wedding, but I never said she was going to be your bridesmaid! He's a nightmare. Shall I get a retraction?'

Tasha made a batting-away gesture with her hand. 'Whatever, babe. It's not as bad as most of the rubbish they print about me.' With her good looks and famous friends, tabloids and websites loved printing stories about Tasha.

'I'll have a word with him anyway,' said Indi.

The girls chatted about Tasha's upcoming wedding plans and were only too happy to let a passing waiter top up their champagne glasses. Indi felt relaxed. After this drink she'd do a circuit of the room with Hollie and try to drum up some new business.

Suddenly, Hollie grabbed Indi's arm tightly and gasped. 'Jesus, Hol, I almost spilt my drink.'

Hollie ignored her. 'Indi, look! It's that fit bloke I saw come in. My God. He is *gorgeous*.'

Tasha followed her gaze. 'Oh, Connor! He's known Nicolas for years.'

Indi froze. She gulped some more champagne and turned around. Sure enough, through the crowd, dressed in beige chinos and a smart black Ralph Lauren polo shirt, with just a tad more stubble around his perfect jawline, was Connor Scott.

'He is the most handsome man I have ever seen,' whispered Hollie. Connor was talking animatedly to his girlfriend, the same tall, thin and extremely beautiful woman he'd been pictured with at the engagement party. She gazed back at him adoringly and Indi noticed every pair of female eyes in the room were glancing at Connor, and most of the men were eyeing up his girlfriend. They made an extremely attractive couple.

'You know that restaurant, Print Room, where Rihanna always goes when she's over here? That's Connor's place,' Tasha continued. 'He does really well for himself. I think Nicolas is investing in some new venture of his.'

'And who's that girl with him?' This from Hollie. Indi was relieved her friend had asked; she didn't want to let on she cared that much.

'Anja? Oh, Connor's girlfriend. She works in Print Room as the hostess, though I think she does modelling, too. I've only met her once and she just talked about herself. She wouldn't leave Connor's side, either. I think she's a bit stuck up, to be honest.'

Anja slinked off in the direction of the toilet, leaving Connor alone.

'Here, I'll call him over,' said Tasha.

'Oh, I'm sure he doesn't want to be bothered,' Indi said hastily, but Tasha was already waving Connor over.

'Hey, Tasha,' he said warmly, giving her a kiss on each cheek.

'Connor, you have to meet Indigo. She has the most fabulous events company and threw our engagement party on Saturday. This is her friend, Hollie. She's a star make-up artist.'

Hollie blushed as Connor said hello and then, 'Oh, I've met Indigo.' He gave a small laugh. 'She fell straight into me last Saturday!' Indi winced with embarrassment. *God, he must think I'm an idiot!*

Hollie, aghast, mouthed to her friend: *'You met him?'* Then, to Tasha, 'My glass is empty. Tasha, why don't we grab us all a round?' As the two went to the bar, Indi found herself alone with Connor.

'How's business?' he asked.

'Great,' Indi replied, and filled him in on her latest projects.

'That's impressive. It's not the easiest climate right now to get work. Investors are pulling out of all sorts of projects, but there are still pots of money to be found.'

'How's the restaurant business?' she asked, genuinely interested, and the two happily talked business until Hollie reappeared clutching three champagne glasses.

'Did I really stumble upon a conversation about profit margins? C'mon, guys, this is a party!' Hollie passed the glasses around as the group laughed. 'Now, Connor,' began Hollie, 'when are you going to invite Indi and me to your famous restaurant with the year-long waiting list?' Classic Hollie, thought Indigo, smiling. No shame whatsoever, but everyone found her adorable instead of rude. At that moment Anja sidled up, placing an arm around Connor.

'Connor, aren't you going to introduce me?' She was

dressed in a short red dress and definitely had the model figure to carry it off. She was almost as tall as Connor and very skinny. Indi felt awkward next to them and took another sip of champagne.

No sooner had Connor made the introductions than they were interrupted by an almighty crash as a tray full of drinks fell to the floor. A flustered-looking woman in her early forties had crashed straight into a waiter. She apologised profusely as the waiter picked up shards of broken glass. Her own loose-fitting long white dress was covered in drink stains.

The roomful of guests stopped talking and stared. The woman looked mortified and ran to the loos, when Anja let out a laugh, not caring if the woman could hear her. 'Jesus, what a mess,' she said bitchily. Connor frowned at Anja, while the other guests gradually went back to their conversations.

'That poor woman,' whispered Indi to Hollie. 'Shall we go and check on her?'

Inside the toilets, they found the woman with her long white skirt draped over the sink. She was mopping it with water. Her shoulder-length blonde hair was frayed, roots showing, and her mascara had run.

'Hiya, are you OK?' Indi asked softly, then tried to lighten the mood by saying, 'The amount of skirts I've ruined with spilt drinks, I can't even tell you. Yours will be fine, I promise.'

'A hundred per cent fine,' chimed in Hollie. 'And at least it wasn't red wine. Do you want to borrow some mascara?'

'No, I bloody well don't,' the woman snapped back.

'I've already made a fool of myself. I don't need a pity party.'

'Excuse us for asking,' muttered Hollie. 'Come on, Indi.'

Indi handed the woman some more tissues, only for them to be snatched from her hand without a 'thank you'.

'What a bitch,' whispered Hollie as the girls went to leave.

'Totally,' said Indi, though she still felt bad for the woman.

Indi knew she should be networking, but the party was so fun with her best friend. They devoured canapés of mini burgers and chips, guzzled champagne, and cheekily asked Cheryl Cole for a picture. She was only too happy to oblige and even asked Hollie where she got her lipstick. As they mingled and giggled, Indi noticed Connor across the room. Their eyes met for the briefest of seconds before they both quickly turned away.

The next day over lunch – a jacket potato with baked beans, cheese and salad to cure the remains of her hangover – Indi idly scrolled through Instagram. Hollie had tagged her in a photo of the two of them with Cheryl. There were various 'likes' from their friends and one comment underneath the picture. *Who are the whores with Cheryl Cole? I'd stab them if they ruined my picture like that, hahahahaha*, it read. Indi was taken aback at the intensity of the comment. The user who'd written it was simple called 'akablush', and its own profile was locked so Indi couldn't identify who it was. But, before she could give it a further thought, the door to her office was flung open and her assistant Ben appeared; she could hear the music coming through his headphones before he'd even walked in.

The office was in an old house that the landlord had converted and rented out to self-employed businesses. Indi and Ben shared one small room with two desks and a meeting table, while the rest of the floor was taken up by a graphic design company, the floor below by a recruitment website, and there was a music studio in the basement. Ben had a crush on one of the male musicians who recorded down there and always hoped he'd catch a glimpse of him. Ben was from a rich family in Buckinghamshire, who funded his studio flat in Oval, but he was a complete sweetheart. Passionate about Glamour To Go, no task was too small for him and Indi loved working with him. Today his blond hair was slicked back and he wore pale pink chinos and a tight navy t-shirt. The boy sure had style. And knew all the best party spots in town.

'How was The Square? I can't believe I missed it, but there was a pool party at The Ned, sooo.' The Ned was a very exclusive members' club in the City, but Ben always managed to get in without being anywhere near a membership card.

'Oh you, know, pretty tame. But I think Hollie has a new best friend in Cheryl. The two were chatting about lipstick to the point where even I was bored!'

'Oh my God, pictures now, please!'

Indi flicked through her phone when she noticed a Twitter notification – Connor Scott was now following her. Ben snatched the phone. 'Who is *that*?' he exclaimed, peering at the profile picture.

34

'You remember him from the Park Lane party, right? Mates with Nicolas and Tasha? He was there last night. We chatted about work for a bit.'

Ben wolf-whistled. 'He is even better looking than I remember. And he just started following you? Indi, he likes you! Marry him immediately. I read an article about him in the *Financial Times*, you know. He's hugely respected in the business world, not to mention the London party scene. Did you know he started Print Room on a bank loan and turned profit in less than a year? And, at thirty-two, a very good age for you, Indi. I recommend.'

'He has a girlfriend, Ben. It's just a friendly business gesture. We're in the same world, that's all.'

'Oh, what a shame.' Ben looked crestfallen.

At that, Indi's phone rang and Ben had no time to argue.

'Indigo? It's Nicolas de Souza.'

Indi sat up straight. 'Hiya, Nicolas! Are you well?'

'Exceptionally well. Indigo, I have a business proposition for you. Are you free for dinner in Mayfair tonight? Cecconi's, seven thirty? We'll be at the bar in case you make it earlier. I'm bringing someone I'd like you to meet.'

'Sure, Nicolas, that sounds great. Can I ask what it's about so I can prepare some notes?'

'No need, see you later,' came the curt reply, and the phone clicked off.

'Looks like some good news is coming our way tonight, Benny-boy.' Indi grinned. Nothing pleased her more than the prospect of new work, and anything Nicolas was involved with meant serious money. Forget Connor Scott, she thought.

Cecconi's was bustling when Indi arrived at seven thirty sharp. Tables were full of suited men and stylish women but, as she followed the hostess to the back of the restaurant, every eye was locked on Indi. She wore a 1960s-style grey shift dress from Zara that came just above her knee and showed off her tanned, toned arms and legs. She had thrown her long hair into a bun on top of her head and finished off the look with patent brown heels from LK Bennett. Simple, classic and elegant. As she approached the candlelit table, Nicolas and his companion rose to greet her and Indi's heart sank.

'Indigo, you look sensational. I forgot that of course you know my friend, Connor?' Nicolas asked, kissing both her cheeks.

Connor extended a hand. 'Hi, Indi, great to see you again. How are you?' Both men looked smart but, where Nicolas's jacket had an elaborate breast pocket with a pink handkerchief poking from the top, Connor simply wore cream suit trousers and a black shirt. His arm muscles rippled through the fabric and she caught the scent of a deliciously rich, woody aftershave. Dammit, she thought. Why does he have to be so sexy? The good men were always taken.

'Fine, thanks, Connor,' Indi replied coolly as she sat down.

Nicolas knew all the staff at Cecconi's and he jovially debated with the manager over which the best champagne

36

was. Connor peered at Indi over his menu and cleared his throat. 'Playing it cool then, are you?'

Indi looked puzzled.

'Not following me back on Twitter yet? I feel quite rejected!' There was his cheeky grin again (and those *eyes*).

'Ha! Sorry, that wasn't deliberate. Here, I'll follow you back now if you're so desperate!' she chided back.

'Please do! Before you leave me hanging any more.' Again, their eyes met for a split second before they both looked away. Indi's heart skipped a beat.

'The steak looks good,' she said, changing the subject. 'Or the seafood risotto . . .'

The waiter came to take orders and the three talked pleasantries before Nicolas's phone rang. He hastily apologised before answering.

'Busy man.' Connor smiled politely.

Indi took a sip of water and cleared her throat. 'Anja seems nice,' she commented. 'How long have you two been together?'

Connor shuffled in his seat. 'A couple of months. We've known each other for a while just through the scene. Then I gave her a job at Print Room a while ago and, well, I don't make a habit of dating co-workers, but . . .'

'Well, I don't think anyone could blame you, she's, like, insanely beautiful. And seems really nice.' Indi didn't quite mean that last bit, but didn't want to seem rude.

Connor nodded slowly, then Nicolas returned to the table. 'Sorry, team. Tasha is freaking out about floral arrangements for the wedding. Indi, she sends you her love, by the way. Now, my phone is off and I believe we should waste no more time, Connor, don't you agree?' Nicolas was extremely direct. He didn't get so far in the investment world by dithering, but it was a quality Indi liked about him. In his early fifties, he was by no means the best-looking man in the room – certainly nowhere near Tasha's beauty – but he was charismatic, intelligent and worldly. When Nicolas talked, everyone listened.

'Indigo, I have followed your work for some time now. And Connor is equally impressed. I am investing in a new club at the top of Degree Hotel. The hotel is undergoing renovation, I'm sure you've heard.' Indi certainly had heard. Degree was a famous hotel in the trendy west London district of Notting Hill, but had lost business over the years. Nicolas and his company had taken over the business a few months ago and had immediately begun modernising it for a grand reopening.

'I've got a PR team handling the hotel, but the top-floor club will be the main attraction,' he continued. 'Connor will be a part-owner and fully in charge of operations. We want to open in September, during London Fashion Week and just in time for the Christmas party season. I would like you to handle the club's opening party and, if all goes well, the Christmas party in early December. And more next summer. There may even be plans to expand in America when Tasha and I move to California after the wedding.'

America!

'Plus, potentially more events throughout next year,' said Connor. 'We're calling it 360 because you'll be able to see panoramic views of London from every side. It's right at the top, on the twentieth floor. There will be a rooftop pool open from May to October and I want pool parties with the best DJs and a huge winter theme for the Christmas party. We'd need to start throwing around ideas as soon as possible.'

Words spilt from Connor's mouth as he talked about the club. It was clearly his passion project. Indi was impressed: it wasn't often she met people who were as enthusiastic about their job as she was. Her own mind buzzed with ideas.

'Well, the opening party could have a Roaring Twenties theme as it's on the twentieth floor, like in *The Great Gatsby*,' she suggested. 'Waitresses would wear flapper dresses and there could even be a cabaret show midway through the night. And we could turn it into a ski lodge for Christmas with hot chocolate with Baileys and huge Christmas trees . . .'

The men beamed at each other and the champagne arrived.

'So, it's settled,' said Nicolas as he gestured to the waiter to pour. 'Indigo, I knew you were the girl for the job. You're young but you're hungry, and that's what I like. A fresh take on things. This will be the biggest job of your career so far, Indigo, and we haven't much time. I want everything ready in four months and the press raving about it. Can you handle that?'

'Absolutely, Nicolas,' she replied instantly. 'I can't wait to get started.'

'You and Connor will be working closely together, so you'd better set up a meeting at Print Room this week.'

Working closely with Connor. The thought couldn't help but excite her. But was it dangerous? Don't be silly, she assured herself. No man had *ever* distracted her from work before.

'Sounds great to me.' Connor smiled.

'Marvellous,' said Nicolas with a nod. 'Now, a toast to 360. And to prosperous times ahead.'

Indi was delighted. She'd gone out for dinner and landed almost a year's worth of work before the starters had arrived! This was going to take Glamour To Go into the next phase, and she'd easily make enough money to put Kyle through college. She couldn't wait to tell Hollie.

The three clinked glasses and, for the briefest moment, her eyes met Connor's and her heart raced. 'To prosperous times ahead.'

Chapter Four

Saskia slumped back in her red upholstered swivel chair at her work desk and rubbed her temples. She was exhausted and her head was thumping painfully. It had been weeks since her mortifying entrance at The Square when she'd crashed into a waiter and his full tray of drinks, but Saskia still felt that it had made her the laughing stock of the industry.

'Sass, I'm off now,' called her cheery account manager, Jo. 'My sister is taking Evie tonight so Stephen and I can have a date-night. I swear, eight months after having our first baby, I don't think we've once gone out for dinner alone!'

'That sounds lovely, Jo, off you go,' said Saskia, still staring at her blank emails and biting her nails in anxiety.

'What are you doing tonight, Sass? I hope not staying here in the office too late . . . It is Friday, after all.'

Saskia shut down her computer. What was the point?

'No, I'll leave now and lock up. Millie's dad has picked

her up so she'll be spending the weekend with him and the Real Housewife of Radlett in their country manor.' Saskia couldn't bear to say the name of her ex's new, surgically enhanced wife. 'Meanwhile it's Netflix and a glass of Pinot Grigio for me tonight.' These days, however, it would be more like a bottle than a glass of Pinot Grigio that Saskia would get through.

Two years ago, Saskia's husband, Charles, a successful banker in the City, had left her after ten years of marriage for his (much younger) blonde secretary. They'd been having an affair for a year and he'd used his and Saskia's holiday fund to buy his mistress a boob job. It was such a cliché.

'You could always join me and Stephen for a drink?' Jo offered.

'Oh, that's very sweet, Jo. But, I wouldn't hear of it. You two go and have a romantic evening. I'm going to have an early night and spend tomorrow pampering myself at the spa. Next week is crunch time. I'm going to get that 360 club account if it's the last thing I do.'

Jo bit her lip. 'Oh, Sass, did you not hear? Glamour To Go landed that account. The press release went out an hour ago.'

Saskia stood up and slammed her fist on the table. '*What?* Indigo Edwards is handling the entire launch of 360? She's barely out of nappies! And how dare Nicolas not even have the decency to tell me himself? Surely he knew I wanted to pitch?'

'I'm so sorry, Sass. She probably only got it because she's mates with Tasha Phelps, who obviously has Nicolas wrapped around her size zero finger.' Jo was trying to be

42

helpful. 'Look, go home and try to forget about it. Have a restful weekend like you planned and, first thing Monday, we'll hatch a plan. You know Andrew always brings fresh ideas to the table. He's so young and hungry. We'll do a big brainstorm and land an even bigger and better account, you'll see.'

It poured with spring rain that night and Saskia was drenched by the time she reached her terraced house in Richmond. After a long bath, she wrapped herself in a white towelling dressing gown. She was debating whether to pour a large glass of wine or a gin and tonic when she was startled by a small figure sitting at the kitchen table, typing incessantly on an iPhone.

'Millie! You scared the hell out of me. What are you doing here? I thought Dad picked you up from school hours ago?'

'Change of plan,' muttered Millie. 'He and Isabella have gone to Paris for the weekend. He said it was the last chance to get away before the baby was born.' Saskia felt a knot in her throat. While they were married, Charles had been adamant he didn't want another baby. But, no sooner had the ink dried on their divorce than the Real Housewife of Radlett had fallen pregnant. But that didn't bother Saskia nearly as much as the bastard letting their daughter down at the last minute. How dare he?

'Oh, darling. I'm so sorry.' Saskia put her arms around Millie, who wriggled away. Saskia knew how hurt Mille would feel at being stood up by her own father. But she was a stubborn teenager and would never admit it.

'Tell you what, let's order a takeaway and stay up late watching movies,' suggested Saskia. 'There's a full tub of chocolate Häagen-Dazs in the fridge and that new Channing Tatum film has just come on Sky Box Office. A treat for both of us! Or we could stick on the *Mamma Mia* DVD?' *Mamma Mia* used to be their favourite film, and singing along to the Abba songs was a pastime that Saskia sorely missed.

'No, thanks, Mum,' said Millie quietly. 'Sadie said I could go and have a sleepover at hers. Can I go? And could you give me a lift?'

Saskia's heart sank a little. 'OK, darling. Whatever you like. Maybe tomorrow you could come to the spa with me and I could treat you to a manicure?'

But Millie was already heading upstairs to pack her overnight bag. 'Can't. Revision,' she called back.

Saskia's day was going from bad to worse. She was furious with Charles. And she couldn't shake her fury towards Indigo Edwards, either, which stayed with her right through the weekend. Even a day at her beloved Blissful Spa in Fulham, including a hot stone back massage, Indian head massage, anti-ageing facial, manicure and pedicure couldn't completely relax her. Saskia was worried for the future of her company, which meant she was worried for her and her daughter's future as well.

After her treatments she went home, uncorked a bottle of red wine and flipped open her laptop. She Googled Glamour To Go, poring over Indi's biography and impressive credits. It wasn't the first time she'd done this. Since Indigo's famous party at Park Lane, and since running into her at The Square, Saskia had become slightly fixated with the young industry starlet and checked her website and social media accounts obsessively – usually after a glass of wine or three – to see what other new work she'd landed. Indi had excitedly tweeted about 360. The tweet had 243 'likes' and responses. Indigo was certainly popular, thought Saskia, noticing that Glamour To Go had 12,000 Twitter followers, 2,000 more than a few days ago. Saskia barely used Twitter, and only had an account because Millie had insisted she set one up for her, but she was determined to master the art of social media, and had been undergoing a crash course in tweeting guided by the youngest member of Sass PR, Andrew. She knew the importance of it as a networking and promotional tool, but constantly felt that the times were moving too fast for her. No wonder she was rapidly losing business. She poured herself a large glass of wine. She thought about phoning one of her old friends for a chat but decided against it. Once the toast of the London party scene, a few years ago Saskia would have organised the most glamorous events in the city – and if not, would have been at the top of the guest list along with her socialite friends. Now they'd all moved out to the country with their musician or footballer husbands and Saskia barely had anyone to hang around with. She'd committed so many years to Charles that she'd lost touch with the social circuit and many of her friends. Glumly, she downed her wine and took her laptop to bed, feeling bitter, depressed and useless, as usual.

'Cheers, daaarling!' Indi and Hollie shouted in unison, putting on fake posh accents and clinking their martini glasses as they giggled. It was Friday night in the middle of June and the best friends had arrived at Print Room, in the achingly cool area of Shoreditch in east London. As always on nights out, the girls had got ready together and were dressed to impress. Indi wore a burnt-orange pencil dress with thin straps, which stopped just above her knees and clung to her figure, showing off her tan and accentuating all the right curves. Indi never went over the top, and the dress was bold enough to make a statement without needing anything else, so she wore no jewellery and just a pair of simple brown leather strappy sandals. She had tonged her long brown hair so it fell over her bare shoulders in sexy waves. Hollie had opted for a cobalt-blue pencil skirt and a crop top that showed off her ample cleavage, bright red lipstick and mounds of gold bangles.

The bar in Print Room was a huge, steel, oval shape in the centre of a room, with blue and green velvet sofas at the edges and low-hanging lamps. It was heaving with pretty women and impeccably dressed men, either air-kissing each other in greeting, glued to their phones or waving credit cards and twenty-pound notes to the bar staff to try to catch their attention. Indi and Hollie sat at the bar on high black leather stools as bartenders in matching polka-dot bowties and waistcoats mixed lavish cocktails in shakers. One winked at the girls as he poured their lychee martinis. 'On the house, ladies,' he said, 'courtesy of Mr Scott.'

'He's trying to impress you,' Hollie said after they'd taken their first delicious glug of quality vodka.

'The bartender?' asked Indi, faking ignorance, as she

knew exactly who her friend was referring to. 'He already has with this cocktail. I could drink these all night!'

'No. And you know exactly who I'm talking about. Connor blatantly fancies you!'

Indi rolled her eyes. It had been almost a month since Indi's Cecconi's meeting with Nicolas and Connor and she'd never been busier. Her contract for working on 360 had been signed, sealed and delivered and, after the press release had gone out, she had been approached by a corporate investment company who wanted Glamour To Go to organise a charity gala dinner they were putting on. She and Ben had been working tirelessly to put it together by July, while prepping for the 360 launch in September. It might be three months away, but Nicolas wanted it to be the biggest, most elaborate and glamorous party of the year. Since their dinner, Indi and Connor had only spoken via brief emails, mainly just ironing out the finer details of her contract, but from Monday morning she'd be working closely with him on the upcoming launch. He'd insisted on hosting her and Hollie to dinner at Print Room beforehand.

'It's a kind gesture, but he's probably got five more tables full of girls he's hosting tonight.' Indi shrugged. 'I'm sure it's more about him showing off than anything else.'

'He's been emailing you every other day for nearly a month!' exclaimed Hollie.

'Only about work. He's very professional over email. I don't think there is anything there. Besides, he's got a girlfriend, remember? And she's probably working tonight, so careful what you say!' Indi would never dream of going near a taken man, but she couldn't deny Connor fascinated her slightly. It was so rare for Indi to meet men as serious about their career as she was about her own, and she respected him for it. She wasn't lying to her friend when she said his emails were entirely professional – always shortly worded, to the point, and never flirtatious. Even when he invited her and Hollie to dinner at Print Room it seemed more like a business gesture than a personal one.

'There's something not right in that relationship,' sniffed Hollie. 'Have you seen his Instagram account? He only ever posts pictures of this place, or him and his mates drinking or at a football match. Not one picture of Anja – don't you think that's weird?'

Hollie was obsessed with Instagram. As a make-up artist she always shared pictures of her glamorous work, but Indi knew she was just as passionate about looking up profiles of hot men.

'That's blokes for you,' replied Indi. 'Work, beer and football clearly take precedence over his girlfriend, so what's new?'

As if on cue, an extremely tall and slim figure sashayed towards the bar, catching the admiring glances of every man she passed. Anja Kovack. She placed one hand on her tiny hip and stretched out the other towards Indi. 'Indigo, right?' she asked in a posh London accent. 'Hi, I'm Anja. If you're ready I'll take you to your table for dinner?'

Indi shook it. 'Hi, Anja. We actually met a few weeks ago at The Square. You remember my friend, Hollie?'

Anja pouted slightly and glanced at Hollie, giving her a quick up-and-down before smiling sweetly. 'Of course.

Silly me for forgetting. You both look great. I wish I had the guts to wear such bold colours. If you'd like to follow me?'

Hollie gave a disapproving look and mouthed the word 'fake' at Indi, who rolled her eyes again at her friend. Hollie could be *so* judgemental. Anja was perfectly civil and professional. She was also disarmingly beautiful, with straight jet-black hair that reached to her lower back, large brown eyes and perfect glowing skin. She wore a minuscule black strapless dress and vampy dark brown lipstick. She was incredibly slender and at least five feet eight inches tall, Indi thought. No wonder she modelled as well as working at Print Room.

The restaurant was smaller and more intimate than Indi had imagined. Tables were close together and overflowing with patrons, arms draped around each other while laughing and knocking back wine or huddled together over plates of food, deep in conversation. Everyone looked fashionable and cool. Indi spotted Brooklyn Beckham in one corner with a small group around him and the TV presenters Laura Whitmore and Caroline Flack laughing over dinner. This was clearly the place to be seen. Print Room was famous for modern European cuisine and had won various 'Best New Restaurant' awards. Anja led them to the only free table, where a bottle of Veuve Clicquot champagne was waiting on ice. 'Compliments of Connor,' she said.

'Is Connor here tonight?' Hollie asked. 'He did invite us, after all. We'd love to say thank you.'

'He's out with friends tonight, I'm afraid. They went to the football earlier and have no doubt been drinking solidly since. Which will be fun for me later!' The girls laughed at her sarcasm. Was that a flash of disappointment that Indi felt? Why did she care so much?

'Anyway, I'd recommend the maple-glazed sea bass. It's to die for. You girls have a great evening and let me know if you need anything at all.'

'See, she's nice,' Indi said after Anja had glided away.

'Hmm. Shame Connor isn't here, though,' said Hollie, as if reading her friend's mind. 'All the more champagne for us! I'm so proud of you, Indi, getting all this amazing work and doing so well. You really deserve it.'

'Thanks, babe.' Indi reached over to give Hollie a kiss on the cheek. 'Now let's get smashed – compliments of Mr Scott!'

The girls did just that. Over the next two hours they polished off the champagne with their starters of delicious fried octopus for Hollie and mini Caesar salad for Indi, followed by succulent salmon and grilled lamb for mains. The girls couldn't decide what to have, so shared both, then divided up a thick slice of vanilla cheesecake served with Amaretto Sour cocktails. It was the perfect meal. Plans for late-night clubbing were scuppered as the girls felt so full. Instead they piled tipsily into a cab and headed back to Indi's flat.

'God, look at us,' said Indi. Having scraped her make-up off she couldn't wait to slip into a baggy t-shirt. 'Friday night. How very rock 'n' roll, eh?'

Hollie, now wearing one of Indi's t-shirts as well, laughed and then stifled a yawn. 'Plenty more nights of fun to be had this summer. Tonight I'm happy to live vicariously through Sofia Vergara! Let's watch some *Modern Family* on my laptop in bed.' But when the girls fell into Indi's double bed, Hollie fell asleep immediately.

Indi flicked through her phone to check any new emails and was notified that she'd been mentioned in a tweet. *Bitch, stop pretending you're something you're not. You look like a cheap dirty little slag. Get a life!!!!* The user was simply titled 'userxx0177xxx' and didn't follow anyone except Indigo's personal account and Glamour To Go's account. The user's account didn't have any followers, either, and no photo. Indi didn't quite know what to make of it, so decided to ignore it. Just as she was about to close her eyes to go to sleep, she got another notification. She angrily snatched up her phone, but this time it was a WhatsApp message. Connor.

'Sorry I couldn't make it over to the restaurant. Hope you had a great time. Looking forward to working with you on Monday. Cx.'

Indi reread the message a couple more times, then swiped her phone off. *He's just being polite*, she thought, and she drifted off to sleep, forgetting all about 'userxx0177xxx'.

Chapter Five

Connor's phone was ringing off the hook. It was Saturday morning but friends, friends-of-friends, ex-colleagues and even people he barely knew were texting him asking for a reservation at Print Room tonight. *No rest for the wicked*, thought Connor as he yawned, pulled away the crisp, white duvet and sat up in his king-sized bed. Beside him, a head of long dark hair stirred and an arm wrapped around his chest.

'Come back to bed,' came Anja's husky voice. She gently tugged Connor back into the sheets.

'I have to get up, darlin'. I'm playing football with the boys then I've got work at the restaurant. It's our busiest night of the week.' Anja nuzzled his neck and whispered for him to stay just another hour longer. Of course it was tempting, but Connor gave her a quick kiss on her head and headed for the shower, leaving Anja pouting.

Connor let the steaming hot water wash over him. His head was banging, and not just because of an afternoon of drinking yesterday, but the growing unease about his relationship status. This was the fourth night in a row that Anja had stayed round and he was feeling claustrophobic. Weren't they supposed to just be having fun? When did it all get so serious? Sure, he liked Anja, but he didn't see what they had as going anywhere. It was only supposed to be a casual fling. Apart from a healthy sex life, did they have anything in common? Anja's only ambition was to get Instagram followers and party all night with a group of models that, frankly, bored the hell out of Connor. Taking selfies half the night and spending the other half in the toilet, powdering their noses, wasn't exactly his idea of fun.

Walking back into his bedroom, he hoped Anja was getting ready to leave, but she was still sprawled out on his bed. 'What do you wanna do tonight, babe? Fancy Kensington Roof Gardens with Tamzina and the girls when you finish at Print Room?'

That was the last thing Connor wanted to do with his Saturday night. He was growing more and more certain that the time was up with their relationship.

At ten on Monday morning, Indi arrived at Print Room dressed in grey tailored shorts and a white blouse. It was a scorching summer's day and she'd been up since six a.m., first going for a run, then answering emails and catching up on work. The bar area, unlike the dim, sexy vibe on Friday night, was now flooded with natural light and full of cappuccino-drinking professionals typing furiously on their laptops at wooden tables. Indi was about to sit when a hand on her lower back startled her.

'Sorry, did I make you jump?' Connor flashed Indi a cheeky smile, motioned for her to sit down and beckoned over a waiter to take their coffee orders. *God, he was annoyingly handsome*, thought Indi as she took in his masculine, neatly stubbled jaw and those intense dark green-brown eyes. He looked positively dapper, dressed in beige chinos and a smart blue t-shirt that showed off *very* defined biceps.

'Hi, Connor,' she replied breezily, and sat up straight to show that she meant business. 'I think we should get right to it. We need to lock down the date for the launch and design the invitation as a matter of urgency so that guests have plenty of notice. Celebrities get booked up months in advance. I think we should aim to get the invitations out by the end of next week. Are we still thinking the sixteenth of September? It's in the middle of London Fashion Week so things will be kicking off, but we won't have to compete with the really massive end-of-week parties. I've already made a guest list. Do you want to have a look and add to it?'

Connor tried not to stare at Indi but, frankly, he couldn't take his eyes off her. Most girls melted at his feet the second they met him (which might be why he got bored of them so quickly), but something told him that Indigo Edwards wasn't like other girls.

He stopped his mind from trailing off even further and snapped into work mode. 'Terrific, Indi. I've actually had my graphics guy come up with a few designs for the invitation already.' Connor flipped open his iMac. 'Let me show you now.'

'Great. We should also start thinking DJs. They'll be getting booked up quickly.'

'I was thinking of a live set as well,' continued Connor. 'Something low key, just a singer and a guitar for a couple of songs before the DJ ramps it up. Ella Eyre is a regular here and would be perfect. Maybe get one of the boys from Rudimental to DJ.'

For the next four hours Indi and Connor barely stopped talking. They had the same taste and vision for the club and bounced ideas off each other easily. With both their laptops open, they researched and brainstormed ideas, nodding and finishing each other's sentences as if they'd been colleagues for years. At two p.m. Connor suggested they break for lunch, but Indi shook her head. He had a girlfriend and she didn't think veering away from business was a good idea. She wasn't quite sure if she trusted him, but, if she was being honest, she didn't quite trust herself, either. There was something so intriguing about Connor (and not just his good looks). He was easy to talk to and made her feel both nervous and relaxed at the same time.

'Thanks, but I should get back to my own office. I'll be on email all week so let's just stay in touch and on top of everything. See you next week here for a catch-up?'

'Sure. Unless you think we need to meet before then? You know, to go over anything . . .' Connor trailed off and he inwardly scolded himself for sounding so desperate. But Indi was enchanting him. Every second he spent with her, he admired her more. Not only was she show-stoppingly beautiful, she was smart. Spiky, even. And wholly mysterious. The fact that she seemed in no way interested in him was also a huge turn-on, but this wasn't just about winning. Indi sparked something in Connor he hadn't felt before.

Indi was already walking away. 'Speak soon, Connor,' she called back breezily.

As day turned into evening, Anja turned up in Connor's office just as he was about to leave for another meeting. 'Hi, babe,' she said, sauntering over to him and wrapping her arms around his waist, reeking of sickly sweet perfume.

Connor pulled away, feeling a surge of guilt. 'Hey, what are you doing here? You're not on tonight.'

'Just thought we could hang out. Go for dinner somewhere?'

Poor Anja. She hadn't crossed his mind once that day, yet he hadn't stopped thinking about Indi. He knew what he had to do. Anja simply had to go. 'I'm running out to another meeting. Look, An, why don't I pop over later? We can have a quiet drink at yours.'

The next few meetings between Indi and Connor were just as productive. Each of them was quietly amazed at how well they collaborated. Indi loved Connor's idea to bring an elegant acoustic set to the opening night, and he'd managed to book Ella Eyre and the musician James Bay to play guitar (both were regular diners at Print Room and personal friends of Connor). Meanwhile, she'd had the invitations signed off by Nicolas and sent out to the agents of TV actors, models, radio presenters and pop stars, as well as some of her own personal connections. She had Davidas Santoro, in her opinion the best florist in London, create bouquets of flowers for the room. Indi always used him for events, as she believed flowers were essential. They'd selected dome-shaped bouquets of peonies and white roses. She kept her meetings with Connor short, sweet and entirely professional, even though she found herself getting more excited to see him before every one.

One Friday a few weeks later he suggested lunch again, outside on Print Room's balcony area. 'C'mon, it's on me. It's almost the weekend and I've been at the gym every morning and working every night. I need a drink and some sunshine,' he said, before his iPhone bleeped furiously. He looked at the text message and quickly stuffed his phone in his pocket. Indi never normally drank alcohol during working hours, but she was starving and reasoned that it was such a beautiful sunny day. Surely just one glass of wine wouldn't hurt . . .

Another bonus for Connor was that sitting outside gave him an opportunity to appreciate Indi's incredible figure from behind his sunglasses. As much as he enjoyed getting work done so efficiently, he'd been dying to get Indi to switch off and not be quite so uptight. And since he'd ended things with Anja and was a free agent again, he was very much looking forward to getting to know her better.

As he pulled up a chair for her, he thought again how truly stunning she was. Those shapely, tanned legs. Her long, thick hair he wanted to run his hands through. And those full, sensuous lips he couldn't stop thinking about kissing. They ordered two grilled chicken salads, a bowl of fries for Connor, sparkling water and a bottle of Sauvignon Blanc, then tilted their faces to the sun. In front of them was a magnificent view of London, with St Paul's Cathedral and the Shard staring right back at them. Indi took a picture of the beautiful view and uploaded it to Glamour To Go's Instagram account. It was a well-curated shot. Ben would be proud of her.

'So, Indi,' said Connor, pouring her a glass of wine before helping himself. 'As thrilling as I find our plans to take over the capital's nightlife scene, are we allowed to talk as friends for once?'

'I suppose that couldn't hurt,' she replied, thinking how delicious the cold, crisp white wine tasted. 'How about this? We get five personal questions to ask each other. You go first. Only five, so make them good ones.'

'You drive a hard bargain, Miss Edwards. OK, I'll start off easy before I probe too much into your personal life. Number one, your favourite film?'

'Good start. *The Departed* followed closely by *Bridesmaids*.'

'Not bad, not bad,' sniffed Connor. 'Standard chick-flick, but I'll allow it.'

'Pah! What's yours? Something really obvious like *The Godfather*?'

'It's a classic so you'd be right,' he argued. 'Number two. Place you most want to visit in the world?'

'Oooh, so many! South America, definitely. I want to do the Inca trail in Peru and see the Amazon rainforest. And I've always dreamed of lying on a white-sand beach in the Caribbean. Heaven.'

'Spot on.' Connor nodded in approval. 'Have you ever been to America?'

Indi's holidays usually consisted of her, Hollie and Tina sunbathing by a pool in Marbella for a week, but she'd been working so hard on the business and saving up money, she hadn't been abroad for years. And as much as she loved drinking cocktails with her girlfriends by a Spanish sunset, she craved somewhere more exotic.

'We went on a family holiday to Florida once,' she replied. 'My brother, Kyle, and I were pretty young, but I remember thinking how amazing Disney World was. I wouldn't mind going as an adult. I hear Miami is very cool.'

They were interrupted by Connor's phone ringing and he excused himself to take the call. 'Sorry, Indi, I hate to be rude but it's a potential investor.'

Indi batted her hand at him. 'Go, go, work is important.' She took the opportunity when he was gone to check her own emails to see if anything needed to be dealt with urgently. There was nothing that couldn't wait a few hours. There was a red notification by her Instagram account. Her picture from Print Room's balcony had already received 42 'likes' but, crushingly, more nasty comments.

'IS IT NICE SCROUNGING OFF RICH MEN FOR A LIVING, WHORE? YOU KNOW HE'S GOT A GIRLFRIEND? IS THE REASON YOU'RE NOT IN THIS PICTURE BECAUSE YOU LOOK SO ROUGH AND HE'S EMBARRASSED BY YOU?'

'What the fuck?' Indi said out loud, but quickly stuffed her phone back into her bag when Connor returned at the same time as the waiter with their food.

'Mmm, I'm starving,' he announced, sitting down. Indi smiled back at him. No need to tell him about the trolling. They'd get bored eventually and she was enjoying herself in Connor's company, so why ruin it?

Connor poured water for Indi before diving into his chips. 'Where were we? Ah yes, Miami. It *is* very cool. I go out there a couple of times a year for the music or art festivals. I'd actually love to have a business out there. I think you'd love it, Indi. Beautiful beaches, amazing food and culture. Saint Lucia is another of my favourite holiday destinations. The people, food and atmosphere are astonishing. I've been many times.'

Art? That was a surprise. Indi didn't have Connor down as a culture vulture.

'Maybe after the 360 launch, you and Hollie can ditch the heels and take a wild tour through the Amazon,' he added.

Indi let out a cackle. The chance of Hollie going on holiday anywhere that didn't have super-clubs, an infinity pool and a luxurious hotel was slim to none. 'You'd have more luck getting Hollie to jump off this balcony than ditch her heels,' she protested. 'Miami does sound cool. So, do you go there with Anja?'

Connor took a large mouthful of salad and shook his head vehemently.

'Don't look so surprised. She is your girlfriend, after all.'

'Nope. Not any more. Not for a few weeks, actually.'

'Oh?' Indi took a slug of wine to try to stop her smiling. So they *weren't* together. Did that mean Connor was single?

'The term "girlfriend" was a little strong even when we were together,' he continued. 'It was just a bit of fun. She's a mate more than anything else.'

'Wow. And she agrees?'

Connor thought back to the awful scene at Anja's flat

60

when he'd tried to let her down gently but she'd started crying and begging him not to leave. He cleared his throat. 'Of course. She's a cool girl, she knew it wasn't anything serious.' He didn't like lying to Indi but she didn't need to know the gory details. Anja knew it was over, that was the main thing. He'd broken up with her like a gentleman.

'OK, Indigo, now we've got that cleared up and you know I'm one hundred per cent free and single, next question. Who was the last person to see you naked?' He grinned and topped up her now-empty glass of wine.

'None of your business, that's who!' laughed Indi, scrunching up her napkin and throwing it at him. Fortunately her sunglasses were so big they shadowed the tops of her cheeks where she was blushing. Connor was certainly a massive flirt, but she bantered right back. And allowed herself to check out his impressive physique, this time without the guilt of thinking she was looking at a taken man. Broad shoulders and strong arms. *Very nice*, Indi thought, thinking she couldn't remember the last time she felt so comfortable around a man. But just seconds later the mood changed dramatically.

'I bet the last person to see you naked was someone really boring like your mum, right?' Connor teased. 'Thinking about it, I bet your mum is pretty fit! Tell me, what does she do when she's not gallivanting around Florida with you? I'd love to see the woman who has you for a daughter!'

At the mention of Lou, Indi felt an intense pang of sadness in the pit of her belly.

'C'mon, show me a picture.' Connor grinned, but his

smile dropped when he saw Indi was holding her head in her hands. 'Hey, Indi, you OK?'

She wasn't. The wine had gone straight to her head. 'Um, I feel a bit dizzy,' she said softly. Connor lightly touched her arm, but the contact made her flinch and pull her chair away.

'Sorry, I just, sorry . . .' Indi bolted up and ran to the ladies toilets before he could see how rapidly her eyes were welling up. She just about made it to the loo before she burst into tears. Her head was dizzy and she felt sickness rise, but she swallowed hard and tried to compose herself. It had been twelve years since Lou had passed away from cancer and there wasn't a single day Indi didn't think about her. While pangs of sadness weren't uncommon, she never normally reacted like this when someone mentioned her mum. The scorching sun had increased the effects of the alcohol and made Indi more emotional, but it was more than that. Something about Connor made her feel at ease. And for a split second Indi, the epitome of a strong, ballsy career woman, had let her guard down.

She caught her breath and stood in front of the mirror trying to compose herself. Her eyes were red and swollen and mascara ran down her cheeks. *Shit*, she thought, splashing cold water on her face and wiping the make-up with a tissue. It didn't do much good, and without her handbag she had nothing to fix her face up with. She blushed at the thought of facing Connor again, who would clearly think she was an insane and emotional wreck. But when she walked out of the toilets she gasped, as he was standing right there holding her bag.

'I've ordered you an Uber in case you want to go home, but if you'd like to stay here I'll get you a tea and you can take a few minutes in my office?'

Indi was so grateful that he wasn't trying to pry into what was wrong. She didn't feel like going back to an empty flat, so she accepted the offer of tea. Connor's office was bright and airy with white walls and two glass desks, one for him and one for Eddie, the general manager of Print Room, neatly arranged with iMac laptops and folders. A striking piece of art – a red canvas with a bold revolver print – hung on one wall, while a huge rectangular mirror hung opposite. As Connor disappeared to get her tea, Indi checked her still-swollen reflection in the mirror and sat on the black leather chair at Connor's desk.

'Thanks, Connor,' she said as he returned, handing her a steaming cup and perching on the edge of his desk, eyes fixed on her. 'I'm so sorry. And embarrassed.'

'Please don't apologise. I feel bad. It's the hottest day of the year and alcohol was definitely not a good idea. No wonder you were sick. I hope it wasn't the salad, though – the last thing I need is for you to sue me for food poisoning!'

Indi laughed. She was grateful to Connor for lightening the mood, but she felt she should be honest with him. 'It wasn't just that.' She took a deep breath. 'My mum died when I was fifteen. We were incredibly close. Usually I don't get this upset when someone mentions her, but when you did it triggered something. Everything that's been going on at work and 360, I wish I could tell her about it. I've just been missing her a lot recently.'

Connor could have kicked himself for being so stupid

and insensitive. Up until now he couldn't imagine anything upsetting Indi so much, she seemed so strong and in control. But now her huge, beautiful blue eyes had so much sadness in them he couldn't help wrapping his arms around her. And Indi, who felt exhaustion sweep over her, leant in to him and rested her head on his firm, muscular chest. She closed her eyes and breathed in Connor's expensive woody aftershave. His body was warm and his arms tightened protectively around her. 'I'm so sorry, Indi,' he whispered, kissing the top of her head. Indi melted into his body and he held her close in silence, before lifting her chin lightly up to his face. 'I'm so sorry,' he said again, cupping her face in his hand. He brushed his lips gently against hers, and then they were kissing. He didn't need to say anything else.

Chapter Six

Indi didn't know how much time had passed when they finally stopped kissing. All she knew was that Connor felt and tasted incredible. His hands held her face and stroked her hair softly, but as their kiss grew more intense he gripped her waist and she caressed his arms, letting him draw her closer. His body felt so good against hers. She eventually pulled away and opened her eyes.

'I've been wanting to do that for so long, Indi,' he murmured.

'I should go,' she whispered back. 'I've still got work to do and a conference call with the caterer. Plus, we've been tucked away in here for so long that people will start talking.' She smoothed down her white silk blouse, which had crumpled up during their embrace.

But letting Indi leave his side was the last thing Connor wanted. 'Why don't we take the rest of the day off?' he said. 'It's nearly four p.m. anyway. Push the conference call to Monday and spend the rest of the afternoon and evening with me. We could go back to mine, stick a film on, let me cook you dinner while you do nothing except lie on the sofa and let me pamper you.' He kissed her neck.

Indi groaned – the thought was definitely tempting – but she walked towards the door shaking her head. 'You don't waste any time, do you? One kiss and you think you can get me into bed.'

'More than one kiss – and who said anything about a bed?' he protested. 'Put it this way, I'm going home for a much-needed night in and cooking myself a huge lasagne as I never got to finish lunch and am bloody starving. That's what I'm doing, and I'd love you to come. No pressure. I'll order you a taxi home whenever you want.' He leant into her again. 'No ulterior motive, Indi, I promise. I just want to be with you.'

Indi thought of the alternative. Hollie was away all weekend at a work event, and Tina would be with her boyfriend, so Indi was looking at either a night on her own sofa alone or heading over to her dad's. 'Taxi home whenever I want?'

'I'll even give you my phone for you to order it, if you like.'

She wrapped her arms around his neck. 'You've got a deal.' She smiled, before another long and passionate kiss.

It was Sunday morning by the time Indi eventually ordered her cab home. Connor had kept true to his word, though, and not pushed her into doing anything more than kissing. *A lot* of kissing. They spent the rest of Friday afternoon sitting on Connor's balcony and lapping up the sun, eating crisps and drinking wine. That night he cooked a feast of lasagne, garlic bread and – on Indi's insistence – green salad. They lay on his sofa and talked into the night. Resting on Connor's chest, Indi fell into a deep sleep. When she awoke on Saturday morning he'd carried her into his bed and slept on the sofa like a perfect gentleman.

Saturday had poured with light summer rain, so they'd spent the day watching back-to-back DVD comedies – *Forgetting Sarah Marshall*, *Ted 2*, *Deadpool* and *Knocked Up* – in between talking, kissing and napping in each other's arms. Indi told Connor all about Alan and Kyle and how close she was to her mum. She shared her concerns about her brother and told him how protective she felt over him. Connor was equally open. She learnt that he had an older brother, Mark, who was a policeman who lived in east London with his wife, Lauren, and daughters who were three and six years old. Connor's face lit up when he talked about his family. He clearly doted on his nieces and spoilt them rotten. He was also incredibly close to his mother, Marion, who had raised the boys as a single mother after their father had abandoned the family. Marion had been pregnant with Connor at the time, so he never knew his father. It was the only time Indi had ever seen Connor look vulnerable. She got the impression that he never normally revealed so much of his personal life, and she was incredibly touched that he seemed to trust her. She had started to feel the same way. That night they slept in Connor's bed draped in each other's arms, but he still didn't try to have sex with her.

'Should I be offended you haven't tried to sleep with

me?' Indi said in mock horror as they finally came up for air from kissing the next morning. She was only half joking. As he was wearing only boxer shorts in bed, she admired his gorgeous body. She wanted to sleep with him so badly, but she didn't want to be just another notch on his bedpost.

'Indi, I'm using every means of resistance I can muster to try not to pin you down right now,' he protested. They were interrupted by the shrill buzz of his phone again. Connor glanced at it, looked momentarily annoyed and turned it to 'silent' mode.

'Everything OK?'

'Just work. Last night was busy and Eddie is hounding me. Honestly, what do I pay him for? Anyway, where was I? Ah yes.' He pulled Indi closer to him. 'I was telling you how respectful I'm trying to be.' Indi kissed him again, feeling slightly smug.

Indi showered in Connor's marble bathroom as he ground up fresh coffee beans. Connor's flat was a typical bachelor's pad. Everything was black, white or dark blue and contained only the minimum – no clutter anywhere. The living room boasted only a huge black leather sofa facing a gigantic flat-screen TV mounted to the wall, a glass coffee table and a bookshelf stacked more with DVDs than with books. His kitchen was pristine white and marble with state-of-the-art everything, including a coffee grinder and espresso machine and a NutriBullet. Everything from the plates to the kettle was either black or dark blue and perfectly clean, thanks to Connor's cleaner, Rose, who came every week.

'Hello, gorgeous,' he said, handing Indi a steaming cup

68

of coffee as she emerged from the bathroom in his huge blue dressing gown.

'I couldn't wash my hair because you've only got boy products,' she said, planting a kiss on his cheek. 'I don't understand how you can have the entire Clinique for Men skincare range and no shampoo or conditioner.'

'The body wash *is* the shampoo and men don't use conditioner,' he said. 'You are, however, the first woman to be given her own brush head for the electric toothbrush.'

'I'm very flattered,' Indi laughed. 'But I can't believe I've been in the same clothes since Friday. Gross!'

'Borrow a t-shirt of mine if you want,' Connor said, reaching into a basket of freshly ironed clothes that Rose had left out on Friday morning. He handed her a black V-neck t-shirt, which actually didn't go too badly with her tailored shorts, although she was going to change the second she got home. 'Are you sure I can't make you some breakfast?' he asked.

'No, I'm fine, thanks. I've got Sunday lunch with my Dad in a few hours. I'll order a cab now. And you've got that football game, haven't you?' Connor, Mark, and Connor's best friend Tom played on a five-a-side football team every Saturday, but because of yesterday's torrential rain, they were playing today.

'But I just want to stay here with you,' he said, wrapping his arms around her and nuzzling behind her ears before his lips made their way to hers. Usually when girls stayed over he wanted them gone after some morning sex and a cup of coffee. The only woman he'd made scrambled eggs for was his mum.

69

'You're doing something to me, Indigo,' he murmured, stroking her back. 'When can I see you again?'

'I'm only free Thursday night this week,' she replied coolly, quite enjoying Connor begging to see her again. It was true, though. Indi had a jam-packed week, what with seeing Hollie for dinner and various work events.

He groaned. 'That's so far away! But I'll take it. We'll go somewhere special.'

Indi hesitated. 'Connor, we have to promise that this won't interfere with work. Nothing means more to me right now than the 360 launch. You understand, don't you?'

This statement only made her more attractive to Connor. She was so independent and sexy. 'We'll keep our business meetings entirely professional,' he said seriously, before breaking out into his signature cheeky smile. 'And our personal meetings entirely *un*professional.' With that, his phone started ringing. 'Shit, I have to take this, babe, I'm sorry. It's the restaurant.'

'Go, go, it's fine,' said Indi, waving him away. 'I'll gather my stuff and order that cab.' But Connor had already disappeared into his bedroom and closed the door. It must've been something serious for them to call on a Sunday morning.

Chapter Seven

During lunch at her dad's later that day, Indi couldn't stop grinning to herself. Connor texted her half an hour after she'd left: *Miss you already xxx*.

'What's up with you? You look weird,' said Kyle through a mouthful of spaghetti.

'You always look weird,' she joked. But she felt like her insides were glowing every time she received a message from Connor. She let Kyle and Alan talk on about the new England manager while she kept thinking back to Connor's perfect kiss. And how she wanted to do so much more with him. She didn't recognise what was happening to her. Hollie was always telling Indi to get out on the dating scene, but the idea of meeting up with total strangers from Tinder was entirely off-putting, while the only men she met through work tended to be gay, and any straight ones were either arrogant or attached. Most of the time Indi was so consumed with work that dating just didn't register. Her phone beeped again and she smiled – Connor was so tenacious! – but, looking down at it, it wasn't a message from Connor, but a notification that she had been tweeted.

It was a tweet from the same account 'userxx0177xxx' that had sent her a vile tweet after her and Hollie's night out at Print Room: *Shagging your way to the top, are you? Pathetic.* Indi frowned. What the hell was this person's problem?

Indi blocked the account so that whoever was behind it couldn't even look at her account, let alone tweet her. She then went to the 'Settings' on her phone menu and turned off all Twitter, Facebook and Instagram notifications. That way she wouldn't be alerted by messages all the time. It was getting seriously annoying, and she was not happy about these bitchy comments. Not happy at all.

On Thursday morning Indi arrived at her office, where a bouquet of flowers and box of Thornton's chocolates were waiting for her. The card read: *Can't wait to take you out later xxxx.* Ben wolf-whistled as he walked past.

'Is he going to send flowers every day? We'll need far more vases if so.'

Indi simply smiled.

After work, she dashed home to shower using her best L'Occitane products. She let her long hair hang in loose waves and wore a sexy satin black playsuit and black high heels (with her new Victoria's Secret black lace underwear underneath). Connor picked her up in his silver Lexus and took her to Sushisamba in central London, a magnificent fusion restaurant thirty-eight floors up and boasting incredible panoramic views of London.

Connor held her hand over the table. 'I haven't been able to stop thinking about you,' he said quietly.

Indi raised her eyebrows. 'I'm sure I'm not the first girl to be showered with this much attention. Tell me, Connor, is this your standard seduction technique?' Then, leaning into him, 'Because it's working.'

She was only teasing him, but Connor genuinely looked a little hurt. 'You think I go to this much trouble for just anyone? Trust me, I haven't wanted to spoil a girl this much since I was in school and took Becky French to Quasar and Pizza Hut!' He sighed. 'Now she really was the love of my life.'

Indi was laughing now. 'Aw, poor baby! I bet you were a charmer even as a teenager.'

'Well, no girl has swept me off my feet quite like this before. And I've only been to this restaurant once for a work meeting. I've been dying to bring someone really special here.' Connor was wearing black trousers and a crisp white shirt; he looked simple, stylish and heart-wrenchingly handsome. Images raced through Indi's mind of tearing his shirt off . . .

Food arrived and it was most delicious sushi Indi had ever tasted. Tuna rolls with chilli and lime, yellowtail sashimi and soy-soaked salmon and asparagus. For dessert Indi just ordered an espresso, but then came a plate of decadent chocolate mousse with her name spelt out in raspberry sauce on a plate decorated with white chocolate flakes.

'You charmer,' she teased Connor, who grinned and raised his whisky glass to her.

'So, do you want me to drop you home tonight?' he asked.

'Only if you're coming with me,' she replied.

They didn't get round to eating the dessert. Connor swiftly paid the bill and whispered in her ear as he held the passenger door of his car open for her, 'I want you so much.'

The second they were through her door they were kissing fervently, hands all over each other. He pinned Indi against the wall in her hallway, lifting her legs so they straddled him and ran his hands up her thighs. His touch sent electric waves through her so intense she thought she'd explode.

'Where's your bedroom?' he demanded, carrying her to the room she pointed at with her legs still wrapped around him. Collapsing on to the bed he whipped off Indi's playsuit and bra, caressing and kissing her breasts as she tore off his shirt and trousers, revealing his huge, very impressive, erection. She lay back on the bed and admired the naked view in front of her as Connor stood over her and put on a condom. He bent down and lifted her legs up so they rested on his shoulders. He slipped off her knickers and started slowly kissing up and down her thighs. It wasn't long before he brought her to a mind-blowing orgasm with his tongue. Then he was inside her, pushing hard and making her gasp in pleasure. It was every bit as incredible as she had imagined and, to her delight, Connor was soon ready to go again. It was hours before they finally fell into a blissed-out, post-orgasmic sleep, each other's bodies entwined together.

'I'm so glad I met you,' Connor said the next morning as Indi got dressed.

'Me too,' she replied, admiring once again his magnificent body. Then they were kissing again and he was pulling her back into bed. Indi glanced at her watch and figured she could be an hour late for work this morning. She did run her own business, after all.

The next few weeks went by in a blissed-out blur. Indi and Connor couldn't get enough of each other. They spent most nights together – even when they'd been out separately, they'd sleep at one another's house, although sleep wasn't the only thing on the cards, as Indi quickly discovered. Sex with Connor was amazing, the best she'd ever had, and he couldn't get enough of her either. At weekends they'd stroll hand in hand through Hampstead Heath, have picnics in Hyde Park and go for romantic dinners in restaurants all around London. Before he owned Print Room, Connor had managed upmarket bars and clubs and had quickly become a fixture in the business world as well as on the London party scene. He knew everyone there was to know. If ever Hollie and Indi fancied a girls' night out, Connor would make sure there was a table and flowing alcohol for them at the best clubs.

One spontaneous Saturday morning, he even whisked her off to Paris for the day. They sauntered by the river Seine and ate at Le Jules Verne restaurant on the Eiffel Tower, 400 feet high (Connor had a thing for heights). Her only complaint was how often he was on his phone, and it had a habit of ringing or buzzing at the most inconvenient times – during dinner or late at night – but he promised to turn his phone off when they went to bed so they weren't disturbed.

'I don't want to get in the way of your job,' Indi said one night over dinner. 'I just think it's important to switch off from time to time. And I can see it stresses you out. I just want you to be happy and relaxed.'

He leant over the table and held her face, kissing her lips softly. 'I'm always happy when I'm with you. Now let's finish up so I can get you home.'

While Indi often cooked for Alan and Kyle, she always joked that, like Carrie Bradshaw in *Sex and the City*, she used her own oven for storage and was always too busy to cook for just herself. Connor, on the other hand, loved to cook and was a fantastic chef, whipping up meals of sea bass linguine or steak with mushroom sauce for them both before they headed to the bedroom. He even made dinner for Indi and Hollie one night, inviting round his best friend Tom as well. As the boys hovered in the kitchen drinking beer, the girls slipped out to Connor's balcony with a bottle of prosecco.

'Seriously, Ind, that man is even more gorgeous than when I first saw him, and he clearly adores you,' said Hollie. 'I knew he fancied you.'

'I'm so glad you like him. Sorry I haven't been around as much as usual. We've kind of just been in our own little bubble.'

'Babe, don't be silly! I'm delighted for you.' Hollie could see how happy her friend was. Since she'd known her, Indi had always been more interested in having a job than having a boyfriend. Her only real romantic relationship was at school doing her A levels. She caught the lad cheating on her at a party and it had left her broken-hearted and devastated. Hollie hadn't known Indi to let down her guard since, and loved seeing her so relaxed. 'You deserve a nice one. Has Connor met Alan yet?'

'No but he says he wants to come for lunch on Sunday! Will you come too, Holl?'

'Of course! You know I can't resist Alan's cooking. And he'll love Connor, I promise.' Hollie glanced inside to where Connor and Tom were bringing plates of homemade pizza out to the table and more bottles of prosecco.

'And not only does he make pizzas from scratch, his mate is well fit, too.'

'It's the first time I've met any of his friends, but he's lovely, right? I think he's a bit of a geek compared to Connor. They've been mates for ever.'

'Hot geeks are my favourite,' giggled Hollie. 'Let's go in and mingle.'

Both Connor and Tom were dressed in jeans and a t-shirt, but where Connor wore a smart blue t-shirt and had just the right amount of neatly trimmed stubble, Tom was scruffier with a beard and the Rolling Stones logo on his t-shirt, but still incredibly handsome and, Indi suspected, a great match for Hollie. He had a warm smile and made Indi feel instantly relaxed. A graphic designer, he'd created the logo and invitations for 360. He had the girls in hysterics telling them about Connor's crush on their headmistress at school, and how he'd even sent her a Valentine's Day card. He and Hollie hit it off immediately. He looked mesmerised as she talked animatedly about her job and they exchanged numbers when he promised to help fix her broken laptop.

Connor, meanwhile, couldn't keep his eyes off Indi, stroking her hand above the table and rubbing his foot against hers underneath it. But then, right in the middle of their perfect evening, as if on cue, Connor's phone rang and his face dropped as he clocked the caller. 'I've got to take this,' he muttered, creeping into the other room.

Tom picked up on the tension. 'His job is so demanding I think it frustrates him,' he said to Indi. 'Don't let it spoil the night.'

'He just seems so stressed sometimes, but he doesn't talk about it,' Indi replied.

'I agree, he seems particularly stressed out recently,' sighed Tom, filling up Hollie's and Indi's glasses with prosecco. 'He's doesn't get overly emotional about anything, but when it comes to work he can be sensitive. He cares so much, I guess. And he isn't great on opening up about it. But don't take it personally, Indi. I know how much he likes you.' He smiled and Indi felt reassured. Connor needed a friend like Tom, she thought. Whatever was on his mind, he'd tell her in his own time. Connor returned, looking annoyed, and mouthed 'sorry' to Indi, who shook her head as if to say, 'It's fine.'

But something told her it wasn't fine.

Chapter Eight

Connor pulled up to the white, expensive town house on the Kings Road in Fulham. He'd been plenty of times before, usually late at night or in the very early hours of the morning, but had never felt as uncomfortable as he did now. It felt wrong even being there. He wished he was in Indi's lovely cosy flat in Manor House. It might not be the richest or poshest area of London, certainly not compared to Fulham, but it had Indi and that was enough for him.

Connor pressed the automatic lock on his car and knocked on the front door of the town house. He'd be in and out in ten minutes, maximum.

'Hi,' said Anja breezily as she opened the door. She was wearing a very short black satin dressing gown. 'Come in, I've just opened a bottle of Malbec.'

'I can't stay long,' replied Connor curtly, walking up the stairs to Anja's living room, already being made to feel more uncomfortable by her inappropriate attire. The town house was owned by her parents, who had split it into two flats. The ground floor was rented out to a couple and Anja shared the top-floor flat with a roommate, another model. Connor didn't know much about the roommate except that she was Polish. His short-lived relationship with Anja hadn't exactly been one where they'd cuddle up on the sofa watching movies and making dinner with her mates. Their dates had been at the expensive restaurants or swanky clubs that Anja had insisted on going to, followed by sex at her house. Until recently, she rarely stayed at Connor's, complaining that she could only sleep in her own bed. Connor seriously wondered what he had ever seen in Anja. She was so high-maintenance, though, as she slinked beside him on to the sofa, her dressing gown showing a hint of cleavage and her bare legs crossed over one another, he remembered the attraction. She was gorgeous – there was no question – but she had nothing on Indi's beauty.

Connor stood up to distance himself from Anja.

'Someone's tetchy tonight,' she purred. 'Why don't I get you a drink and you can relax a bit? Chilean Malbec, that's your favourite, right?'

'I haven't got long, Anja. I came to tell you that all the phone calls, the messages, they have to stop. I'm with Indi now. And she's going to guess that something is up, so I want all this to stop before it gets out of hand.' Anja looked hurt. Connor sighed and sat down next to her, speaking more softly now. 'I'm sorry. I don't mean to sound so cold. But it's just got to end, Anja. You're calling me in tears all the time, begging me back. It's been over for weeks now. Even if I weren't with Indi, you and I just wouldn't work out. I've told you this.'

'But why, Connor?' Anja's eyes filled with tears. 'Didn't we have fun together? You certainly had fun in my bedroom. I'm pretty sure you were very much interested in me then.'

Connor shifted uncomfortably. 'Well, yeah . . . But you said yourself you didn't want anything serious. I told you I wasn't ready for a relationship. I thought we were on the same page.'

Anja gazed up at Connor. As their eyes met she ripped off her dressing gown to reveal her supermodel figure wearing a tiny cream thong and see-through lace bra. She pounced on Connor's lap and started kissing him, using all her force to hold him down, but he easily pushed her back on to the sofa and shot up to stand. Anja, not giving up, tugged at the flies on his jeans. 'I know you want me, Connor, just kiss me!'

He wasn't tempted, even for a second. All he could think about was being with Indi. He shook Anja off like a pesky insect. 'This is fucking ridiculous. I never should have come here. You need to pull yourself together, Anja. It's over, do you understand me? OVER.' And with that he ran down the stairs and out of the door to his car. He couldn't get away from her quickly enough.

'Do I look all right?' Connor asked Indi. They were outside Alan's house and she was searching through her bag for her keys. It had been days since his encounter with Anja, and he hadn't told a soul, not even Tom. He wanted to pretend it had never happened. Unfortunately going to see Anja had only encouraged her, and her messages were getting more extreme. In one she had told Connor she couldn't live without him.

Indi stopped to look at his outfit again: smart cream chinos and a pink Ralph Lauren t-shirt. There weren't many men who could carry off a pink t-shirt but, with Connor's body – defined muscles and bulging arms but not body-builder buff (a look Indi hated) – he looked utterly masculine. His short, dark brown hair, scruffy except for a slick of wax, and green eyes only made him look more gorgeous. Indi herself was wearing a wispy floral dress and gold sandals, her long glossy hair tossed up in a bun.

'You always look sexy, but it's only lunch at my dad's; he's not expecting black tie.' She smiled. 'I think it's sweet that you're nervous, though.'

'Not nervous,' Connor replied defensively.

Indi kissed him softly. 'Found my keys. Come on.'

As she suspected he would, Connor fitted into her family easily. She appreciated it was nerve-wracking for a man to meet the father of a girl he was dating, but Alan was so gentle and lovely it was impossible to be intimidated by him. Alan welcomed Connor with a warm handshake and a cold beer. Connor remembered Indi saying that brandy was Alan's favourite drink, so he'd brought a bottle as a gift. 'Nice to meet you, Mr Edwards,' he said, handing him the bottle. Indi suppressed a laugh. *So cute!*

Her dad patted Connor's arm. 'Call me Alan.'

Kyle and Hollie were already in the kitchen arguing over who should be evicted from *Celebrity Big Brother*.

82

Alan turned to Connor. 'Any idea what they're talking about?' Connor laughed and shook his head.

'Right, you two,' Alan called. 'Food's almost ready. Kyle, get over here to say hello to your sister and meet Connor.' Kyle shuffled over, looking slightly nervous as he always did when he met new people.

Indi gave him a quick reassuring hug then introduced the pair. 'You know David Beckham was in Connor's restaurant the other day, K?' Kyle's gaze lifted and instantly the two men were deep in conversation. Indi went over to say hello to Hollie, who nodded her head towards the boys.

'He's slotted into the family already,' she said. 'And, guess what? I've got a date with Tom tonight!'

'Amazing! What are you going to wear?' Indi was delighted for her friend, who of course had already made a Pinterest board of date-outfit inspiration for the girls to analyse.

Conversation between the five flowed for hours as they ate Alan's signature roast chicken – the summer version with salad and sweet potato wedges. Connor and Kyle got on particularly well, Indi noticed. At one point she looked at the group and considered how lucky she was to have such amazing people in her life. Of course she wished Lou was alive to meet Connor. Her mother would have adored him, and would probably have taken Indi and Hollie to one side by this point to get all the gossip about her daughter's new relationship. That was one of the things Indi remembered most vividly about her mum; she loved a laugh and a good schoolgirl gossip. There had never been a dull moment when Lou was around.

Later, Hollie left to get ready for her date with Tom, and Connor and Indi eventually said their goodbyes, too. Connor thanked Alan profusely for the meal.

'You're welcome back, any time,' Alan said, giving Connor a hug goodbye and pat on the back. He winked at Indi, a sure sign of approval, as Connor and Kyle exchanged numbers. Indi even overheard them arrange to meet up to watch a football match – and she smiled to herself. The afternoon couldn't have gone better. Once outside he pulled Indi in for a tender kiss. 'That was lovely. Are you OK, though? I thought you looked a bit distant.'

She shook her head. 'It's silly. I was just thinking about how much my mum would've liked you. Flirted with you, probably, knowing her.'

He held her closely. 'I bet I would have loved her. I want to hear more about her. I know how much you miss her. I have to say I have a bit of a man-crush on your dad, though, what a legend! And Kyle is awesome. It just convinces me even more that you're the perfect girlfriend.'

Indi shot him a look of mock-horror. 'So I'm your girlfriend?'

He stared her straight in the eye, a look that made Indi's legs weak. 'If you want to be? I don't want to be with anyone else, Indi.'

She snaked her arms around his neck. 'Me either.'

Three weeks before the opening party of 360, Indi and Connor were frantically busy.

As co-owner, Connor's job was to keep Nicolas and the investors satisfied that everything was going according to plan, and to work closely with the manager of 360 he'd hired and the managers of Degree Hotel to make sure everything was in order. The launch party was a huge night, but it was up to Connor to ensure the club would be the best in London every night after that. He hired mixologists for the bar and brought in a luxury vodka brand to sponsor the launch party and create bespoke cocktails. He was constantly on his phone or on email and in and out of meetings, and Indi updated him frequently on how things were going. It was by far the biggest event she'd worked on, but she thrived on the challenge and loved every second of planning the launch and designing the entire look of the club with its 1920s theme.

Indi had commissioned a set designer to make a huge chandelier to be the centrepiece, hanging over the bar, with hundreds of droplets of Swarovski crystals. There was also the mammoth task of making sure plenty of celebrities and journalists were coming, and Indi had hired two interns whose sole job was to book cars to pick up and take home the glitterati. One diva reality TV star, Leonie Parr, said she'd only come if hair and make-up was provided. All the celebrities wanted to look camera-ready the minute they stepped out of their car, but most hired their own hair and make-up if they wanted it. Even the real A-listers like Tasha wouldn't make such demands but, as Indi knew, generally, the smaller the celebrity, the bigger their demands. But Leonie was dating a high-profile football player and had recently won *Celebrity Big Brother*, so the press attention she'd attract was huge. It was also the perfect opportunity to throw some work Hollie's way, and her friend was delighted with the gig.

Every member of the media was dying to get an exclusive invitation to the hottest new opening in town, and Indi was inundated with requests. In her own office, she and Ben whittled down the guest list.

'Obviously Sally from *Glamour* magazine, Jenni from the *Mail Online* and Claire from the *Evening Standard*,' said Ben, eyes fixed to a spreadsheet in front of him on the round white meeting table.

Indi sat opposite, pen in hand, and Starbucks iced latte in the other, ticking off and crossing out names. 'Miles Horner too,' she added. 'He's been emailing every day.'

Ben scrunched up his face. 'Desperado.'

'He's certainly persistent,' Indi sighed. 'But he has to be if he writes for a tabloid website, I suppose. And they get so many hits it would be brilliant exposure.'

Persistent was putting it mildly. Not only had Miles been hounding Indi for several VIP tickets to the 360 launch for his mates, he'd been begging her for a date as well. Indi had always brushed off his advances as a silly crush, but he'd certainly become more intense since she and Connor had become an official couple. Earlier that month, she'd run into Miles at another party and he'd tried to warn her off Connor. 'It's only because I care about you, Indi, but that man has got a reputation,' he'd said. Indi suspected that Miles didn't really care about anything except getting the latest scoop for his website. But, anyway, between Miles and Connor there was no contest. Miles was a boy, Connor was a man.

'I appreciate the concern, Miles, but I can look after myself,' she'd told him.

'It'll end in tears, Ind,' he sighed.

Indi contemplated this as Ben talked about the guest list. 'You're too soft on him, you know,' Ben said with raised eyebrows. 'He completely went behind your back with the Bella Hadid thing. You gave him a great story, above everyone other journo, and he still pasted a lie on to it. I know he's your mate, but I don't trust those tabloid hacks. Most of them would screw over their grandmother for an exclusive.'

'Miles hasn't got a grandmother.' Indi shrugged.

Ben lowered his eyes to her as she laughed. 'Don't worry about him, Ben, honestly. I can handle Miles Horner.'

'Just keep him away from Tasha Phelps,' Ben replied.

'Yeah, and the free bar!'

'Oh, Nicholas has sent more names for the list over, too. Who's Saskia Taylor?'

Indi recognised the name and filled Ben in. Saskia was prominent in the events world. She thought back to the clumsy woman who had knocked the tray of drinks over at The Square's summer party and had been so rude to her and Hollie. Nicolas had later told her that it was Saskia. Indi wondered what she was up to now as she rarely saw her out and about.

'She probably wants to come and check out the competition,' said Ben. 'See what the young blood is up to. Knock yourself out, babe. See how it's really done!'

Indi smiled, but she never liked the prospect of showing off. As far as she was concerned, there was more than enough room in London for plenty of event planners. If anything, Saskia could be someone great to know. They might even hit it off.

Chapter Nine

When Saskia breezed into her office at 10.30 a.m, Jo and Andrew were already at their computers. Saskia was of the 'old school' PR mentality that the working day didn't really start until mid-morning. Despite one too many glasses of wine last night at home, she was ready for a new day, and wearing her favourite bright red trouser suit and chunky silver bangles. 'What's news, guys?' she said, switching on her computer and glancing over the front pages of the newspapers that Andrew had laid out for her, as he did every morning. 'I see Tasha Phelps has made the cover of the *Daily Mirror* again. Are we any closer to signing the deal for her new sunglasses range?'

Saskia was desperate for that account. Ever since the humiliation of losing out on the 360 launch to that child Indigo Edwards, she was more motivated than ever to make sure she didn't miss out on anything else. The decline in business recently had meant that Saskia had had to let go of two senior members of Sass PR's staff. The company had retained some loyal, core clients – a skincare brand called Revival, the annual Dublin Fashion Awards and Essex Fashion Awards, and the odd party for a few older celebrities who Saskia had known from her wild noughties days. There could always be more work, however, and she relied on one-off launches, opening nights and glamorous events to bring in big bucks.

'Still no word from her manager,' replied Jo.

Saskia tutted. 'Have you tried Nicolas de Souza? He must have some influence and God knows he owes me a favour.'

Jo shook her head. 'No reply. But we've got some new pitches we're working on and Andrew has completely revitalised our Twitter and Instagram accounts.'

'OK, you need to give me another refresher lesson in all that, Andrew,' said Saskia, thinking how much time Millie spent on social media, and wondering whether she'd be impressed if her mum started following her on Instagram. 'Let me have a coffee and go over some emails and we'll run through everything. Andrew, darling, would you mind running to Starbucks for me?' She handed him a five-pound note. 'The usual: soya latte, extra hot, and a banana.'

Andrew obediently scuttled off. Saskia skimmed over her emails when one in particular caught her eye.

Hi Saskia,
Hope you're well. You may remember we met very briefly at The Square a few weeks ago and I've been meaning to get in touch since and properly

introduce myself. Please find attached an invitation for you and two guests to attend Degree Hotel's 360 club launch on 16 September. I would be honoured if you could attend and very much hope to meet you properly.

Very best wishes,
Indigo Edwards
Founder and Director, Glamour To Go Events

'That was nice of her,' Jo said after Saskia read the email aloud.

'Huh. So she can gloat over winning the account and rub it in my face,' Saskia replied bitterly. 'And three weeks before the event? It's either that I'm a last-minute thought or she's left all the invitations until this late. Either way, it's insulting.'

'Well you have to go regardless,' snapped Jo, impatient with her boss's childish attitude. 'It's the biggest launch of the year.'

Saskia sulked and returned to the newspapers. Underneath them was *Flash*, the weekly industry magazine for PR professionals. Right there on the front was a profile interview with Indigo. Saskia couldn't believe it. The headline screamed out: *Blue Steel: How Indigo Edwards is the toast of the town.*

Saskia was furious. Who *was* this girl? 'Just make sure we bag something brilliant before September, Jo. Indigo might be the new toast of the town, but I don't want her thinking for a second that she's any better than me. She's just a child who got lucky. I've been in this industry – this town – for decades!' She scowled. Who did Indigo Edwards think she was, anyway?

As the launch drew closer, Indi spent more time at the venue at the top of Degree Hotel, finalising plans with Ben. She had a walk-through with the security team she'd hired, going over where the entrances, exits and sealed-off VIP areas would go. Often Connor and Nicolas would be there to make sure everything was going according to plan and fitting in with the vision all three shared. Needless to say, Nicolas was thrilled at everything Indi had done. She and Connor were never touchy-feely in front of him, or anyone else for that matter, as they both hated the idea of looking unprofessional. But one early evening, after a soundcheck of the club's equipment, Ben and the music technicians had left and Connor and Indi found themselves alone. Indi stood at the bar, engrossed in a huge file of documents and spreadsheets, when she felt Connor's hands slide around her waist from behind and hug her closely to him, burying his face in her neck.

'I can't wait for this to be over so I can take you on holiday and have you all to myself,' he said softly, kissing her neck. 'Turn our phones off for a week,' he continued. 'Let a waiter bring us cocktails while I look at you in a bikini all day.'

Indi turned around to face him, wrapping her arms around his torso. 'Hmm, a holiday sounds nice. Although, knowing you, you'd have me naked the entire week.'

Connor groaned softly and hoisted Indi up on to the bar. 'Now that is something to think about,' he said, hands creeping under her summery red dress and reaching for her underwear.

'Connor, not here.'

'No one's here,' he replied. 'I locked up.'

Indi had to admit the danger turned her on, but not nearly as much as Connor did. As his fingers slipped inside her she bit her lip in pleasure and realised resistance was futile.

'Good thing we haven't got the security cameras installed yet,' joked Indi later as they walked hand in hand through the streets of Notting Hill, feeling extremely smug and satisfied. 'Which reminds me, we still need to get that done.'

'I'll sort it tomorrow,' he replied, attempting to hail a taxi. 'Right now I just want to get you home.' And he stopped in the street, kissing her firmly, and lifting her up with one strong arm. Indi giggled, but the moment was interrupted by a buzz from his trouser pocket. Connor jerked away and whipped out his phone, reading a text message. His face turned to stone.

'What's wrong?' she asked.

He dropped her hand and stormed up the street. 'Nothing, come on. Let's just go home.'

'Connor, what is it?'

He was still marching as she ran to keep up with him.

'Connor! What the hell is wrong with you? Stop right now and tell me what's going on.'

Connor halted and turned around. 'I'm sorry, Indi. It's just . . .'

'What?'

'Nothing. I'm sorry, really I am. Let's just go home.'

But she didn't move. 'Nope. I've had enough of this. Every time your phone goes off you get cold and distant. Unless it's a message from Tom – and I know when it's from Tom because it's generally a video of a bloody dog playing football that you find hilarious somehow – who the hell is texting and calling you to make you so angry? And don't tell me it's Eddie, because I'm not buying it.'

'Indi, let's not do this here. We're in the middle of the street.'

She was angry now. 'Oh, so it's fine to kiss me in the street and shag me in a bar? I'm not walking an inch until you tell me what's going on. Are you cheating on me, Connor? Is it another woman?'

Connor looked at the ground and said nothing. For a few seconds, Indi's heart froze over.

'I would never cheat on you, Indi,' he said sternly. Another pause, then he let out a sigh. 'It's Anja. Nothing is going on, I *swear*. I told you I broke up with her months ago and that was the truth. But she couldn't accept it. She rings me all the time. At night she gets drunk and calls me, crying, saying she loves me, or sends me messages saying what a dickhead I am. A few weeks ago she threatened to kill herself if I didn't speak to her.'

He held out his phone to Indi, who saw dozens of long blue blocks of texts on Connor's iMessages. 'See? I kept telling her it's over and that I am with you. Now I just ignore her, as anything I say gives her fuel, but it's getting completely out of control. Even when I switch my phone

94

off at night I wake up to messages. But I also feel guilty. I mean, if she did do something stupid, I'd never forgive myself.' Connor didn't just look irritated, he looked genuinely upset. 'She keeps saying how I ruined her life and used her. We went on a few dates over a couple of months. It wasn't anything. I never wanted to hurt her, I just thought it was a bit of fun.'

'Jesus, Connor, why didn't you tell me?'

'I just thought it would blow over. I try avoiding her. Like the night you and Hollie came to Print Room. I was dying to spend the evening with you, Indi, but couldn't deal with her evil eyes staring at us all night. She'd be raving with jealousy; she's jealous of you as it is. If I'm at Print Room I can generally get away with avoiding her, but then she gets drunk alone or with her model mates and the texts start. I feel sorry for her.'

Indi didn't. What the hell was Anja playing at? She knew Connor and Indi were an item. 'Do you want me to say something to her?' she asked.

'No, definitely not. It will just make her worse. I'll talk to her.'

'You need to, Connor. You need to tell her once and for all that you're with someone now and if she's going to keep working at Print Room then she needs to accept that.'

Connor looked uncomfortable. 'I know. I will, I promise.'

But the rest of the evening was filled with tension. It was the first time since Indi and Connor had become an item that they spent the night together and didn't have sex. Indi blamed it on a headache, but secretly she was still fuming that Connor hadn't been honest with her in the first place.

And as much as he tried to cuddle and assure her that nothing was going on with Anja, there was an uncomfortable feeling that she still couldn't shake. Was Miles right? Could she really trust Connor?

Chapter Ten

'I've got a surprise for us,' Connor said over coffee the next morning. Indi was exhausted and had slept in until nearly 11 a.m., by which point Connor had already played football with his mates and collected the Saturday newspapers, fresh coffee and muffins.

'Oh yeah?' she yawned, still unimpressed by last night's revelations. Her phone had died and she'd forgotten to charge it overnight, so she plugged it into the wall by Connor's kitchen table.

'Yep. I remembered how you said you'd always dreamt of a holiday to the Caribbean, soooo, how would you like to go to Saint Lucia? Just you, me, a beach, and flowing cocktails. My treat.' Connor bent forward to kiss Indi on the cheek and she caught a waft of his delicious scent. Fresh out of the shower and smelling of Bleu de Chanel body wash, he was dressed in jogging bottoms and a tight white shirt. Indi, wearing only his West Ham t-shirt, looked him up and down appreciatively and sipped her coffee.

Saint Lucia! She could think of nothing better than a hot holiday right now but, before she had a chance to reply, her iPhone woke up and started beeping furiously, alerting her that she'd got dozens of missed calls and unread messages.

'There's a couples-only hotel I know right on the beach,' he continued. 'All you have to do is decide when you want to go and pack a bag.'

But Indi wasn't listening. She read through the messages on her phone but it took her a minute to focus on what they were saying. 'Oh my God,' she exhaled.

'What's up?'

Now Indi was on the phone. 'Dad? I'm so sorry, my phone died and I've just switched it on. What happened? Is he OK? Where is he now?' A pause, as Indi listened intently to whatever Alan was saying. Her face had turned pale and she bit her lip in angst. 'I'm on my way.'

She hung up and dashed to Connor's bedroom. Connor followed and stood in the doorway as she scrabbled to get dressed. 'Kyle's been arrested for arson,' she told him. Her tone was matter-of-fact, but her face was etched with worry. 'There was a fire at his old school last night. It's not burnt down or anything, but there is considerable damage. A witness says she saw Kyle running away from the school.' Kyle had been in trouble with the police in the past for starting fights in his old school and, even once, threatening a teacher. That particular incident had been very soon after Lou died and he had clearly been lashing out. Plus, Indi knew that particular teacher was a real battleaxe and had probably provoked the vulnerable Kyle – his diagnosed behaviour problems and the fact that his mum had just died meant that he needed special treatment, but not everyone there had been prepared to give it to him. He hated school as a result and had had run-ins with some of his teachers, often getting into trouble. Even though that was years ago, the police probably thought he had every motive to start a fire back at the school. Indi knew he never would. Not in a million years.

'They came to my dad's late last night and searched the entire house, turning Kyle's room upside down and confiscating his phone and laptop,' she continued. 'Dad said they wrapped plastic bags over his hands and took him away. He's in a custody suite at Edmonton Police Station.' Indi's voice started trembling. 'My phone was off, Connor. Dad had been trying to ring me and my phone was off! What if something had happened to him? I wasn't there, Connor. I wasn't there for him!' She was crying now, hot tears spilling down her face as she threw items in her handbag and pushed past Connor, heading straight to the front door. Instantly Connor's arms were around her. 'It's going to be OK,' he said, but she wiped her face and pulled away. 'I have to go. Shit, my phone, it's going to die again any second.'

'I'll drive you, come on. You can charge your phone in my car.'

Connor raced through traffic. Indi stared anxiously out of the window, unable to stop fidgeting. She remembered Kyle telling her how difficult it had been for him to find a job with his behavioural problems. This could be seriously damaging for him. He must be so scared, she thought. And poor Alan must be going out of his mind with worry, too. Connor placed his hand on hers. 'It will be OK, I promise.' She was about to snap back at him – how could he possibly know that? – when her phone rang again. She answered instantly.

'Dad? Tell me. What? They can't do that, surely? Just sit tight, I'll be there soon.' She threw the phone down and held her head in her hands for a few moments, trying to compose herself. Connor waited for her to speak.

'Kyle had a screaming fit in his cell,' she said. 'I'm sure he would have told the police that he needed medication for his ADHD, but blatantly they didn't listen. I knew he'd be vulnerable in that confined space. It obviously got to him. Now they're not letting him out. They gave him a solicitor this morning who sat in with him on an interview and they're now saying they're keeping him for thirty-six hours.'

Indi did the maths in her head. Kyle had been arrested at eleven p.m. and held in custody from approximately two a.m., according to Alan, so he had already been detained for ten hours.

'The solicitor says there is nothing he can do and it's all perfectly legal. Dad thinks he is a useless lawyer. He's not helping him at all!'

Connor frowned. 'I think they can keep them up to twenty-four hours, but thirty-six sounds excessive.' Then he was typing furiously into his phone with one hand, the other on the wheel.

'What are you doing?' Indi asked.

Connor spoke urgently. 'Mark? It's me, mate. I need Gerald but his number is in my other phone. Can you phone him for me?' A pause. 'Right now. Like, *right* now.' Another pause. 'Edmonton Police Station. I'm on my way . . . Any minute now . . . No, not for me, it's . . . Just get here, will you, mate? OK, see you soon. Cheers.'

Indi looked at him, puzzled, but before she could find out what was going on Connor skidded up to the front of the police station. 'Go and see your dad. I'll park the car and be right in.'

Indi couldn't get inside fast enough. The police station was a long brick building with grey walls. It was a balmy August day outside but somehow the police station's reception was freezing. A coffee machine stood in one corner; there was also an interview room and a window counter. Indi assumed the cells were downstairs. Alan rushed over to her. His eyes were red and bleary from sleep deprivation and he looked overwhelmed with worry. Indi hugged him in silence for a few seconds, then pulled herself together and clicked into business mode. Now was not the time for her to lose it. 'Where's the solicitor?' she asked firmly.

'He's just gone but said he'll be back in a couple of hours. He said that the officers who interviewed Kyle told their superintendent that they believe Kyle should be detained for another twenty-four hours. I assume it's because of this fit, but he didn't hurt anyone! If only they'd talk to me more.'

'And have they found any evidence linking him to this fire?'

'Just the witness, the solicitor told me, who says she recognised him, but he was wearing blue jeans and a black hoodie jumper. It could have been anyone, for God's sake!

'Have you seen him?'

'No. He's over eighteen so they're not obliged to let me see him.'

'It must have been horrible when they came to the house, Dad. Jesus.'

'I was asleep, Kyle was watching telly. It was like a scene from a film when they led him away. All the neighbours were watching.'

'Don't worry about them. Was Kyle watching telly earlier when the fire took place?'

Alan shook his head forlornly. 'That's the problem. He went to the cinema alone and threw away the ticket before coming home. That would have been his perfect alibi.'

'Surely there are witnesses who can vouch for him? Why haven't they found them? Why haven't they asked?' Indi was furious. 'Where is the superintendent? I want to speak to him right now.' She marched to the front counter but she was told to sit quietly and that someone would be with them shortly. Huffing, Indi paced up and down while Alan sat, head in hands. Suddenly Connor burst through the door with two men. One looked very similar to Connor, with the same deep green eyes and dark features, but he was slightly bulkier and his dark hair was greying. The other man was tall and lanky, probably about fifty years old, with curly hair and a slight bald patch and glasses. He was carrying a briefcase.

'Where's the solicitor?' Connor asked Indi.

'I don't know. He's gone. Dad says he'll be back but we're waiting for the superintendent. What's all this?'

Connor motioned to the bulkier man. 'Indi, this is my brother, Mark.' The policeman, Indi remembered. Connor pointed to the tall, lanky man. 'And this is Gerald Mackover. He's worked with Mark on many cases and his firm represents my company, too. You can trust him. They're both here to help. If you need it, that is.'

Mark stepped in and placed a hand on Indi's shoulder. 'Gerald is the best lawyer I know.'

Indi and Alan looked at each other, stunned, before Indi turned to Connor. 'Oh, Connor, we can't afford—'

'Ms Edwards, we consider any friend of the Scott family a friend of ours.' This from Gerald. 'I won't charge you a penny for now and will give your brother my undivided attention. If it goes to court, we can come to some arrangement but, as I understand it, the boy hasn't even been charged, is that correct?'

Indi didn't know what to say so simply nodded. Gerald marched up to the counter and returned a few seconds later. 'The superintendent is coming out now.' Turning to Alan, he said: 'Mr Edwards? Would you like to tell me your version of events? And do you believe the boy has been treated fairly here?'

Alan sat down with Gerald and Mark, who both listened carefully as he spoke. Connor placed an arm around Indi. Two minutes later the superintendent appeared and

103

Gerald demanded to know why Kyle was still being detained.

'Those are not sufficient grounds for a thirty-six-hour detention,' he said firmly. 'I'm representing Kyle Edwards. The boy is on prescription medication, which you have ignored. I could sue you. You're to release him on bail at once.' The superintendent muttered and went back to speak to her interviewing officers. An hour later she returned to the group in reception, agreeing to let Kyle out on bail. She read out the terms.

'He's not to leave the country, be within 500 metres of the school, or have any contact with the witness, direct or indirect. Also, we're setting a curfew between eight a.m. and eight p.m., unless he works nights, which we don't believe is the case.' She glanced down at Kyle's notes and turned to Alan. 'He works part-time at your building company, sir, I believe?'

Alan was about to answer when Connor interjected. 'He's actually been hired to work as a full-time bartender at my new club, 360. It's opening in Notting Hill in two weeks and he needs to do several evenings' worth of training beforehand, so that curfew won't work. The contract is being drawn up as we speak. I can have it over to you by the end of the day if you need to see it.'

Indi was speechless. Connor was really putting his neck on the line to help Kyle. Gerald nodded and there was more talking. The superintendent agreed to lift the curfew, but Kyle was required to sign in at his local police station twice a week until further notice. Then he was free to go. By the time Kyle was actually released it had been four hours since Indi had arrived at the station and Kyle had been detained for fourteen. As he appeared in reception he looked completely deflated, wearing washed-out grey tracksuit bottoms and a t-shirt that the police had provided. They'd taken his own clothes to run tests on. Indi and Alan rushed to hug him. 'Let's get you home, son,' said Alan, holding back tears of relief at having his boy returned to him.

'How're you feeling now?' Indi handed her brother a cup of tea and settled on the sofa next to him as he aimlessly channel-surfed. Alan had retired to bed and she'd just got off the phone to Hollie, who had rung to offer her support. They had been home for hours, Kyle not saying a word. 'Look,' Indi continued, 'everything is going to be OK. You can start working at 360 soon and that'll give your employment record a great boost. We'll write your college application too. Last night and today will soon be forgotten.'

'How are we going to write a college application, Indi? They took my laptop, remember? After I was fucking framed for something I didn't do!' He was shouting now, hands clenched into fists, but Indi didn't flinch. He had every right to be irate. She let him get it all out. 'Do you have any idea what I've been through? Having my room turned upside down, arrested in front of all the neighbours? They'll dine out on this for weeks. I didn't do anything wrong!'

'I know you didn't. There's no evidence. They've got nothing to go on and we've got the best lawyer on the case. I promise, this will pass soon.'

'Easy for you to say,' he spat back. As much as Kyle loved his big sister and knew she meant well, the last thing he wanted right now was a pep talk.

Kyle sank into the sofa and closed his eyes. Indi could tell that he was thoroughly exhausted but doubted he'd be able to sleep. This time yesterday he had been here, at home on the sofa, when the doorbell had rung and he had found himself facing a team of policemen. Indi shuddered at the thought. It was enough to make her feel terrified; she could only imagine how frightened Kyle would have been. At that moment, Alan's house phone rang and Indi rushed to the kitchen to pick it up.

'You won't believe it,' Indi ran back into the room with a grin on her face. 'That was Mark, Connor's brother. He's been working on your case all day with Connor and Gerald. They asked around all the shops in town to see if anyone recognised you and could come forward to provide an alibi. At the cinema, three attendants confirmed you were there last night. Why they had to do the police's work for them, I have no idea. But they also got hold of CCTV footage from the petrol station opposite the cinema, showing you there at the exact time the witness claimed she saw you running away from the school! Gerald reckons he can get the charges dropped! I mean, it's not certain, but it's a massive step forward.'

Kyle leaped up from the sofa and hugged his sister. 'I can't believe they'd do that for me. I don't even know how to thank Connor.'

'Well, the 360 job still stands, so I say you go to training next week and be the best damn bartender that ever was.

And we *will* get you into college next year. That I can promise you. I'm going to wake up Dad and tell him the good news.' Indi made for the stairs then hesitated and turned back to Kyle. 'Everything is going to happen for you now, bro. Things will only get better.'

Chapter Eleven

Connor cracked open a bottle of Beck's and slumped on his sofa, resting his laptop on his knees. It was Saturday night, one week before the 360 launch, and he would have loved it if Indi were with him for a cosy night in, but she was with her family and there was no question that was where she needed to be. The past week had been a whirlwind. The police had finally stepped up and accepted Kyle's alibis and even found the real culprit – the arsonist was an embittered student who'd been expelled for drug-dealing and wanted revenge. The charges against Kyle were quickly dropped and Indi had gone to the station with him earlier that day to collect his phone, laptop and clothes. She phoned Connor frequently to update and thank him for everything he'd done, saying that her family didn't know how to repay him. But he assured her that he was only too happy to step in. It was the least he could do for the girl he loved. And, though he hadn't yet mustered up the courage to tell her, he really did love her. He'd realised it the day Kyle had been arrested. Connor could think of nothing else except doing whatever he could to help the Edwards family. He'd offered to go to the station with Indi earlier but she maintained that she had it under control.

Connor decided to make the most of his day alone and hit the gym after playing football with his mates. He ran on the treadmill and lifted weights before coming home to work. There were the account books of Print Room to check and dozens of emails to answer and queries to deal with about 360. There was a business trip to Miami coming up that Connor needed to plan, too.

Connor's flat was in Hoxton, just a short walk from Print Room. Since he was a teenager, his dream had been to own a bachelor pad, and the style was exactly how he wanted it – clean and minimal. He loved to tease Indi about her own living room, with magazines scattered everywhere and cushions in clashing colours.

Connor rarely stopped working. Before Indi swept him off his feet, his weekends had generally consisted of playing football, watching football, visiting his mum and hanging out with Tom, but he always factored in a few hours of work. And dating, of course. Connor wasn't a particular fan of one-night stands, but he found it so hard to resist a girl who threw herself at him, as they frequently did. Truth be told, he liked the idea of having a girlfriend, someone to spoil and care for, but he got bored easily. He'd usually date a girl on and off for a month or two before growing tired of her and engrossing himself in his business, much to their annoyance. The best-looking girls tended to be quite dull, he realised. Or, worse, clingy. But not Indi. Not only was she drop-dead gorgeous, she was also smart, funny, and had her own thing going on. She never hassled or nagged him. But, at the same time, Connor knew she wouldn't put up with any crap from him, a quality he found unbelievably sexy. And he got the impression that she rarely showed vulnerability to anyone except Hollie, yet he'd seen another softer, more authentic side to her over the past few weeks and it only intrigued him further. He wanted to be with Indi all the time.

His thoughts turned to Kyle and what a great kid he was. Connor was only too happy to give him a job if it would help him. Though he'd never known his own father, he and Mark were incredibly close, and he liked the thought of having a little brother-figure to mess around with. He texted Indi again to check she was OK and tell her he couldn't wait to see her. Then his imagination went into overdrive, thinking exactly what he'd like to do if Indi were with him now . . .

His thoughts were interrupted by the shrill ringing of his phone. 'Hiya, Mum,' he answered. 'You all right?'

'Hello, sweetheart. How are you? What news from Indigo?' Marion hadn't even met Indi yet, but knew every stage of her family's ordeal from her sons and was deeply concerned for her.

'She's fine, thanks, Mum. Gerald to the rescue, as usual.'

'The poor family,' she said. 'Well, it's over, thank goodness. She's lucky to have you.' Connor was always a hero in Marion's eyes. 'I've got some pasta on the go if you'd like to pop over?'

110

Connor glanced at his watch. Six p.m. He'd been working solidly since midday and hadn't eaten anything except a protein smoothie. 'Sounds perfect, thanks, Mum. Want me to bring anything?' It was a ritual when Connor arranged to go to his mum's house that he'd ask whether he should bring anything; she'd say no, and he'd turn up with some sort of treat anyway, such as a bottle of wine, chocolates, flowers or bubble bath. There was only one woman in Connor's life that he cared about more than Indi, and that was his mum.

Marion always put her sons' needs above her own. She was from Donegal in Ireland originally, but had come over to London in her early twenties with friends. She had met Connor's father, George, and had quickly became pregnant with Mark. Connor had followed five years later. One day, George had gone out to buy cigarettes and never returned. Having babies out of wedlock disgraced Marion's family back in Ireland, so she stayed in London working two jobs to support her family. The first thing Connor and Mark did when they started making money was to buy her new furniture and make sure she never had to spend a penny on them again. His past had instilled a strong work ethic and fierce independence in Connor. The reason he had gone through so many women wasn't just that he tended to grow bored of them, it was a fear of abandonment. He made sure he left before anyone else had a chance to, and felt, deep down, that if women never got too close to him, he'd always be protected.

After thirty-seven years in London, Marion still hadn't lost touch with her roots; her voice was soft but had a strong Irish accent. 'Just bring yourself, sweetheart. Mark, Lauren and the kids are here too. And can we expect Indigo as well? Sorry, Indi. Such a beautiful name. Is she a beautiful girl, Connor? I bet she is.'

Connor laughed. Marion would adore Indi. 'She's with her family now, Mum, but of course you'll meet her soon. And she's the most beautiful woman I've been out with.'

'Well, I wouldn't know, would I? You never bring them home to meet me.'

'This one's special, Mum. I'll see you soon.'

He checked his watch again and had an idea. He picked up his phone and called Indi. She picked up after two rings. 'I was just thinking about you.'

'All dirty I hope!' he replied cheekily. 'How are you? How's Kyle doing?'

Indi sighed with relief. She was so glad this week was over and she could start relaxing around Connor again. She'd been so preoccupied, but realised now how much she missed him. 'He's doing great, thanks to you. He's completely shattered, so just went to watch a film in bed. He didn't even want me to make him dinner. But he can't wait to start bartender training on Monday night. The job is exactly what he needs, Connor. He'll meet new people and have some fun. I've not seen him so excited for years.'

'I'm happy to help, honestly. Hell, I need more staff I can trust, so he's doing me a favour. And Alan, is he OK?'

Indi glanced at the armchair next to her where her dad had dozed off. 'Yeah, he's good. It's just me sitting here, bored, watching some crappy drama on telly.'

'Fancy some dinner?'

Indi paused. She had planned to stay at her dad's in case he or Kyle needed moral support, but they were both fast asleep and seemed perfectly all right now. 'What did you have in mind?' she asked.

Connor was already getting in his car. 'It's a surprise. I'll pick you up in half an hour.'

An hour later, Connor pulled up outside Marion's two-bedroom semi-detached house in Leyton clutching a bottle of her favourite white wine. 'I wish you'd let me go home to change,' pleaded Indi. She was dressed in blue ripped jeans and a pink V-neck t-shirt and a faded black leather jacket. Hardly the outfit she'd planned to wear to meet Connor's mum!

'I told you, my mum won't notice or care,' assured Connor. 'Besides, you always look gorgeous. She just really wants to meet you, and I really want you to meet her.'

'You sure she won't mind me just turning up?' Indi felt nervous, but Connor couldn't wait to bring her into his life.

'Last minute and informal is actually pretty perfect,' he said, planting a kiss on her cheek and letting them into his mum's house with his own set of keys. 'Mum! I'm home!' he called.

A familiar smell of garlic wafted through the hallway, and the elder of his nieces, Izzy, ran towards him. 'Uncle Connor!' He scooped her up in his arms.

Lola, the toddler, shuffled behind and greeted Connor by attaching herself to his leg. 'Herro, Uncle Connor!' she shouted. Connor introduced the girls to Indi and they were completely mesmerised by her.

'Are you a model?' asked Izzy, her bright green eyes fixed on Indi.

'Er, no, but that's very sweet of you to say! I like your pretty dress.'

'Will you plait my hair, Indi?' asked Lola, but before Indi could object, Izzy announced that Indi had to do her hair first because she was the oldest and a squabble ensued.

'Sorry, but I think they're quite taken with you,' laughed Connor.

At that, Marion appeared in the small hallway, but stopped in her tracks when she saw Indi. 'Connor Scott! Don't you tell me you've brought home this beautiful girl and I haven't even had a chance to do my hair?' Marion was tiny at five foot three inches; she was wearing blue leggings and a pink jumper with rolled-up sleeves underneath an apron. Her black hair, peppered with grey, was tied into a ponytail, and a pair of glasses rested on her head. Connor gave her a huge hug and kissed her cheek.

'I'm so sorry to intrude,' gushed Indi. 'Connor didn't tell me where we were going until we were actually on our way and, well, I really hope it's no trouble.'

But Marion had already hugged Indi warmly and led her into the living room. It was lovely and cosy, with cream carpet, bright yellow sofas, and a wooden dining table laid with plates, cutlery and a huge steaming bowl of spaghetti. Mark and his wife Lauren were already sitting down drinking wine, but bounced up when Indi came in and greeted her warmly, Lauren with an affectionate hug and Mark with a polite kiss on the cheek, though Indi gave him a huge hug and thanked him once again for everything he'd done to help Kyle. Marion ushered everyone to sit down at the table, while she settled Izzy and Lola on the sofa and made them mini-bowls of pasta.

'Mum, sit down, will you?' said Connor, beckoning his mum to a chair. Turning to Indi, 'She always does this, you know. Won't feed herself until we're all fed.'

True to his word, Marion made sure everyone had food and the adults all had wine before she finally took off her apron to join them. Over dinner, she and Lauren practically fell over themselves to ask Indi questions. Where did that stunning name come from? Tell us about your job? Where did you grow up?

'Mum, leave her alone,' laughed Connor, even though he knew it was no use telling the women in his family what to do. He glanced at Mark, who laughed and shook his head, knowing that fact all too well himself. Mark was the strong and silent type. Fortunately Indi didn't seem to mind the interrogation, and was her usual enchanting self.

Lola and Izzy begged Indi to read them a bedtime story before Mark and Lauren drove them back to their family home, just ten minutes' drive away, but Lauren insisted it was way past their bedtime and bundled her family into the car, hugging Indi as she left. 'Thank God he met you.' She winked. 'Next time I'll get Mark to babysit while we have a girls' night out. All my friends are boring mums and, from the sounds of it, Hollie is someone I have to meet!'

Indi laughed. 'Any time! And so lovely to meet you, too. See you soon, I hope.'

Connor and Indi finally left at around eleven p.m.,

Marion showering them both with kisses and making them promise to come back soon.

'Well, they're in love with you, but that's hardly a surprise,' Connor said in the car. 'Thanks for coming tonight, Ind. I'm sorry for putting that on you last minute, but I was so desperate for them to meet you. I'm not too much of a dick, am I?'

'They're amazing, all of them,' replied Indi. 'We've both met each other's families now, so we really are a proper couple! Scared yet?'

Connor took her hand and kissed it. 'Happier than ever.' He looked into Indi's huge blue eyes and was about to tell her that it wasn't only his family who'd fallen in love with her, but something in Connor hesitated. He'd never said the Three Big Words to any woman. It wasn't that he doubted his feelings for Indi. On the contrary, he loved her more and more every day. Then why couldn't he just say it? What was holding him back? Instead, he gave her a cheeky smile and came up with another, much safer sentence. 'Now let's get home so we can go to bed.'

Unfortunately for Connor, sex was out of the question as, back at his flat, she fell asleep the second her head hit the pillow. Connor was about to crawl in next to her when his phone rang. Indi was in such a deep sleep she didn't even stir. Connor crept into his living room. Normally he ignored Anja's calls, but this time decided to pick up. 'What do you want? And it's Saturday night, shouldn't you be working?'

116

But Anja was crying down the phone. 'I just want to talk, Connor, please.'

'You always just want to talk,' he snapped back, emphasising the last four words. 'But last time we met up, you threw yourself at me. How many times can I tell you, Anja? It's over. I'm with Indi. She knows you've been messaging me almost every day now. If she knew I came to meet you the other week, she'd go completely ballistic.'

She really would. With everything going on with Kyle, Connor figured the last thing Indi needed to hear was how Anja had tried to seduce him, so he had kept the incident to himself. He continued ranting down the phone, but in a whisper so that Indi wouldn't wake up. 'I'm sorry I hurt you, Anja, but how many times can I apologise? I don't know what else I can do. This has to stop. The drunk phone calls, the messages. I think you need professional help.' And with that, he hung up. He'd tried being polite. He'd tried being kind. Now, he had to take Indi's advice and be firm with Anja, no matter what the consequences.

Chapter Twelve

It was the night of 360's launch party at Degree Hotel, Notting Hill. Indi and her team – Ben and several experienced interns she'd hired – had been at the venue all day, but the first guests were due to arrive any minute and Indi was frantically getting ready in a suite Nicolas had arranged for her so she could shower and get ready on site, and sleep there instead of going home. Before rushing to Leonie Parr's house to do her make-up, Hollie came to the hotel early to help Indi get ready. 'Do you really have to wear this ugly headpiece?' she asked with a look of disgust. 'It hardly screams "glamour" and completely ruins the look I'm going for with you.'

'It screams "professional", though, Holl, and I need it to keep in contact with Ben and the security all night.'

Hollie sniffed and made the finishing touches to Indi's bold red lips. 'Well, I still prefer you without. Now then, if I do say so myself, I've accomplished a work of art here. Connor will *die* when he sees you!'

Indi smiled. Hollie certainly knew how to bring out her best features. She'd given Indi fresh, dewy skin with a light foundation and subtle shimmer, thick black mascara to open up her already big and glowing blue eyes, and bold red lipstick which gave Indi a bee-stung pout that Rosie Huntington-Whiteley would be jealous of. Indi tonged her hair and styled it to the side so it cascaded down one shoulder. Her dress was spectacular. Pulling out all the stops and dragging Hollie to Selfridges earlier that week, she'd splashed out on a House of CB floor-length sleeveless silver gown with a plunging neckline. The look was vampy, gorgeous, retro glamour. 'Thanks, Holl. Now I'd better get down there. Wish me luck!'

'Good luck, babe, make it a night to remember!'

'Tasha! This way, Tasha! Over here!' Flash bulbs popped furiously and photographers yelled the model's name as she posed casually on the red carpet, expertly turning this way and that and blowing a kiss to the cameras. Nicolas waited patiently at her side, shaking hands with guests as they arrived. Tasha's model friends attracted the same attention, as did the slew of actors, footballers and TV personalities who graced the red carpet, sending the photographers into overdrive.

The red carpet had been laid out in the lobby, with a backdrop screen boasting logos for 360 and the vodka brand that was sponsoring the party. Journalists had arrived early to mark their territory on the carpet and interview the stars as they walked by. Several lifts were situated in the lobby, but the two at the end flew directly and exclusively up to 360 on the twentieth floor. Here, burly security guards stood with clipboards. Famous guests were ushered in with more security, and non-famous guests had to show their golden invitation or be ticked off the guest list. Nicolas was adamant that 'no blaggers' should be allowed, and he had given Indi a huge budget for security. Getting celebrities to an A-list event such as this was a military operation, and Indi had hired several more interns to act as chaperones on the red carpet, while Ben had the essential and enormous task of overseeing car bookings. Once the celebrity was safely in their car and en route to the venue, the driver would text Ben, and then alert him once again as the car approached the carpet so Ben could make sure there was a chaperone to walk them through.

As the lift doors opened to 360, guests were greeted to incredible views of west London and beyond through floor-to-ceilings windows. Waiters in white jackets held trays of champagne and bespoke vodka, gin and elderflower cocktails. Cream leather sofas and gold tables were dotted by the windows, and the ceiling was shiny gold, too. Keeping with the 1920s theme, low-hanging chandeliers hung everywhere. The huge circular gold bar stood in the centre of the room, surrounded by cream leather retro bar stools. The enormous Swarovski centrepiece hung above it and Davidas's flower-domes sat on every table. Waitresses in flapper dresses circulated the party with trays of mouth-watering canapés – lobster rolls, salmon on wafer-thin seaweed crackers, aubergine and goat's cheese pastries, tiny doughnuts dusted with flower petals and sugar-coated pear served with caramelised walnuts. Everything was opulent, rich, elegant and extremely glamorous. But Indi had ensured there were elements of fun, too. In one corner stood a photo booth and a box of 1920s props, such as feather boas, top hats, gloves and wacky, oversized sunglasses. If there was one thing party revellers loved, it was playing dress-up and posting pictures of themselves on Instagram and Snapchat.

Indi circled the venue to make sure every single aspect was going according to plan and under control, stopping to greet her guests and thank them for coming. She'd been so occupied she had barely spoken to Kyle all night, he was busy behind the bar, mixing up cocktails or chatting up pretty girls. She dashed over.

'How's it going, bruv?' she yelled over the music. Kyle swept to the end of the bar so they could talk a little more easily.

'This is mad! You've done a proper good job here, Ind.'

'You think so?'

'Oh yeah! All my mates are going to be well jealous!'

'You managing all the cocktails, OK? I know it's a lot to learn. Are the other bartenders being nice to you?'

Kyle laughed. 'Yes, Mum. All the other boys in the sandpit are playing with me.'

Indi softly punched her brother in the arm and they both laughed, then Kyle's eyes widened. 'Woah! I wouldn't mind playing with her for a bit.'

Indi turned to see who he was talking about and her smile dropped. Anja sauntered past the bar and had the nerve to wink at Kyle, who beamed as if all his Christmases had come at once. She certainly looked beautiful in her tiny black sequined dress, which left nothing to the imagination.

'Urgh, Kyle! She's way too old for you and a complete nut job. Stay well away.'

'Whatever, sis. Listen, I'd better get back. Bars getting pretty jammed.' He kissed his sister affectionately on the cheek. He seemed completely in his element in this job.

Indi greeted a few more guests and spied Nicolas, in a typically jolly mood, talking to the PR and ex-It Girl, Saskia Taylor, who looked polished in a loud pink trouser suit. Indi started to make her way over to introduce herself properly to Saskia, but Connor intervened and stole her away for a kiss. All night he'd been equally busy mingling with guests, shaking hands with investors and business associates or talking to Eddie, who he'd moved over from Print Room to manage 360 as well, but every chance he got he tried to take Indi into a quiet corner.

'You look unbelievable,' he told her. Connor looked undeniably handsome in a perfectly cut grey chequered three-piece suit, white shirt and tie. Knowing Connor, he would have had it tailored at Savile Row or ordered from Hugo Boss. His style was simple but expensive. Indi couldn't resist kissing him. 'You scrub up pretty well yourself! But stop trying to grab my waist, I've got to enchant my guests!' She gave him another quick kiss and left him smiling. It was then she noticed Tasha sauntering towards her. The women greeted each other with a warm hug. Tasha was accompanied by an extremely attractive group of actors and models. Indi recognised one as the handsome British actor Elliot Blake, who was famous for starring roles in gritty British gangster films. Tasha insisted Indi join them at their table for a glass of champagne. Indi normally shied away from drinking at her biggest events, but one glass surely wouldn't hurt, and she didn't want to seem rude to Tasha.

'Fabulous party, honey! Have you met everyone? It's extra celebrations tonight as Elliot has just been cast as the lead in the new Guy Ritchie film.' Tasha made introductions and Indi blushed as she felt Elliot's gaze rest on her for a few seconds. She could see why his acting career was taking off: he had an incredible body, handsome face, and she'd seen him in a few films – he could actually act, too. He'd even had a short-lived role on *Game of Thrones* as an evil and philandering prince. Indi and Hollie had swooned over him, as *Game of Thrones* was one of their favourite shows.

'Nice to meet you, Indigo.' He smiled cheerily at her. He seemed genuinely nice. 'This is officially my new favourite club. I'm supposed to be organising a stag do for a producer I know; it would be great to do it here if you'd organise?'

'Sure!' she replied, mind whirling on ideas already.

'Nicolas is milling about talking to people, but he told me to congratulate you and that you must relax and enjoy yourself,' said Tasha, pouring Indi a drink. Indi chatted happily to the group, but her smile dropped when she saw Anja stroll past her and give her a patronising smile. Indi couldn't manage a smile back, so turned her attention to the group again. Tasha had clocked her expression.

'Urgh, Anja Kovac. My friend saw her at a casting last

123

week and said she was a total bitch – rude to all the other models but sucking up to the casting director.'

'Hollie got a bitchy vibe off her too,' replied Indi. 'I tried giving her the benefit of the doubt, but since she's continually trying to fuck my boyfriend, it's hard not to hate her.' It was an unusually sharp comment from Indi, who was normally the epitome of calm and reason. She remembered that she'd eaten nothing but a slice of toast hours ago, and the champagne had gone straight to her head.

'She *what*?' exclaimed Tasha. Indi filled her in on the constant messages to Connor. When she finished, Tasha was gawping. 'So, she's a stalker as well as a cow. Oh God, speaking of stalkers, here comes your favourite journalist.'

Indi turned to see Miles making a beeline for their table. 'Aw, he's an old friend, and not too bad, I promise. Can he have a drink with us? I promise, if he's inappropriate I'll throw him out personally.'

Elliot leant over and joined their conversation. 'Oh, I know Miles. He's all right. Did a profile on me for News Hub when I was starting out, and no other journalists were interested. I'll keep his prying eyes away from you, Tash, don't worry!'

Tasha shrugged. 'Fine, as long as he behaves himself.'

Indi beckoned Miles over. 'Great party, Ind,' said Miles, sitting down at once. He actually looked quite dapper, Indi thought, in a black suit and black shirt. His normally messy hair was slicked back with gel.

'Very smart, Miles. How many glowing stories are you going to put up on News Hub about my party, then?'

'I'm still hoping to go with the headline: "Gorgeous events planner says yes to date with tabloid hack",' he said with a grin.

'Oh my God, do you ever give up?'

He stared at her. 'Indi, you know I've fancied you since the first day we met. Connor may have more money and better suits than me, but I knew you in Fresher's Week when you drank pints of cider and WKD and were sick on your shoes outside the Walkabout bar. And I *still* fancy you, so if that isn't real love, I don't know what is!'

Indi held her hand to her face. 'Ha! Oh God, cringe!'

A few minutes later, Miles and Elliot were deep in conversation about Elliot's new movie and Tasha seemed at ease, so Indi decided to check in on Ben to make sure everything was OK down on the red carpet.

'Everyone's in now and we've closed the carpet, Ind,' he told her. 'Now it's just a matter of relaxing for a few hours before making sure all the cars arrive whenever the celebs want to leave, but we've got that more than under control here. Just enjoy yourself.'

'Thanks, Ben. I'll stay upstairs and do another circuit of the party to make sure everyone is happy.'

The party was in full swing. Ella Eyre had just finished her acoustic set to raucous applause and now one of the members of the famous dance producers Rudimental had taken to the DJ decks. Leonie Parr and her footballer boyfriend were all over each other, much to the delight of the photographers, and their table was packed with other celebrities. Indi glanced around and couldn't see Connor anywhere, but the club was packed with five hundred guests so she just assumed he was mingling. Indi checked in with all the house photographers to make sure they were getting plenty of pictures of everyone, and did a round of the other journalists to make sure they had plenty of positive news to write about. Then it was a quick dash to the ladies to touch up her lipstick.

Coming out of the toilet, however, she came upon a sight that made her heart stop. Connor, standing against the wall, and Anja quite literally throwing herself against him, forcing a kiss on his lips. Connor pulled away, looking gobsmacked.

'What the *fuck*?' screamed Indi.

Anja ran off. Connor rushed to Indi and held each of her arms. 'Indi, listen to me. We were talking and she just threw herself at me. I mean, you saw that, right?'

Indi had seen, but she was still livid. Had Anja made a move because he'd led her on somehow? She stormed off but Connor chased after her, grabbing her hand to make her stop. 'Sweetheart, I'm sorry. You must have seen, I pulled her away from me the second she came on to me.'

But Indi still couldn't shake the image from her head. It might have just been for a second, but seeing Anja and Connor kissing right there in front of her had made her feel nauseous. She couldn't look at him.

'I'm sorry,' he pleaded again. 'You know what she's like.'

'Then why the fuck were you talking to her, Connor?'

'She came up to me and apologised! She said she knew you and I were together; the next thing I knew she was throwing herself at me. Literally! She's off her face on something.'

126

Indi looked down at her phone. There was a text from Tasha: *Hey hun, we're all going off to The Square. There's a car outside. Miles and Elliot here. Wanna come? Meet in lobby now if so.*

Indi replied instantly. *I'm coming down now.* She was sick of being proper, sensible Indi. She'd worked her arse off for months getting this party together; it was a major success and Ben had everything under control. She wanted to let her hair down and not deal with any stupid Connor/ Anja drama. And, as amazing as the last few months had been, she didn't need to be with Connor every second. She had been an independent, single girl for years beforehand, after all.

'OK, Connor, whatever. It's just a whole lot of shit on a night that's a huge deal for me. I just want to go out with my friends and forget work and what I just saw.'

'OK, I'll come with you.'

'No. I don't want to talk about it or think about it tonight, so I think we should just do our own thing and catch up tomorrow.' Connor looked hurt but she stood her ground. 'I'll call you tomorrow.'

'Indi, you're upset. I don't like the thought of you—'

'For God's sake, Connor, I don't need you to look after me! I was fine before you came along and I'm fine for a night without you.' She knew she was snapping at him, but didn't care. That champagne really had gone to her head.

He was pissed off too now. 'Fine. Just at least text me later to let me know you're home safely, will you?'

'Fine,' she muttered on her way to the lift. As the door opened, she came face to face with Saskia, returning to the party after nipping outside for a cigarette. Saskia looked

Indi up and down and pursed her lips. 'Ah, Indigo Edwards, isn't it?'

'Yes, hi, Saskia.' The timing made Indi more annoyed. Half an hour ago she would have thrived on networking, but she *really* wasn't in the mood for a meet-and-greet right now.

'What a delightful party,' said Saskia. The comment was tinged with sarcasm. 'A great effort, though with all the money Nicolas threw at it, I'm sure it didn't need much planning.'

The passive-aggression didn't go unnoticed. Indi was at boiling point as it was and wasn't about to tolerate this stuck-up attitude. 'Actually, Saskia, it's been months in planning, but maybe you've been so out of touch you've forgotten what it takes to put on an event of this magnitude. Excuse me.' And with that, Indi stormed into the lift and slammed the lobby button, leaving Saskia speechless. All she wanted to do was get the hell out of 360.

Chapter Thirteen

Indi didn't know how many times her phone had rung. Half asleep, she had swiped the red 'cancel call' button every time. At 11 a.m. she finally rose with a yawn and looked at the missed calls. Six from Connor, two from Hollie, one from her dad. Bleary-eyed, and with a pounding headache, she dialled her dad immediately. 'What's happened, is Kyle all right?'

'He's fine, love. Are *you* all right?'

Indi stepped out of the king-sized bed and into the en suite of her hotel room. She was wearing an old t-shirt of Connor's she'd taken to sleeping in every night. 'Oh God,' she said out loud as she clocked her own reflection in the bathroom mirror. Her hair was wild and curly, and dried mascara was clumped to her lashes and smudged all around her eyes. 'I'm fine, Dad, why? Well, apart from the raging hangover and fact that I slept in my make-up.' She yawned again.

'Ah. You haven't seen the papers.'

Indi was so hung-over she'd momentarily forgotten that last night had been the biggest event of her career to date. Slowly, a succession of dramatic memories unfolded in her mind . . . Connor and Anja kissing, the run-in with Saskia, storming out, an after-party in The Square's hotel penthouse, lots of dancing and a whole lot of vodka. Indi barely remembered her taxi ride back to the suite Nicolas had booked for her at Degree, but she doubted it was before four a.m.

'They have written about the party, haven't they?' she asked with a mouthful of toothpaste. If there wasn't a smidge of coverage about the club, Nicolas would hit the roof.

'I think you'd better see for yourself, love.'

Indi spat out her toothpaste. This didn't sound good. 'Dad, please tell me this cloak-and-dagger routine is a ruse and you phoned to tell me the club landed a front-page scoop saying it was the greatest party of fashion week? There were so many journos there it must have got *some* press? In fact I remember Ben phoning me to tell me he stayed until the last guest left and there was no drama, and I've got a text from Kyle saying the night went brilliantly.'

Alan cleared his throat. 'The club is on the front page all right, sweetheart. Of the *Sun*. And so are you. It suggests that you're . . . getting intimate with some married actor called Elliot Blake. You're coming out of the club with your arms around each other.'

Indi squinted as she had flashbacks of leaving 360. She had been so upset; Elliot had put his arms around her as the group left the hotel. Of course paparazzi were waiting outside, Indi had made sure they would be, but to take pictures of the famous people, not her. There had been so many flashbulbs going she'd assumed they were for Tasha. '*Intimate?* For God's sake. We were just leaving the club. It was nothing. I don't even know the guy.' She spared a thought for Connor and how furious he must be. Her hangover really wasn't in the mood for another row with him. 'I'll ring you later, Dad.'

'OK, sweetheart. Take care of yourself. If there's no truth to it, then it will be forgotten by tomorrow. What is it they say? Today's newspaper, tomorrow's fish 'n' chip paper?'

As soon as Indi hung up she flipped open her laptop and scanned the news, knowing that anything from the papers would be online. Sure enough, on the *Sun*'s homepage was a picture of Elliot leaving Degree, arms protectively around Indi. She was tucked into him. It looked intimate but, at the time, Indi had been so overwhelmed by all the paps that Elliot momentarily drew her into him. It was for a second but, of course, it was the shot they went with. The headline above screamed 'El of all right!' The story explained that Elliot – married, who knew?! – and the 'brunette beauty' had been partying at 360 most of the night, 'getting very close, according to a friend', before heading back to an after-party at The Square. It didn't even mention that Tasha, Miles or anyone else from their group were with them. Indi scanned through News Hub, the website Miles worked at. They had the same story, credited to the *Sun*. In fact, the story had reached most of the gossip sites. Miles wouldn't have tipped off the *Sun*.

He'd have wanted to break such a story himself and, besides, he might have an ambitious streak, but he would never screw her over like that. Thankfully Leonie Parr had made headlines as well, as had a number of the other star guests, but the 360 coverage was overwhelmingly swayed towards Indi and her apparent 'close friendship' with Elliot. She needed some reassurance, so she called the person she always went to in a crisis.

'Holl? Have you seen the papers? I look like a total slut! I just met that guy that night, I don't even know him!'

'Hey! I tried to phone you this morning. Oh my God, Indi, you're famous!'

'I don't want to be famous! Especially for cosying up to a married man, even though that's nowhere near the truth.' She brought Hollie up to speed with last night's events. As usual, Hollie saw the best in the situation.

'Babe, calm down. Everyone knows Elliot Blake is a massive player and cheats on his wife all the time. It will be another girl next week and, besides, this is amazing coverage for 360. It's mentioned everywhere, and have you read the story on News Hub? They say it's the best club in London. Oh man, I wished I'd been there, but those girls took so long with their make-up I was completely shattered and it was all the way over in Essex, so took me hours to get home.'

'I wish you'd been there too, Holl. And Connor has phoned me six times already, probably to break up with me.' Indi was dreading that call.

'It serves Connor right for being such a prat,' argued Hollie. 'He should stay away from Anja, who by the way I always knew was a massive bitch. Are you at the flat? Why don't I come round and we can order pizza and watch movies all day?'

That sounded like complete heaven to Indi, but she had fires to put out first. 'Thanks, babe. But I'm still at Degree. I'm going to get myself together, speak to Ben, Connor, Nicolas, and do something about this hangover. Come over this afternoon?'

'Perfect. You know my fail-safe cure – two paracetamol, salt and vinegar crisps and a Diet Coke. And, Ind? Don't worry. It's just tabloid rumours and you did an amazing job.'

'Thanks, Holl, call you later.'

No sooner had she hung up than Ben phoned. Just like Hollie, he assured Indi that all press was good press. 'Elliot is big news at the moment because he's just been cast in that Guy Ritchie film, and any small story about him, they're going to blow up,' he said. 'All the photos are up on our Instagram and Facebook pages and, by the way, we got about 2,000 new followers overnight. Look on the bright side!'

'That's great!' Indi replied cheerily, hanging on to every bit of good news she could. 'You've been fantastic, Ben, as usual. Take Monday off and let's regroup on Tuesday and run through everything. Connor and Nicolas will want a breakdown of the night and we've got a meeting with them on Tuesday afternoon.'

'Well, they'll be completely thrilled. Congratulations, Indi.'

Indi was starting to feel better. Maybe Hollie and Ben were right. All press was good press, right?

The only person left to speak to was Connor. He answered on the first ring but, before he had a chance to speak, Indi launched into a rapid, unprepared speech. 'I know how it looks but I swear, *nothing* is going on with me and that actor,' she began. 'I literally met him for two minutes then, after our fight, I left with him and Tasha, but there were loads of us, a massive group. We all went back to his penthouse at The Square, but loads more people came and there was a party. I came back to Degree because all my stuff was here and I didn't answer your calls because I was hammered and still a bit pissed off after our fight, but I swear, I *swear* nothing happened.'

'Indi, stop,' Connor said gently when he finally got a word in. 'I understand.'

'You – you do?'

'Ind, I own a bar, don't you think I know a blown-up story when I see one? I was ringing you so many times to check you were OK because I was worried about you, and I wanted to say how sorry I was again for the whole Anja debacle. I've blocked her from my phone and on Monday I'm going to get Eddie to give her a formal warning. One more strike and she's fired. I don't want her interfering with us.'

Indi slumped back on the bed in relief. All this time she'd been pacing around the hotel suite, still in Connor's t-shirt and a face caked in last night's make-up. 'Thank you, Connor. That means a lot to me. Can we just forget about all this and move on?'

'Deal,' he replied. 'I don't want anything to come between us. I also just got an email from Nicolas who is delighted with how the night went.'

'Really? That's amazing!'

'I don't think he reads the tabloids, to be honest. All his investor pals and corporate colleagues had a great night, and I told him there was loads of press coverage so he's over the moon. We'll go through it all in the meeting on Tuesday. But please don't worry. More importantly, when can I see you? I missed you in my bed this morning . . . '

'Me too. I know it didn't look like it but I did. Hollie is coming over this afternoon to watch some films, but come round tonight?'

'See you later, gorgeous.'

Two hours later, Indi was freshly showered and back in her own flat with Hollie, putting pizzas into the oven. Hollie had wanted to order in but, still delicate from last night, Indi had insisted they walk to the big Tesco's supermarket in Finsbury Park taking a long route so she could get some fresh air to rid her of her hangover. It did the trick, but she didn't count on the ringing in her ears from Hollie complaining!

'See, now isn't this better? We've got some exercise, saved some money and gone for the healthier option.'

Hollie shot her an unamused look. 'I suppose shop-bought pizza is less calorific than Domino's. You know how I feel about walking, though!'

Indi laughed at her friend, who busied herself with selecting a DVD while Indi scrolled through her laptop, making notes of all the stories about 360 and trying to ignore any mention of her and Elliot Blake. She then gazed at the Instagram pictures on Glamour To Go's feed.

Ben was right, there were thousands more followers. There was one shot of Indi that Ben had insisted on putting up, even though she'd maintained that no one cared about her. But it was a shot of her and Connor, and it was, she had to admit, striking. It had been taken at the beginning of the night beside the gold bar, and Indi's dress shimmered beautifully in the light. She and Connor were looking at each other laughing. There was no denying it, they looked completely in love. Underneath, Indi's friends had posted heart emojis in the comment section, but some other comments caught her eye, too. *Her parents should be ashamed. Disgusting dress, bag of bones but fat in the face! Clearly a botched boob job and dodgy face-fillers. He could do so much better lol.* They were from an account simply named, 'akablush'. Indi tried to click on the account's own profile, but was blocked. She thought back to The Square's summer party months earlier. She remembered that the same account had written 'whores' underneath a photo of her, Hollie and Cheryl Cole. She told Hollie.

'Trolls,' Hollie muttered as she popped some Haribo sweets into her mouth. 'That just proves you've made it into the big time. Take no notice, hun, they're just jealous.'

Indi felt uneasy. 'I feel like someone's watching me or something. They must really hate me. Who would write that?' Then Indi remembered the night after she and Hollie had been out at Print Room. She'd received some foul tweets then, too, hadn't she? Indi scrolled back through her Twitter accounts notifications. Sure enough, there were the comments including, *Bitch, stop pretending you're something you're not,* but they had been from a different account, 'userxx0177xxx', which she had blocked some time ago. It was very strange.

'Block the other one as well,' suggested Hollie. 'It's probably psycho Anja. I wouldn't put it past her. She sounds completely bonkers.'

Indi took her friend's advice and blocked the account, so 'akablush' couldn't write any more comments to her, 360's or Glamour To Go's account. But, even after doing so, she couldn't shake the anxious feeling. Would Anja really do that? Whoever it was, Indi thought, they really hated her.

Chapter Fourteen

Connor came over later as promised, clutching a box of cupcakes for Indi and bag of Waitrose shopping to make her dinner. Indi appreciated all the effort he was making, but still couldn't shake the image of him and Anja kissing, even if it was just for a second. The nasty online comments and everything in the papers made her feel on edge. To his credit, Connor did everything possible to make her feel relaxed, including running her a bath and two mind-blowing orgasms in bed.

'I really haven't got anything to worry about, have I?' asked Indi as they lay naked afterwards. 'With you and Anja?'

Connor took her in his arms and stroked her head. 'Indi, I promise you, nothing will ever happen with me and Anja. Now that things are calming down, let's pick a date for that holiday. At this time of year, Saint Lucia is almost as exquisite as you are.'

Indi kissed him back. She had to trust Connor.

*

Things settled down over the next couple of weeks. Indi and Ben made a detailed success analysis report to present to Connor and Nicolas, and Nicolas congratulated Indi profusely, booking her to organise 360's Christmas party. Mercifully – and as everyone had predicted – the press got bored of Indi pretty quickly. Elliot Blake was still making headlines, however, for boozing around town with his actor pals. Connor booked a romantic holiday to Saint Lucia for early October, which couldn't come fast enough as far as Indi was concerned. She avoided Print Room at all costs, in case she ran into Anja, and threw herself into another work project – a party for one of her beauty clients, bareMinerals, who were launching a new range of lipsticks. It was a relatively easy and straightforward event and a nice pay-packet before her holiday with Connor. Indi started to feel strong, powerful and like herself again.

Kyle, meanwhile, loved working nights at 360, and still helped Alan out with jobs on the odd afternoon, so money was coming to him thick and fast and he seemed to be growing in confidence, too.

'I think he's got a girlfriend, you know,' Connor said to Indi one day. 'We were meant to go see the new George Best documentary and he bailed. A man only ever bails on something football-related when there's a woman involved.'

Indi frowned. 'Nah. Kyle's not interested in girls. Apart from Hollie. I'd be the first he'd tell if he was seeing someone.'

'You think a 21-year-old lad as good-looking as that,

and who works in the hottest club in London, isn't interested in girls?' Connor laughed.

But Indi shook her head. Kyle was just loving his new job and making new friends.

One Friday evening, Indi was in her usual routine of applying make-up at her office desk before meeting Hollie and Tina for drinks. Opening the door to leave, she found herself face to face with the last person she ever expected to see on her doorstep.

'What the hell are *you* doing here?'

Anja looked sheepish. Instead of her trademark dark, seductive lipstick and short skirt, she was fresh-faced and make-up free, wearing blue jeans and a white jumper. Despite her dressed-down look, Anja still looked stunning. Indi was grateful she had on her killer pink Louboutins and an elegant grey pencil dress. But somehow, compared to Anja, she still felt underdressed.

Anja bit her lip. 'Can we talk, Indigo?'

'I'm on my way out to meet friends,' Indi snapped. 'What do you want, anyway?'

'Please, just two minutes? I want to apologise . . . For everything.'

Indi sighed and, without a word, stepped back to let Anja in. She motioned her to sit on one side of her white round meeting table, while she sat opposite, arms folded and legs crossed.

'Well?'

Anja stared at the ground and took a deep breath. She spoke in a posh west London accent. 'I know you hate me.

I don't blame you after the way I've carried on. I've been . . . not been very well. Connor broke my heart when he dumped me, Indi.' Indi simply stared, waiting to hear the rest.

'We've known each other for years, you know. We'd see each other at parties and had this flirty thing going on. Then, a couple of weeks after I started working at Print Room, we got drunk one night, ended up back at his and, before I knew it, we were a full-on couple.' Indi winced at this. That certainly wasn't how Connor would have described their – what was it – *fling*?

Anja went on. 'I really fell for him. He was so romantic, whisking me off my feet and taking me to the best restaurants in London. Then you came along and everything changed.'

Indi didn't like the not-so-subtle accusation that she was the reason Connor had dumped Anja. And she really hated the thought of Connor being remotely romantic towards her. *He'd better not have taken her to anywhere he took me*, she thought bitterly. She was about to object but Anja kept talking. 'All the men I meet are old sleazes. I live in a flat in Fulham with another model who barely speaks English, my parents live round the corner and still never have time to see me, and all my friends are married and not interested. When Connor paid me all that attention it was so flattering. He called me every day and was always buying me little presents.' At this, Indi winced again. 'I thought he was falling for me too and then . . . He told me he didn't have time for a relationship. It came completely out of the blue and I was heartbroken. Completely devastated. I'm used to men leaving me the second they get what they want, but I thought Connor was different. I loved him.' At that, Anja's brown eyes welled up. 'I begged him to come back. I thought if I just could explain . . . Well, you know the rest.'

'But you know he's with me, Anja. All the text messages, phone calls. It's erratic behaviour. It's not right.'

'I know. I was so embarrassed after throwing myself at Connor at 360. I was wasted, Indigo. One of my mates gave me some coke and there was all that free booze. I can't believe what I did. I'm so sorry. I know you hate me but I really am sorry.' A tear slid down her delicate cheekbone.

Indi softened slightly at the sight and reached in her bag for a tissue. They sat in silence as Anja cried. This wasn't a scornful woman, Indi realised, she was a broken one. And, despite all the drama Anja had caused, she was here now, apologising.

'It must have taken a lot to come here and apologise,' said Indi gently. 'How did you even get my address?'

Anja blew her nose and took a few deep breaths. 'I looked online. I really like your website by the way. I could never do what you've done, starting your own business. But I just wanted to say that Connor hasn't spoken to me since the party and I'm going to stay away from him, from both of you. I'm going to cut out the booze and drugs and see a therapist. I know I need help.'

Indi could only imagine how lonely it must be not having any friends. She didn't see the world of modelling being very welcoming. 'That sounds like a good idea, Anja. You don't need to put that rubbish up your nose. And thank you for apologising. I appreciate it.'

142

'So, does that mean you forgive me?'

'Well, let's just say that I'm glad you're getting the help you need. I'd much rather things were cool between us and we just forgot all about this and moved on.'

The girls shook hands and Anja smiled, kindly for once instead of the fake, patronising smile Indi was used to receiving. 'Thank you, Indigo. I can't tell you how relieved I am.'

'And call me Indi, for heaven's sake!'

'Thanks, Indi. I'll let you get to your friends now.'

Indi wasn't one to hold a grudge and she believed in second chances. She'd keep her guard up around Anja for a while, but it was a relief not to have the worry of her and Connor at the back of her mind any more.

'What do you think, darling, green or blue?' Saskia held up the two bold dresses but her fifteen-year-old daughter Millie was more interested in her phone.

'Hello! Earth to Mille! Can I prise you away from that thing for one minute to give your dear old mother fashion advice before you go to school?'

Millie sighed and looked up. 'What's the occasion?'

'I've got a drinks meeting after work followed by a little party for bareMinerals make-up. Hey, maybe you could come with me? It's at that new club, 360. They'll have goody bags.'

'Goody bags? Really?' Millie looked genuinely interested for the first time in months. Saskia knew how to work her daughter. 'Oh wait, no. It's Friday, remember? My weekend with Dad? He's picking me up from school and we're going to the IMAX cinema in Waterloo to see the new *X-Men* movie. He hasn't bailed on me yet, so I suppose that's a good sign.'

Saskia's heart sank. For a fleeting moment she thought she'd have an evening out with her favourite girl. 'Of course. Well, have fun, sweetheart. Do you want me to drive you to school now?'

'Nah, it's OK, I'm going to walk with Sadie. Hey, I saw that Andrew has rebooted your Twitter account by the way. Looks great. I love the new profile pic of you.'

A compliment from her daughter! This was a good start to Saskia's day.

'Thanks, darling. And I even remembered when you taught me to Twitter all those months ago!'

'Tweet, mum. The phrase is tweet. God, you're old.'

Saskia knew Millie only meant to tease her, but that last comment still hurt.

That evening Saskia arrived late at the bareMinerals party. Her previous meeting at a wine bar in Soho had been cancelled at the last minute, but Saskia was already there, so swiftly polished off two large glasses of Chenin Blanc.

As the lift opened on to 360, she was greeted by a waiter and tray of champagne. 'Don't mind if I do,' she said to no one in particular, downing one glass before reaching for another. Surely there was some business she could drum up here? She noticed Nicolas in the corner of the bar talking intently to a brunette girl. Saskia made a beeline towards him, but when the girl turned around she saw that it was Indigo. She should've known anything to do with

360 would now involve this girl. She was probably sucking up to Nicolas – or about to suck him off somewhere, thought Saskia bitterly. Surely that was the only reason she was doing so well.

Saskia decided to wait for Nicolas to be alone before cornering him. The pair went back years and she'd known Nicolas long before Indigo had arrived on the scene. Suddenly, the lift doors opened, and a woman in black patent boots with sky-high heels, skinny jeans and a peroxide-blonde bob stormed over to Indigo with a furious look on her face. A look that said she meant business. She grabbed Indigo roughly by the arm, in full view of the party, which stopped abruptly to witness the dramatic scene.

'Who the fuck do you think you are?' hissed the woman.

Indigo looked terrified. 'What? Who the hell are you?'

'The wife of the man you've been screwing! Or did you forget he was married?'

Indi was wide-eyed. '*Connor?*'

'Not Connor, you stupid tart. Elliot Blake. *My* husband.'

Indi tried to pull her arm away but the woman's grip was firm. Saskia looked on in glee.

Nicolas wedged his arm between Indi and the intruder.

'Now, now, ladies, I'm sure this can be settled *quietly* somewhere. Shall we all step outside and take a moment?'

'I'm not going anywhere with her!' protested Indi. 'Let go of me.'

But the woman's grip became tighter, a look of pure rage in her eyes. Her long acrylic nails dug into Indi's arm, making her wince in pain. 'You stay away from my husband, do you understand?'

Kyle, who'd been stationed behind the bar, rushed over, but Indi held out her other hand to signal him not to intervene.

'Listen to me,' she said sternly to the party's gate-crasher. 'I met your husband once. Here. He failed to mention the fact he had a wife at all, but nothing happened and nothing would ever happen, and if he's been playing around you need to look elsewhere, so back the fuck off!'

The women stared each other out for a few seconds before Elliot's wife finally let go of Indi's arm.

'If I *ever* see or hear of you sniffing around him again I will finish you, do you understand?' And at that, she turned sharply on her heels and stormed out.

Indi was completely mortified. And shocked. The 360 party had been two weeks ago. Had this woman been planning on confronting her all this time? It didn't seem like a premeditated confrontation, more like an impulsive decision. Indi wondered whether it was her who'd been responsible for all the trolling. Kyle put an arm around her while Nicolas ordered a waiter to fetch a brandy.

The sight of everyone fawning over Indi made Saskia sick. She couldn't help herself.

'Well, well, well, not so perfect after all, are you?' she snarled. 'I knew Little Miss Toast of the Town wouldn't last. You're just trying to screw your way to the top, aren't you? I've got news for you. It doesn't work like that. Some of us worked damn hard to get where we are and—'

'Oi, don't speak to my sister like that,' interrupted Kyle, who called out for security. He kept his arm around Indi, who stared at Saskia in disbelief. She had no idea where this vitriol was coming from.

Then it was Nicolas's turn to step in. He was red with embarrassment at all the commotion in his club. 'Saskia, control yourself! You're drunk. As usual, from what I hear. Come on, I'll walk you out.' He took Saskia by the arm, but she was still shouting back at Indi as he dragged her towards the lift, accompanied by a security guard who'd just appeared. 'You're finished, Indigo! Finished!'

Chapter Fifteen

'Another pina colada, Miss Edwards?'

'Yes please.' Indi handed the waiter her empty glass and reclined on her sun lounger as he obediently scurried off. She gazed at the view ahead of her: the deep blue ocean, glistening under the sun. There wasn't a cloud in the sky and Indi closed her eyes, listening to the waves crashing softly. Sun beat down on her face and the rum from her last pina colada took effect, about to send her into a blissful, lazy slumber, but she wanted to take in the incredible view again. And a good job she did. Emerging from the sea wearing only black swimming shorts was by far the sexiest man on the island of Saint Lucia. He ran his hands over his dripping wet face and stalked across the sand, right up to Indi's sun lounger, excess water dropping all over her as he leant in for a kiss.

'Connor! I'm all wet!'

He flashed her a cheeky grin and pulled on one of the strings of her purple bikini, just one of the new purchases she'd made before their trip. Holidays in October were ideal, she realised, as all the summer clothes in the shops were on sale. She'd picked up three new bikinis in bright, bold colours to show off her tan, some silver Kurt Geiger wedges and five new dresses from H&M for her romantic Caribbean excursion with Connor.

'Oi!' Indi giggled and let him kiss her again before they were interrupted by the waiter returning with her drink. Connor ordered a beer and reclined on his lounger next to Indi's.

'Hollie would love it here,' she commented. 'She's made me send her pictures pretty much every hour on the hour.' Connor simply laughed and closed his eyes.

'She and Tom seem to be going strong,' Indi continued. 'Really?'

'Yeah, he met her parents last night. He must really like her, then?'

Connor nodded, his eyes still closed. 'Yeah, I guess so.'

'Well, what's he said?'

'Dunno. That he likes her.'

'*And?*' Indi was desperate to get the gossip from Connor. It was proving useless. Naturally, Hollie had given Indi specific details of each and every one of her dates with Tom.

'Boys don't really talk about that sort of stuff.'

Indi raised a suspicious eyebrow. She highly suspected Connor and Tom told each other just about everything, but that he was adhering to some sort of boy code that even she couldn't penetrate.

'You're no fun,' she teased.

'Yeah, yeah. Well, all I know is that Tom hasn't met a

149

girl's parents in a long time. Now, can we forget them so I can concentrate on how perfect this view is?'

They were halfway through their week-long holiday and it had indeed been perfect, consisting largely of swimming, sunbathing, eating and drinking. When they could tear themselves away from their bedroom, that is. Connor had booked a deluxe suite featuring an enormous four-poster bed, stand-alone bath, rainforest shower and a hammock on the terrace, which the couple crawled into every evening with a glass of wine before dinner. They'd made a rule not to look on social media or the news for the week so that they could escape entirely and switch off completely. It had worked: Connor was completely laid-back and most of the stress and tension from Indi's last few weeks had drifted away; however, there was still a niggling feeling she couldn't quite shake. She didn't know if it was because of her ghastly encounter with Elliot Blake's wife just last week, the alarming abuse from Saskia Taylor, or the online troll who loved to post bitchy remarks on Glamour To Go's Instagram and Twitter accounts. Indi didn't know if it was the same person she'd blocked previously just using a different account, but whoever it was she blocked them as well, and tried to ignore them. But the worrying fact remained that she was racking up a list of enemies – and she couldn't fathom why.

As if reading her mind, Connor looked over. 'You're not still thinking about that social media scum are you, sweetheart? I told you, you're so successful and high profile now that haters come with the territory. It's just kids messing about. Don't give them a second thought.'

Indi twirled a strand of dark hair around her finger and sipped her pina colada. 'I wouldn't exactly call myself high profile. But I guess after everything with Kyle and the police, I'm just a bit more sensitive than usual.'

'High profile in the events world and, trust me, that's something to be proud of. You've been completely run down, so it's only natural that everything seems worse than it is, but by the time we come home everything will have blown over. And, hey, no Anja to worry about. That deserves a toast, surely?' He raised his beer glass towards her. 'To us.'

That was true, at least. Indi was thankful that the whole Anja mess was behind them. In fact, the last time she and Hollie had been at Print Room for dinner, Anja had been genuinely friendly, and even Hollie had admitted that Anja seemed to have turned over a new leaf.

Indi clinked her glass with Connor's. 'To us!'

After an afternoon of sunbathing in the glorious heat, Indi and Connor joined a few other couples from their hotel on a boat trip and went snorkelling. One of the other guests took a picture of Indi and Connor, hand in hand, jumping off the boat, and they swam for an hour, exploring the astonishing sea-life below the water. Small reef sharks dashed past them and hordes of electric-blue and stripy fish spun around them. Indi loved to swim, though this sure was a step up from the pool at her gym!

Back at their hotel, Indi and Connor fell on to their bed and made love for hours before finally showering and heading down for dinner. Connor threw on a light shirt,

Indi a short pale pink dress, which made her tan look even darker. Her skin was sun-kissed and she radiated a post-orgasmic glow, so she didn't bother with make-up, except a slick of black mascara, and let her hair hang naturally tousled.

'I love you like that, all natural, sexy and shagged out.' Connor smiled as he led her down to the beach that the hotel backed on to.

'Babe, where are we going? I thought we were having dinner at the hotel?' Indi was starving.

'I've got a surprise.'

'If it's skinny-dipping again, can we wait until after I've eaten? I'm craving one of those Caribbean steaks.'

Connor put a finger to his lips and continued down the beach as Indi moaned about how hungry she was. But when he stopped walking, the sight in front of her shut her up. There was a single table on the sand, with a white cloth over it and a bucket of champagne on ice next to it. A tree next to the table was covered in fairy lights and, a metre away, there was a small crackling bonfire. Connor pulled out a chair and motioned for Indi to sit down.

'Connor . . . You did all this?'

'Yep. We've got our own private waiter for the evening, but I took the liberty of pre-ordering us steak and lobster to share. I hope that's all right.' He popped open the champagne and poured her a glass, then one for himself.

'It's more than all right, it's amazing! But you didn't need to go to all this trouble. I don't know what to say.'

'I do.' He took her hand from across the table and looked into her eyes. 'I love you, Indi. I think I've probably loved you since the first time I saw you. And I'd do anything to make you happy, I hope you know that.'

Indi was smiling so much her face started to ache. She leant over the table to kiss him. 'I love you, too.'

'It's freezing!' exclaimed Indi as she and Connor waited for their bags at Heathrow Airport. She had stepped on to the plane ten hours earlier in shorts and a t-shirt, but stepped off it having changed into jeans and one of Connor's fleece jumpers underneath her leather jacket, but she was still shivering. It was almost midnight. 'I can't wait to get home and have a cup of tea.'

Connor was glued to his iPhone. 'Babe, a story about you has just gone up on News Hub. They've taken pictures from your website and run the photos of you and Elliot leaving 360 again, claiming you two are now sleeping together.' He paused and kept reading. 'I didn't even know that thing with his wife had made it into the papers at all, but a week later it's still getting hits and they've followed it up with this big exposé.' A pause again. 'They've . . . they've mentioned your mum, Ind.'

Indi grabbed the phone off him to see for herself. There indeed was a feature all about, 'Indigo Edwards: The blue-eyed brunette who's swept Elliot Blake off his feet and away from his wife.' The writer, Gilly Davis, had mentioned Alan's building company and written that Kyle had a 'troubled history with the law'. She read more.

'Someone who lives across the road from the school is a named source,' Indi said. 'She blatantly phoned the website to make a quick buck as soon as my name was making

153

headlines and dished the dirt on poor Kyle.' What was even worse, the article featured Indi's Facebook profile picture, which was a shot of Lou and Indi taken when Lou still looked young and healthy. Indi was on her lap, they were hugging and both beaming to the camera. 'Are they allowed to use this?' she asked abruptly, showing Connor the photo.

'If it's for public view then, yes, I think so.'

'I'm closing my Facebook account down,' Indi said, pulling out her own phone. As much as she hated the intrusion into her life, bringing up her family was crossing a serious line.

'Apparently I'm a "single, party-loving career girl, just the type of no-strings fun Elliot loves". Honestly, where do they get off writing this crap?'

'You don't think it's that journalist mate of yours being an anonymous source, do you? Doesn't he work at News Hub?'

Indi shook her head. She was racking up enough enemies and she really hoped Miles wouldn't need to be added to that list. 'No. He's ambitious but he's not ruthless. I'm going to talk to him first thing anyway and see if he can get them to stop writing about me and my family.' Indi was worried for her father. Alan only used his computer to watch documentaries on BBC iPlayer and email invoices. He was traditional, and liked to read his news from a newspaper or hear it on the radio, never the Internet and certainly not tabloid websites like News Hub. He wouldn't have seen the story, but it was only a matter of time before someone alerted him to it. Kyle would probably see it first tomorrow morning. It was horrible for Kyle but he would most likely shrug it off. Alan, on the other hand, was a private man, and would hate the intrusion, not to mention all the references to Lou, which would devastate him.

Connor planted a kiss on Indi's cheek. 'I'm sorry, sweetheart, it's horrible that they are doing this to you. I'm sure it's a slow news week and they like you because you're pretty and an easy target. They'll get bored of it when they realise nothing is going on and it will be another sorry soul next week.'

'I hope you're right,' Indi grumbled.

Chapter Sixteen

'But, Miles, why can't you just tell them nothing is going on with me and Elliot? You were there that night at 360, you were talking to him far more than I was and you know the truth.' Indi was feeling desperate now. She'd been unable to sleep after arriving home from the airport, tossing, turning and ruminating about the tabloid stories. She had sent a text to Miles at seven a.m., not caring how early it was. He was already on the way to his office for the early shift and phoned her as soon as he got in.

'I *have* told them, but until they find another girl to blame the affair on, they want to go with you. A pretty girl gets interest, what can I say?'

Just as Connor had predicted. 'But surely the truth matters more than a poxy story?' she pleaded.

'It's not my call, Indi, I'm just a writer. I've had nothing to do with this anyway, they've got me shadowing Leonie Parr for a "Week in the Life of" feature. I just do what I'm told.'

Indi slammed her coffee cup down and the contents spilt on to her desk. She was jittery. She'd left her house early to go to her office, spotting a pap lurking outside her building and dashing into an Uber before he could get a picture. She looked online to see if there was any law against what the website was writing, but however nasty she felt, everything they'd published about her family was the truth; they hadn't slandered them in any way. Connor suggested she phone Gerald to see if she could sue the website for the defamatory accusations that she and Elliot were sleeping together, claiming damage to her reputation. But not only would that cost be extortionate, Indi didn't love the idea of relying on Connor for help again. No, she had to figure this out for herself.

'I do have one idea,' said Miles slowly. 'Let me interview you. Sell your side of the story. Tell the world that there is nothing going on with Elliot and say how scared you were when Helen had a go at you. That'll get everyone off your back and drum up some sympathy. And you know you can trust me.'

'I'm not sure, Miles.' Indi hated the idea of being featured even more heavily on News Hub. Even though she was feeling desperate, she still hoped Connor's theory that it would all blow over soon would prove correct.

'Where is Elliot in all this anyway? Even if we were sleeping together, why is it that the girl gets all the heat while he's still seen as some sort of lovable player? It's sickening. He likes you, Miles. Can't you get him to deny any involvement with me?'

'He's just landed back from Los Angeles, actually. I could

call him. He won't make any statements to me on the record – I've tried – but maybe I could arrange a meeting between the two of you for this afternoon and maybe you might have more luck persuading him? You get to clear your name and I get an exclusive quote.'

This made Indi feel relieved. 'Yes, please. The sooner the better.'

'I'll call him now and set it up. Keep your phone close to you and I'll text you with a meeting point and time.'

'Thank you, Miles. I really appreciate it.'

'Anything I can do to help. But at least think about giving your own interview.'

'OK,' Indi replied. But she knew she wouldn't.

Miles texted back quickly and said Elliot was free to meet Indi an hour later. Elliot had suggested a quiet café in Primrose Hill. Indi got there early and sat at a table at the back. She was on her second espresso by the time Elliot arrived, looking every inch the rock 'n' roll movie star in dark blue jeans, battered leather jacket and Ray-Ban sunglasses. His face was unshaven and his hair messy. He slid on to a chair opposite Indi, greeting her with a kiss on the cheek that she quickly pulled away from.

'Woah, sorry, babe,' he said, holding up two palms.

'I'm just trying to be discreet. I've had a pretty rough day what with this exposé about our apparent affair.'

He sighed. 'I know, babe, my publicist filled me in. It comes with the territory having my personal life splashed all over the Internet, but it shouldn't be happening to you.'

'So, can you tell Miles that it's all bollocks? That there is absolutely nothing going on?'

'Look, Indigo, I'm truly sorry for you. I am. But my publicist says the way to handle this rubbish is to do a Kate Moss.'

Indi looked at him incredulously.

'You know, "never complain, never explain"? Giving them more to go on will only drag this all out longer. If everyone just stays silent, they'll get bored soon enough and move on to another story. Besides, I don't mean to sound like a dick, but I'm really trying to make things happen in Hollywood, and speaking to a tabloid wouldn't be great for my reputation.'

'What about my reputation?' hissed Indi, so angry she almost spat out the words. The tiredness and coffee overload were making her short-tempered. 'Elliot, please. There was a pap outside my house this morning. And probably my dad's house too.'

Indi still hadn't spoken to her father, but could only imagine how distressing this was for him. It was just the sort of thing that could trigger his depression; it had come on after Lou's death and had a nasty habit of reappearing every now and again.

'Why don't I pay for a holiday so you can get out of town for a bit until this all blows over? I want to help, Indigo, but I can't talk to News Hub. That's the one thing I can't do.'

Indi took a deep breath and held her head in her hands. This was getting her nowhere. 'I can't afford to be away from work right now,' she said.

'Look, if the stories get worse and more personal, maybe you can get an injunction so they can't write about you any more? I can help get it done behind the scenes and get my lawyer to deal with it all, OK?'

'You can do that?'

'Sure. But I honestly don't think it will even come to that. Give it a couple of days and it will be old news.'

Everyone was telling Indi this. She wished she could believe them.

'The press get bored quickly, trust me,' he added. 'I'm getting a coffee, do you want one?' Indi nodded and stared out of the window. When Elliot returned he placed a dish of pastries in front of Indi.

'I figured you'd want something sweet after the morning you've had,' he said. But Indi didn't feel at all like eating. There was a long pause as they sipped their coffees. Indi was trying to work out what her next move would be in this whole mess, but was too tired to think properly.

'It's not true what they've written about me either,' Elliot finally said quietly. 'I'm not this shagger they're making me out to be. My publicist tells them that to give me an image, but there's only one girl I've been having an affair with and I love her. Problem is, I love my wife, too.'

Indi shot him a look as if to say, 'Yeah, right.'

'I don't expect you to believe me. Helen and I were married so young, at eighteen. We were together all through school. People change, you know what I mean? She doesn't care about acting or movies. The only thing she watches is *This Morning*. We've just got nothing in common any more. She's like my best friend, but the spark went years ago. Then I met this other girl . . . She's sort of in the industry too. She gets it. It's not just sex either, I really care about her. No one knows this, but I've moved out and into a flat across the road. Helen is livid, of course, but I told her I needed space. I didn't want to keep lying to her.'

'Why are you telling me this, Elliot?'

'I guess I care about what you think of me. That's the trouble with us actors, we're all pretty insecure when it comes down to it.' He half smiled. Indi picked at an almond croissant.

'You're still being unfaithful,' she said. 'You need to tell your wife.'

Elliot nodded. 'I suppose I've ruined your relationship as well, have I?'

'Thankfully, it seems I have the greatest and most understanding boyfriend in the world and he doesn't believe that tabloid crap for a second.'

'Sounds like he's a keeper.'

'He is.'

Elliot checked his phone. 'I'm sorry, I've got to go. I will sort this mess out, Indigo. I'm going to speak to my publicist later and see if she can do anything with News Hub to get them off your back. It's not fair. And if it gets worse I'll get my lawyer on the case, I promise.'

Indi was so tired she didn't even notice that Elliot had come over to hug her. 'Keep me updated and call me if you need anything.'

'Thanks, Elliot. It's not your fault. But I do appreciate it. Anything you can do.'

'I'm not the bastard they think I am.'

Indi nodded. 'I'm not the home-wrecker they think I am, either. Although your wife still is certain I am, so it would be marvellous if you could straighten that out. It might not be the easiest thing to do but it's the right thing.'

Elliot looked at the floor. 'Sorry about the way she kicked off at you by the way. Anyway, talk later.' He gave her one big hug and Indi allowed herself to hang on a few seconds as it was so comforting. She didn't even notice Elliot kiss the top of her head just before he left.

'Hi, Dad, I'm sorry it's taken me all day to call you. I've been trying to sort this mess out and get the journalist to stop writing about us. I'm in Primrose Hill now, I've just had a meeting, but I can drive straight over.'

Alan sighed. 'There're some photographers outside the house.'

"How are you, Dad?'

'Well, you know I'd never read that rubbish, but Kyle showed me this morning. It's . . . well, it's very difficult, darling.' Alan's voice broke and he took a deep breath. 'They didn't have to mention your mum, that's all. It was hard to see, sweetheart.'

Indi struggled to hold back her own tears. Hearing her father so upset hurt more than anything a pathetic tabloid website could write about her. Of course her business and career meant the world to her, but nothing compared to how protective she felt towards her father and brother. She decided then and there that she had to be strong for them and not let anything break her. 'Dad, I will fix this, I promise.' But the truth was she didn't know how.

Indi tried to distract herself with work all afternoon. Her big project now was starting to put together the Christmas party for 360 in two months' time, another Christmas party for a new fashion client's staff, and Connor wanted her to help him plan a New Year's Eve party for Print Room. Creative ideas normally flowed from Indi, but today she was tired, jet-lagged, cranky and couldn't concentrate. It was a far cry from twenty-four hours earlier when she'd been lying on a beach in Saint Lucia. She just couldn't shake the horrible News Hub feature from her mind, or the pain in her dad's voice. Kyle phoned Indi offering to beat the journalist up, whoever it was, but Indi laughed quietly and told him not to dare. At least Kyle wasn't upset. In fact he seemed cheerier and stronger than ever these days. Indi was grateful for his support. Hollie called too and offered to come straight round, but Indi thanked her and assured her that she was best at work, distracted.

But things got worse still that afternoon. Blocking the vile trolls from Indi's social media account had made no difference, and she was still getting hateful comments underneath pictures on Glamour To Go's Instagram account.

Man-stealing whore. Watch your pretty little back because people are out to get you. The truth ALWAYS comes out, bitch, read one of the comments.

Indi didn't know where all this was coming from. Who could hate her so much? But the comment that really disturbed her came later that day. After scoping out lunch venues online for the bareMinerals Christmas function, she logged on to her personal and business Twitter accounts to see if anyone had replied to her shout-out for any set designers who could make or donate sledges to decorate 360 for its Alpine ski lodge Christmas party theme. There was a message on Twitter.

Hey @GlamToGo, heard about your mental brother burning down his school. Lol!! Looks like mental runs in the family. Did u get it from ur Mum?!

And, on her personal account, *@IndiEdwards needs to die.* They'd added a menacing skull emoji at the end.

Indi's hands shook as she read and reread the comments. Of course, the user was anonymous, so clicking their profile gave her no clues as to who it was. She blocked them straight away, but knew that it only took a few minutes to create another account. Whoever was trolling her didn't seem to want to stop any time soon. And not only were they getting nastier, they were getting threatening. Indi decided they weren't going to get away with it. She copied and pasted the tweet in a text to Connor, then sent another: *Can you give me Mark's number?*

She expected him to phone or text her back straight away, but there was radio silence. She called him, but there was no answer. She tried Hollie and her dad. No answer there, either.

Indi spent hours obsessively checking her phone before going for a long swim at her gym to try to clear her head.

Connor finally called at seven p.m. when Indi was watching TV but unable to stop fidgeting.

'Sorry for not calling sooner,' he said. 'How are you? I'll text you Mark's number now, you definitely need to call him.'

'Where have you been, Connor? I've been going crazy.'

He paused. 'Something came up at 360. But anyway, forget that, I'm worried about you now. Phone Mark and get the police to look into that awful troll and then call me back, I'm here.' Indi was surprised that he hadn't offered to come round to her house immediately, but brushed the thought away and dialled his brother's number.

'Unfortunately, there's nothing the police can actually do,' Mark said after she'd explained the reason for her call. 'I'm sorry, Indigo, I know it must be very unsettling getting a message like that. You did absolutely the right thing blocking them. Can't you make all your accounts private so that no one can comment or tweet you without permission?'

'I've closed my personal ones down now, but the others are for business,' replied Indi. 'I want everyone to see what we're posting. I'm just worried it looks unprofessional otherwise. Don't you have some sort of technology you can use to track where the tweets are coming from and arrest that person?'

'I'm afraid not. The threats aren't direct or – sorry – serious enough. I know they must be upsetting for you, but with people like this, their bark is generally worse than their bite. They want a reaction, a rise out of you. My best advice is to ignore them and wait for it to blow over. Trolls get bored. Believe me, we see a lot of it. But if they start threatening you further, or you feel unsafe, call me straight back.'

Indi thanked him and hung up. But the truth was she did feel scared. She waited for Connor to call back but he didn't. Of course she could have called him, but she was sulking somewhat that he hadn't at least checked up on her. Then she felt angry with herself for being so needy. What was happening to her? Normally the epitome of cool, calm, collected and in control, today she felt the exact opposite: on edge, anxious and tense.

At nine p.m. she decided the best thing was to turn her phone off, take a long bath and go to bed, but it was a night of interrupted sleep, waking every hour with a racing heart and a head full of worry. The jet lag didn't help, either.

She finally fell into a deep slumber at four a.m. and woke up groggy five hours later. Turning on her phone, there was a WhatsApp message from Hollie, apologising for not answering (she'd been on a romantic date with Tom), and a voice message from her dad saying that the photographers had finally left the house, probably knowing they weren't going to get any comment or juicy picture from either him or Kyle. There was nothing from Connor. Furious, Indi phoned him, but before she had the chance to lay into him, Connor began speaking.

'Sweetheart. I'm sorry I didn't phone you last night. I really wanted to but I had to take care of some business here. Can you come to 360, Indi? Now. I'll explain everything. See you soon. I love you.' And with that he hung up.

166

Indi was livid. How dared he not even let her speak? Expect her to come running to wherever he was? This was *not* the relationship she'd signed up for. She jumped out of bed, showered and dressed in black cropped trousers, a black shirt and her Tory Burch flats, threw on a beige trench coat and headed out to 360. At least the adrenalin from being so angry kept her from tiredness. Connor was about to get a piece of her mind.

Chapter Seventeen

Indi burst out of the lift on the twentieth floor. The club was empty, apart from a cleaner hoovering the carpet and a barman taking a stock-check of bottles from behind the bar. On a corner table by one floor-to-ceiling window she saw Connor, wearing dark blue trousers and a white shirt, deep in conversation with Eddie. As Indi marched over he sprang up to give her a kiss and ask how she was feeling.

'I've been better. Any chance of a coffee?'

'Let me get it,' Eddie replied and disappeared.

'I'm just going to come out and say this,' Connor began. 'Some money was stolen from the safe here while we were on holiday – £8,000, to be exact. It was an inside job as the thief knew the safe's code, but they didn't realise there was a hidden camera in the office, so fortunately we know who it was.'

Indi had no idea why Connor had called her all the way down for this. She shrugged and raised her eyebrows, impatient for her coffee.

Connor cleared his throat. 'It was Kyle.'

Indi snorted with contempt. 'For fuck's sake, Connor, don't be ridiculous.' But he slid a brown A4 envelope over. Inside, Indi found several black and white photographs, taken from the CCTV video. They were grainy, but there was no mistaking what they depicted: Kyle opening the safe, Kyle reaching inside for bundles of £50 notes, Kyle looking around nervously, Kyle closing the safe.

'Well there's obviously a reasonable explanation,' she snapped. 'Kyle would never steal so much as a bag of peanuts.'

'I haven't called the police yet,' replied Connor. 'I wanted to tell you first and give him a chance to return the money. Only Eddie and I know, and you now, and I want to keep it like that. I wanted to give you the chance to talk to him first and foremost. It would be better coming from you.'

'*Police?* There's no need to call the bloody police!'

'That's what I'm saying. I don't want to involve them. I'm hoping to resolve this quickly and quietly. I didn't know you guys had been having money troubles, Indi. Why didn't you tell me?' Connor spoke quietly, trying to remain reasonable even though Indi was livid.

She jumped up. 'You patronising wanker! You think I'd get my brother to steal from you? Because we're a poor little family? A charity case?'

'Hey, that's not what I said. I just meant—'

'I know what you meant. You immediately assume the worst. Well, I know there's an explanation for all this.'

'I'm just trying to help.'

'We don't need your help!' She was shouting now. 'Stop trying to be the fucking hero all the time. I don't *need* you, don't you understand that? I don't even want to see you. All you do is try to make me into a victim so you can swoop in and feel like the big man.'

'Hey, listen!' Connor stood up too now. 'I don't need this shit from you. I'm doing your family a favour. Again. God, Indi, you've turned into a crazy woman.'

'It's *you* that's making me crazy! I was doing fine before you came along, we all were. I'm sorry we're all so much trouble for you.' Indi was shaking with rage now and could feel hot, furious tears welling up. She ran to the lift, leaving Connor speechless. She managed to get out of the hotel lobby and around the street corner before tears fell down her face. She quickly composed herself, wiped away the tears and hailed a cab to take her to her dad's house. She needed to focus and make sense of what was happening. She called Kyle but there was no answer. A text came through from Connor: *What the fuck just happened?* She deleted it without replying. He was the last person she wanted to speak to. All her attention was on Kyle and what the hell would have possessed him to do something so stupid.

Indi didn't have her keys for Alan's house on her, so she rang the doorbell, hoping that Kyle was in. Thankfully there were no pesky paparazzi there today. Indi hoped that they were bored already. There had been no new stories about her and her family on News Hub since the big feature, but that one was still getting attention and there were reams of hateful comments about Indi underneath. She couldn't bring herself to look at it any more.

Alan answered the door and ushered Indi in. He saw that she'd been crying, a very rare sight for his daughter. Usually it was Indi looking after him, being the strong and capable one. He was so surprised that the only thing he could think to do was give her a huge hug and say, 'I'll stick the kettle on.'

The quintessential British sentiment made Indi laugh through her sniffling. 'You seem a bit brighter than when I last spoke to you at least, Dad.'

Alan laid out cups and placed teabags in a blue, chipped teapot. Indi made a mental note that she needed to buy him a new one, as he would never remember to do it himself.

'Cat and Tim came round last night,' he said. 'We cracked open that bottle of brandy Connor brought round.'

The mention of Connor clearly did something to Indi, so Alan rested his hand over hers. 'What's wrong, love?' he asked. 'If you're worried about me, you mustn't be. The photographers have gone now, thank God, so we can go outside again. And nothing they say about us means anything. We've got our memories of your mum and that's all that matters.' He held Indi's hand tightly and she squeezed his back.

'I'm so sorry, Dad. Everyone keeps saying it will just blow over, so I'm hanging on to that. Is Kyle in?'

'He's doing a light-fitting job for me but should be back soon. He's been out most nights, I don't know what he's been up to. He never tells me anything.'

'What, stayed out all night?'

'Says he's been staying at a mate's, but there's a spring in his step and if I know my son, I bet there's a girl involved,' Alan said with a wink.

Indi frowned. Connor had said the same a few weeks ago. Kyle was certainly flirting with pretty girls at 360 that night, and he had always had a crush on Hollie, but aside from that he'd never shown much interest in actually having a girlfriend. She struggled to imagine it. He might be twenty-one but, to her, Kyle would always be her baby brother. Anyway, there were more pressing matters she needed to discuss with him.

'So, do you want to tell me what's wrong?' asked Alan again, pouring them both tea.

Indi didn't want to tell her dad about Kyle before speaking to her brother directly, so she just replied: 'Connor and I had a big fight.'

'I thought so.' Alan shifted uncomfortably in his seat. Boy advice wasn't his strong suit. 'Do you, er, want to talk about it?' Then, more seriously – 'He hasn't hurt you or anything, has he?'

'No, 'course not. It was just a stupid fight. I've been a bit on edge recently with work and the whole News Hub thing.'

'That makes sense. Didn't you have a nice time in Saint Lucia, though? You still haven't told me about it. Hollie popped round while you were gone and the pictures she showed me looked lovely.'

In all the commotion of the past two days, Indi had forgotten all about her holiday. The Caribbean paradise seemed like a distant dream. Now she was back to cold, harsh reality. But to pass the time until Kyle got home, and avoid any more awkward questions about her fight with Connor, she gave Alan the highlights of her holiday. She was in the middle of describing their boat trip when Kyle came through the door, carrying a toolbox, and slumped on a chair in the kitchen.

'All right, sis? What are you doing here?'

'I just came for a chat. We haven't caught up in ages and I wanted to see how you were doing.' Spending time in her familiar, cosy home, and in her father's company, had Indi feeling significantly calmer and more herself. Alan, sensing that Indi wanted to talk to Kyle alone, disappeared into the garden.

Kyle cracked open a beer. 'So, what's up?'

'Are you in some sort of trouble, Kyle?'

'Huh?'

'Is there something you'd like to tell me?'

'No. What are you talking about?'

Indi sighed. 'I've just come from 360. Connor says eight grand was stolen from the office safe over the weekend and,' she paused, 'he says it was you. In fact, you were caught on CCTV. He showed me the pictures. I told him there had to be some mistake, and then came straight here to see how and why he would have concocted such a ridiculous story.'

Kyle froze. He and Indi stared at each other for a few seconds before he dropped his shoulders and looked to the floor. 'There's been no mistake,' he said quietly. 'I took the money.'

Indi squinted and furrowed her brow. It was so strange

for Kyle to be lying about this. 'What are you talking about? If this is some sort of joke you and Connor have thought up, I have to say, it really isn't funny. Well, I don't get it, anyway.'

Kyle sighed. 'I took the money. It's not a joke.'

Indi shot up in her seat. '*What?*'

'Sssh, Indi! Calm down!' Kyle hissed, glancing nervously outside to where Alan was watering the garden, blissfully unaware of the conversation that was taking place between his children.

'What on earth would have possessed you to do something so stupid? You've jeopardised your job, your whole future! Not to mention the future of Connor and me. He will probably want nothing more to do with me after the way I've just spoken to him. How could you be so stupid, Kyle? What the fuck were you thinking? After everything Connor has done for you.'

Kyle yanked Indi back on to the chair. 'It's not what you think. The money isn't for me, it's for someone else – but Connor knew all about it. At least, I thought he did. Some wires have been crossed, clearly, so I just need to get to the bottom of it, that's all. I'll talk to Connor and explain everything, I promise.'

'What do you mean he knew all about it?' Indi was shaking her head in disbelief. 'You could go to jail! *To jail, Kyle.*' She emphasised the words for effect.

'You've made your point.'

'I don't think I have. I think I deserve much more of an explanation, as does my boyfriend. If he still is my boyfriend. He stuck his neck out for you, you know.'

174

Indi felt terrible about the way she'd flown off the handle earlier. Connor had been nothing but calm and reasonable and, just like he said, she was acting crazy. She owed him one big apology.

'Look, I can't talk about it,' said Kyle. 'I know you're angry, but you really are just going to have to trust me on this. I've already said too much. The club will get the money back, but I'm begging you, please tell Connor not to call the police.'

'He says he won't if you return the money.'

'Thank God for that. Do you promise you'll leave this for me to sort out?'

'I don't know, Kyle. I'm really worried about you. If you've got yourself into trouble with someone dodgy, I need to know. I can help you, but only if you tell me the truth.'

'Please, don't worry. I've got this. If things get out of hand you'll be the first person I tell, I promise you that. But for the time being just give me a couple of days to sort this out and Connor will have the money back, I swear.'

Indi stared at him, chewing on her bottom lip. She did not like the sound of this at all, but Kyle kept promising her he had things under control. He certainly seemed calmer than she was.

'OK, fine. Just sort it out.'

Kyle nodded. 'I have to go and make some phone calls. Promise me you won't say anything to Dad? He'll only worry.'

Indi *was* extremely worried, but Kyle pleaded with her to trust him, and reluctantly she made a promise not to tell Alan. 'Just get it sorted. Quickly.'

Indi declined her dad's invitation to stay for dinner. She was thoroughly exhausted and wanted to go home and phone Connor to apologise. She'd offer to cook him dinner, go round to his flat, anything to make up for the vile way she'd spoken to him earlier. He was only trying to help, and had done so much already for her and her family. Anyone else would have phoned the police and reported Kyle by now. And how did she repay him? Screamed and swore at him. Her anxiety worsened, knowing that the next day she had to be in work mode for a meeting with Nicolas at Print Room. She still had a day's worth of work emails she'd been ignoring.

That night, Indi phoned Connor five times before he eventually answered the phone. 'Hello? Indi?' He had to shout. Deep, low-tempo music and the sound of a dozen conversations, including some high-pitched female laughter, blasted from wherever he was.

'Connor? Where are you?'

'I'm in the bar. Whasssssup?' He sounded hammered. This was not the big apology scene Indi had in mind.

'Can you step outside so we can talk?'

'Huhhh?'

'I said, go outside so you can hear me. I want to apologise.'

'Can't talk now, babe, too loud,' Connor slurred, and with that his phone clicked off.

Indi was furious, but reasoned that she was still technically in the wrong. She decided a text was the best way forward.

Just phoning to apologise for earlier. The way I spoke to you was completely out of line and I'm so sorry. Please let me make it up to you. Have a good night and I'll call you tomorrow. I love you xxx

She slumped off to bed, exhaustion washing over her. They'd make up, Kyle would return the money and everything would be OK, she told herself as she drifted off into a deep sleep.

Chapter Eighteen

Indi's meeting with Nicolas the next morning was to go over a few details of the 360 Christmas party. Nicolas loved the Alpine ski-lodge theme, with faux-fur blankets everywhere, sledges, and small ski lifts that doubled up as photo booths, boxes wrapped in ribbon under a ten-foot Christmas tree, frosted glasses, dry ice and fake snow. During the meeting Indi glanced around but Connor was nowhere to be seen. She'd also tried calling him that morning but his phone had been off.

Nicolas rose to leave and then stopped, remembering something. 'Oh, Indigo, before I leave, I wanted to check you were OK about that whole nasty Saskia Taylor business. The way she spoke to you was damn well out of line.' Nicolas spoke formally, but Indi appreciated his compassion.

'I've tried to not to think about it, but it shook me up, I have to say. I just don't understand where that all came from.'

'I might have something to do with it. Saskia and I go back a long way. She handled parties for all my ventures when I started out. Oh, the times we had – long liquid lunches at the Groucho Club; those were the days.' Nicolas chuckled. 'I think she was probably expecting that I'd bring her on to 360. But you see, things have changed now. Connor is the young blood who's shaking things up and I wanted someone on the team like him. Ambitious and hungry. It wasn't anything personal against Saskia – business is business.'

Indi nodded. It didn't excuse Saskia's behaviour but she understood why Saskia might feel resentment.

'I've been meaning to reach out to her, to see how she is,' continued Nicolas. 'Word on the street is that Sass PR is on its last legs. A shame, Saskia was a talented woman. A lot like you, in fact. Anyway, don't take it too personally.'

'Thanks, Nicolas. I really appreciate that.'

Nicolas left and Indi was about to head off as well when she heard someone call her name. Anja. She had on her standard work uniform of a short, slinky black dress with a high neck and no sleeves.

'Hi, Anja.'

'Indi, I saw in the books that you had a meeting with Nicolas here today. I came in early to speak to you. I – I – I need to speak to you.'

'Are you OK? You haven't been taking coke again, have you?'

'Please, Indi. I don't want you to find out from anyone else. I feel so terrible.' She started crying, and dragged Indi over to a quiet sofa in the corner of the bar.

'Anja, what happened to you?'

'Oh gosh, I feel so terrible,' Anja repeated. 'Before I say anything just please, please believe me that I didn't mean for this to happen. We didn't mean it. It just . . . I mean, we have this past and . . .'

Indi froze and spoke slowly. 'What didn't you mean to happen?'

'We never wanted to hurt you. I deleted his number so I couldn't text him. I really thought I was getting over him. I even met someone else, someone lovely. But he and I have this thing . . . This chemistry . . .'

Indi knew the 'he' Anja was referring to, but wanted her to say it anyway. 'You and *who* have this chemistry?'

Anja wiped away a tear. 'Connor. He came here last night; he'd been drinking. He was upset. We talked and he told me about your fight. He said . . . I'm sorry, Indi, but he said he knew he'd made a mistake being with you. Then we had another drink. One thing led to another and then . . . We were back at his place.'

Indi blinked. 'You had sex with him?'

Anja spoke through tears. 'We spent the night together, yes. It just all happened so fast but he kept saying how right it felt. He said that he'd never really got over me, and I felt the same. I guess something started a few weeks ago when he came round.'

'When he *what*?'

Anja looked at the floor, red with guilt. 'You know, when he came over to mine a few weeks ago? Nothing happened then, we just talked, but maybe his feelings started for me again, I don't know. He didn't tell you?'

'No. He didn't tell me.' Indi spoke quietly, firmly, trying to make sense of what was being said to her.

Anja kept talking, apologising, explaining, and giving lurid details of her and Connor's reunion. But by now it just sounded like muffled noise to Indi. A sudden headache hit her and she felt nauseous. She held her hand up to signal that she'd heard enough. She needed to get out of Print Room right now. Without saying a word to Anja, she picked up her bag and walked out.

Connor's flat was situated in a private building near Hoxton Square. Guests needed to be buzzed in through the main entrance, but when Indi arrived, a woman with a buggy was coming out. Indi held the door open for her and then marched in as if she lived there.

Once at Connor's door, she banged her fist on it so hard her knuckles started bleeding. Eventually, Connor opened the door. His eyes were half open, glassy and red, and his face unshaven. He was wearing only boxer shorts. Indi put his dazed and confused attitude down to a hangover and the fact he'd clearly just woken up. She stood in the doorway, unable to step inside the scene of the crime. All her happy memories of being there with him, tucked away in their own little private world, had been shattered. At first, she couldn't bring herself to speak, just stared at him with a pained look on her face, wishing so much that crazy Anja had fabricated the entire story. Finally she spoke. 'Tell me it isn't true.'

Connor rubbed his eyes and yawned. 'Huh? What isn't true?'

'Tell me. It isn't. True.'

It took a few moments for Connor to focus. Indi could see him piecing together last night's events in his mind. Clearly he'd been completely wasted, not that that was any excuse. He groaned and fell back so he rested on the doorframe. 'Indi, I don't remember what happened last night.'

'Really? Do you remember spending the night with Anja? Telling her how much you loved her and that I was just a mistake?' Indi was crying now, and with the last word punched his chest.

'Anja . . . Anja was here, yes. We were talking. I was so drunk.' Connor held his face in his hands. 'We were kissing. The next thing I remember is waking up thirty seconds ago. I don't even remember taking my clothes off. But I didn't have sex with her! I'm telling you, Indi, I didn't.' He tried to take her in his arms but she stepped back, tears streaming down her face. He started rubbing his head again. This was some hangover.

'How could you possibly know that if you can't remember anything?' she screamed. She started hitting his arms and chest as hard as she could but Connor didn't even flinch. Instead he grabbed her arms to keep her still.

'Because no matter how hammered I was, I would never do that to you.'

'Oh, but stripping down to your boxers and kissing her is all right, is it?'

'No, of course not,' he replied desperately, looking Indi straight in the eye. 'But it was just a drunken kiss, I swear! Last night was a mistake. But we'd had that huge fight and

I was upset. And, besides, you're one to talk! You started this whole mess. Now you rock up here . . .' He was trying to get his words out, but he was so hung-over he had to stop to hold his head again.

'And what about a few weeks ago when you went round to her flat, Connor, hmm?' Indi spat out the words in fury while Connor, again, took a few moments to think before he spoke.

'A few weeks ago? Oh God, no. That was nothing. I went round there to tell her to back off and she threw herself at me!'

'So, it's true? It's fucking true!'

'I didn't tell you because I didn't want to upset you and—'

'Oh, well done for not upsetting me! You complete and utter wanker. You make me sick.' Indi's hands were shaking, her lips trembling. 'I hate you!' she screamed, storming away.

'Fuck this, Indi. We're over,' he shouted after her.

'Good!' she shouted back, before she heard his door slam shut. She couldn't believe she'd been so stupid as to trust Connor Scott. Miles was right. He had broken her heart and it had ended in tears.

Indi got the tube home in a daze, not quite believing what had happened. It was all so surreal. She played images in her mind over and over again of him and Anja in his flat, kissing, laughing, making love. The thoughts made her feel sick but she couldn't escape them.

Indi made it through her door before bursting into tears.

*

Saskia waited outside Millie's school. It had been two weeks since her drunken outburst at 360. Journalists who had witnessed the explosive scene had been tweeting about it, and Saskia's name had even made it into the online story about Elliot's wife, 'psycho Helen Blake', although the real focus was the war between Helen and Indigo. Saskia was so embarrassed she had shunned work entirely, spending days feeling depressed and nights drinking alone. But today she was seeing her girl. Millie had allowed her mother the privilege of letting her take her on a shopping trip after school.

Saskia planned to buy Millie the coat from Miss Selfridge that she knew her daughter had her eye on, and some fabulous silver sequined leggings from Forever 21. Most mothers rolled their eyes at their teenage daughter's fashion sense, but not Saskia. Millie could do no wrong in her eyes, and Saskia adored the fact that her daughter had clearly taken after her in the wardrobe department and loved loud, bright clothes. Though Millie was much cooler than Saskia ever was, with gorgeous blonde hair hanging down her back and a beautiful figure.

Saskia was so excited that she arrived at the school gates bright and early, eagerly anticipating much-needed quality time with her daughter.

'Sass?'

Saskia turned to see Felicia Fitzpatrick. 'Darling, hi, how are you?'

The two air-kissed. Felicia was a celebrity publicist from the 'good old days', who used to be one of the most important names in the industry, famed for her high-profile clients. She was still very successful, and represented a few ageing but iconic rock stars and actors, but was trying to spend more time with her twins, who went to Millie's school. Saskia ran into Felicia now and again and the two loved to catch up and gossip at the school gates.

'Run ragged as ever!' exclaimed Felicia. 'Rod Stewart wants me to sign his wife and Emma Thompson has a string of new films out next year that I haven't even begun to make a press proposal for. It's just me and my assistant Ashley now after Bethany left.' Bethany had been Felicia's co-partner in the business, but had quit the entertainment industry and moved to the south of France with her family. 'I hate turning down work, but two people can only do so much.' Felicia was tapping away at her phone while talking.

'Horrendous,' muttered Saskia, wishing that she was so inundated with work. Sass PR seemed to be heading nearer and nearer to bankruptcy.

'Sweetie, by the way, I read about the awful scene at that club thing on Twitter. They made you out to be totally insane!' It sounded like a rude comment, but Saskia knew Felicia well enough to know she was simply direct and had no filter. The two were old friends.

'Yes, it was quite a low point,' Saskia replied awkwardly.

'If you ask me, Helen Blake is the crazy one. What was she thinking, making a huge scene like that in a roomful of journalists? And that poor girl she accosted. You know who he's really having an affair with, don't you?' Saskia shrugged. 'My assistant! I told Ashley, never get involved with a married man. It only causes heartache and the

185

mistress never wins. But it's been carrying on for months, Sass, and she won't listen to me, the fool. She thinks she's completely in love – and the problem is, he says it too. Says he's going to leave his wife. *Please.*'

'But he shags everything that moves, doesn't he?'

'Apparently not any more. Ashley says his publicist goes around town telling that to anyone who listens to boost his bad-boy image, when really he's like a lovesick puppy.'

'What about Indigo Edwards?'

Felicia shook her head. 'Barely knows her. Trust me, I've seen his and Ashley's relationship play out. Utterly scandalous, of course. And you've seen the latest story about Indigo, haven't you? Oh dear, they've done a proper hack's job. Dug up things about her brother – he was arrested recently – and her dad, who's this sad, lonely widower. It's just awful.'

'Widower?'

'Yes! You didn't read it? Oh, Sass! Indigo's mother died of breast cancer when she was just a teenager. Honestly, you must read it. Ashley and I are simply addicted to the story. It's so tragic! How are you anyway, sweetie? How's work?'

Saskia was stunned. Up until now her only regret from her drunken outburst was about how it had looked to Nicolas. She hadn't given much thought to Indi, but suddenly felt consumed with guilt. How could she have said those awful things? What had Indigo ever done to her? Sure, she was an ambitious young starlet in the world of events, but hadn't Saskia been exactly the same fifteen years ago? She remembered their first encounter at The

Square's summer party. All this time, Saskia had thought Indi had been trying to patronise her, get one up on her, but the reality was she was just a girl. And to have her life unpicked and splashed all over the papers ... Saskia wouldn't wish that on anyone. For a fleeting, agonising second she thought about Millie and what it must feel like not to have your mother around as a teenager. It was too much to bear. Indigo didn't deserve all this. Suddenly, Saskia burst into tears.

'Darling, whatever is the matter?'

'I'm a terrible person,' sobbed Saskia.

Just then, the bell rang, signalling school was finished. Saskia wiped away her tears before Millie could see. Felicia put an arm around Saskia.

'How about a coffee tomorrow? You can tell me all about it.'

Saskia was grateful. God knows she needed a friend right now. But how could she ever forgive herself for what she'd done?

Chapter Nineteen

'You have to eat something, come on.' Hollie shook Indi lightly and handed her a bowl of tomato soup. Indi was slumped on her sofa wearing pyjama bottoms and one of Kyle's old hooded jumpers. Her greasy hair was scraped back in a ponytail. Hollie had let herself in, armed with groceries. She flung back the living-room curtains and opened a window, exclaiming that the flat hadn't seen natural light or fresh air in days.

'I don't feel like eating,' grumbled Indi, but accepted the steaming soup anyway. It did smell good. And the only things to pass her lips had been a bit of mouldy cheese and a bag of Dairy Milk buttons. Hollie took a baguette out of the oven, slathered it in butter and handed it to Indi on a plate, then set about picking up the scrunched tissues that surrounded Indi's sofa on which she had been stationed for three days. As if her personal life being in tatters wasn't bad enough, bareMinerals had dropped Indi, backing out of their contract. It turned out the CEO of the brand was close personal friends with Helen Blake. According to Ben and his friendships with all the other assistants on the party-planning circuit, she was bad-mouthing Indi all over town and making it her mission to destroy her.

Indi reacted by shutting down completely, setting an 'Out of Office' automatic reply on her emails stating that she was off work sick, and switching her phone off so as not to be tempted to check Connor's Instagram feed to see how much fun he'd probably been having without her. Social media was toxic to a break-up.

Hollie placed her hands on her hips and looked down at Indi, who was watching *Loose Women* on the TV even though she didn't seem remotely interested. She was fed up. As if things with Connor weren't bad enough, Kyle had gone completely off the radar and she had no idea if he'd ever managed to return the money to the club, or even where he was. He never answered her calls and replied to text messages simply to say he was 'fine' and 'everything was under control'. Indi despaired. She felt she was losing all the people who mattered to her, and felt sick with worry for her brother. She was petrified that he was in serious trouble with some nasty people, although she tried to reassure herself that if things were that bad, Kyle would tell her. He had promised he would, after all. But why the sudden distance?

Up until this point, Hollie had done everything she could think of to comfort her friend – telling her over and over again how great she was and that she'd get through this, sticking on Indi's favourite films, bringing gallons of ice cream and providing unlimited cuddles – but so far nothing had worked. Now she was trying the 'tough love' approach.

'You do realise you're in the same spot on the sofa you were in when I last came round, right? Two days ago? And the same clothes. And I'm assuming you haven't showered or run a brush through that hair, either?'

Indi glanced up, then turned her attention back to the TV. 'What's the point of showering if I'm not leaving the house?'

'The point is, this isn't doing you any good, honey. I know Connor hurt you, but you can't hide away here for ever. Wallowing in your misery isn't the answer. Also, it's gross. No offence.'

Indi shrugged. 'Hurt' was an understatement. She felt hollow, as if someone had torn out her heart. The few times she had managed to sleep, she'd wake up, blissfully thinking everything that happened had been a bad dream, but then, a few seconds later, realisation would hit hard, like a dagger to her heart.

Hollie slumped on the sofa next to her. She didn't know anything about the money situation with Kyle, so assumed Indi's glumness was all down to Connor. 'Have you talked to him?'

Indi shook her head.

'You know, I think Connor really feels terrible for what he did. Tom hasn't even seen him, says he's gone completely AWOL, which only happens when he's properly upset. Maybe if you just called him . . .'

'And say what?' Indi spoke in a whisper, her voice raw

190

and husky from sobbing. 'He slept with someone else – the worst, most vile person he could sleep with; someone who, if you can believe it, I was actually starting to warm towards – and then tried to blame it on me!'

It was all such a mess. That fateful morning Indi had confronted Connor at his door, he'd scornfully told her she'd 'started this whole mess'. She had no idea what he meant and the words repeated in her head. Also, how long before he'd call the police about her brother? Surely that was going to happen any day now.

'What? How's he figured that one out?' Hollie asked indignantly. Thank God for best friends, thought Indi. She'd been going over and over it in her head. The only thing she could think of is that Connor reckoned *she* stormed out on *him* after he told her about Kyle stealing the money. But that hardly justified him jumping straight back into bed with his ex. Indi hated keeping things from Hollie but it didn't feel right to tell her about all this until she had spoken to Kyle again. Hoping the conversation would wrap up soon, she simply shrugged and bit her lip.

'Maybe he didn't actually have sex with her, though?' Hollie continued. 'He said he couldn't remember what happened, and he was wasted, right? Maybe they just kissed and then Connor passed out drunk. That's still not ideal, but better that and Anja's lying about them sleeping together? You know what a manipulative cow she is.' Hollie, too, was ashamed for believing Anja's show of friendship since she'd apologised to Indi, but her instincts had been right all along. She was a nasty piece of work.

'I don't see why he'd go so far as to kiss her with no

clothes on and then not go all the way,' Indi scoffed. 'This is Connor Scott we're talking about. The reputation clearly precedes him. And have you forgotten that he went round to hers a few weeks ago, too? He admitted that one all right. I should have listened to Miles all along. At least he tried to warn me about Connor. Anyway, I don't know why you're taking his side.'

'Of course I'm not taking his side. I'd punch him for what he did to you. But I also do believe that Connor really did – correction, *does* – love you. Tom is convinced of it too and he knows him better than anyone. I just think things aren't always what they seem, and maybe there's some sort of explanation.'

'Hollie, even if they didn't have sex, the minute we have a fight he's with her, drinking, kissing and sleeping in the same bed. That's bad enough, if you ask me; and even if he was sorry, which he clearly bloody isn't, how could I ever trust him again? I can't even bear to think about him, but then again it's all I can think about.'

Hollie sighed. 'I know, honey. It just feels like something isn't right. Things don't add up, to me. The way Connor felt about you . . . '

But, in Indi's mind, there was nothing that could be done.

'Hey, I've got an idea,' Hollie said brightly. 'Why don't we go to Brighton tomorrow? It's been ages since we stayed with Matt and James and they'd love to see you. We could have a day and night there, then come back the next morning?'

Indi loved going back to Brighton for the odd weekend

with Hollie, who often used to visit Indi at weekends and also fell in love with the coastal town. One of their best friends, Matt, lived there with his boyfriend James, and the girls always stayed with them just minutes' walk from the beach. Brighton held so many memories for Indi and, despite being just an hour outside London, it somehow felt like a world away. The pace of life was much calmer. Most importantly, there was no Connor, no Anja, no Print Room and no 360. Indi smiled for the first time in days and hugged her friend tightly, overcome with affection. 'That sounds perfect.'

'I'll text Matt now. He'll be over the moon. Have you spoken to your dad or Kyle? I bet they've been trying to phone you.'

Indi shook her head and wondered again if Kyle was at home, safe and sound, or if he was in trouble.

'Well, if it makes you feel any better, there haven't been any more stories about you on News Hub, so I think the press are getting bored now.'

Indi sat up. 'Thank God for that. Although everyone still clearly has me down as a home-wrecker. Did you see all the comments on the *Mail Online* stories about me?'

'You know only crazy, bored, sad people leave comments online. And about people they don't even know. Pathetic! How's the trolling situation now, have they stopped?'

'I can't bring myself to look. The last thing I need are more death treats and strangers telling me how ugly and useless I am.'

'Fair point.' Hollie nodded. 'Best to stay away and ignore them.'

A pause, then Indi said, 'Can you believe Elliot wouldn't tell the press the truth?'

Hollie frowned. 'Urgh! He probably likes having a rep as a bad boy. Forget about him. You've got your own successful business, remember? Though don't you think it might be an idea to answer a few emails? Maybe have a shower? Go for a walk outside?'

Indi raised her eyebrows. 'You're not leaving until I do, are you?'

'Nope! And to show how proud I am of you, I'll even blow-dry your hair. Now hop to it! I'm going to book us some train tickets to Brighton for tomorrow. It'll do you the world of good, I promise.'

As usual, Hollie was right. The minute their train sped out of Victoria Station the next morning Indi felt more relaxed. Fifty minutes later they arrived in Brighton, where Matt and James greeted them at the station with open arms. The four hugged each other in a group and Indi instantly realised how much she'd missed being here. Matt was a nutritionist and James a physiotherapist. They were both incredibly fit and had buffed physiques, but loved a night out as much as Hollie and Indi did.

'We thought we'd dump your bags at ours then go straight for a nice stroll around town and stop for lunch at Côte,' said Matt as they all walked arm in arm away from the station.

'Then go to Revenge tonight, of course!' chipped in James. Revenge was the biggest gay club in Brighton and the four had spent many a messy night out there.

194

'Ooh but Indi is newly single, so we have to get her out to No. 32 for a few drinks first,' insisted Hollie. 'It's so fun in there and *always* full of hot men.'

'Yes to No. 32 but no to hot men,' corrected Indi. 'It's too soon.'

The boys and Hollie shot each other glances. 'We'll see about that,' said James.

Indi knew they were trying to cheer her up, but there was no way she could even look at another man. She'd have been happy to stay in and catch up with her friends over a few bottles of wine. She still felt exhausted from the emotional turmoil of the past few days, and she couldn't stop thinking about Connor and Kyle. Kyle had responded to her last text only to say that everything was under control and, no, the police hadn't arrested him. No text from Connor. Indi couldn't believe he hadn't been in touch yet. She didn't talk about it with her friends, though, as she didn't want to ruin the happy vibe. Besides, they'd just tell her to forget him; that he wasn't good enough for her and she was better off without him. Maybe that was true, but it didn't feel like that to Indi at all. Connor had broken her trust completely by sleeping with Anja. Were Anja's claims true: that Connor had always been in love with her, that being with Indi was a mistake? Hollie certainly didn't think so, but Indi wasn't sure. Was that why Connor had gone quiet all those times Anja had rung him? Maybe he wasn't angry with her at all, but in love with her. Or, worse still, having an affair the entire time? Despite all the pain these thoughts caused Indi, she couldn't deny the fact that she was still madly in love with Connor. That's why it hurt so much. Her head might be telling her to move on, but her heart was burning for him, and some flicker of hope said that it wasn't true, that he hadn't had sex with Anja; that it was just one messy, drunken fumble and everyone makes mistakes. Indi was so confused, she didn't know what to think.

She tried to put all thoughts of Connor out of her mind. Her friends were going to so much trouble to cheer her up and she didn't want to seem ungrateful. As Hollie had predicted, the excursion was just what Indi needed: fresh sea air, a different environment and being with close friends made her feel secure and loved. Matt and James were the perfect hosts and Hollie sensed when Indi didn't feel much like talking, so would regale the group with gossip about snotty customers at House of Fraser but constantly asked her if she was OK. She also took Indi's phone for the day, to avoid the risk of drunkenly phoning Connor, who still hadn't made any contact since their break-up. Hollie really was the best friend a girl could ask for. By the time she'd done Indi's make-up (a classic smoky eye, of course) and the group had drained a few cocktails at No. 32, Indi was able to put on a brave face, but deep down she felt hollow, as if a piece of her heart had been torn out and would never be replaced.

'My head is banging,' muttered Hollie the next morning, folding up the double sofa bed in Matt and James's living room. The boys were getting dressed in their bedroom. Indi had cooked a full English breakfast for the four of them, even though she'd had no appetite since the break-up and only managed a slice of toast. 'You still have my phone, right?' she asked Hollie. 'I better check that I haven't missed anything from Kyle.'

'Kyle? Why, what's up with him now?'

'Oh, nothing,' Indi said quickly. 'I just mean that I don't want to miss anything from home.' She switched on her phone and read a text from her dad saying that he hoped she and Hollie were having fun. Nothing from Kyle. Then, Connor's name flashed up and Indi gasped.

'Holl, there's a message from Connor. Shit, will you read it for me? I don't think I can.' Even mentioning his name gave Indi anxiety. What on earth could he want? Whatever it was, Indi couldn't face it. Hollie took the phone and read aloud:

Just thought I should let you know that I sacked Kyle yesterday. I'm sorry it had to happen but under the circumstances I'm sure you'd agree I had no choice. I've given him three more days to return the money, otherwise I will have no option but to call the police. Connor.

Hollie paused. 'What money? What's he talking about?'

Indi grabbed her phone back. 'I'll tell you on the train. Let's say our goodbyes and get out of here.' After thanking Matt and James profusely for being such great company and promising to visit them again soon, Indi called Kyle as soon as she stepped outside. She half expected him not to pick up, as the phone rang out for so long, but as she was about to hang up he answered.

'Kyle, what the fuck? Why haven't you given him back the money? You keep telling me you've got this all under control, but it sounds anything but. You could've kept your job. You know he's going to call the police, don't you?'

197

'Indi, I'm sorry. I didn't want you to worry. But I don't have the money. I tried to get it back, I failed.'

'Get it back off who? What is going on?'

'I'm sorry, I can't break my promise. I have to take responsibility for this myself.'

'Promise? Promise to who? Kyle? *Kyle?*' But it was too late. The phone went dead.

Chapter Twenty

Indi was restless all the way back to London. She phoned Kyle repeatedly but his phone was turned off.

'Have you thought about telling your dad?' asked Hollie, after Indi had brought her up to speed with Kyle's drama.

'Kyle made me promise not to.' Indi had never broken her brother's trust before. 'And I don't want to worry him. Kyle says he'll fix it himself, but he's in way over his head, Holl. Do you think he's in some kind of trouble with a loan shark? Dad says he's got some new girlfriend. Maybe he borrowed money to try to impress her? You don't think it's drugs, do you?' All sorts of images flashed through Indi's mind.

'I'm sure it's not drugs. Kyle is young but he's not stupid. I can't imagine why he'd get involved with a loan shark. Wouldn't he just ask you if he needed money?'

'He's very proud. You know I'm saving up to put him through college, but he doesn't like the idea of relying on me – on anyone, for that matter.'

'Sounds like someone else I know,' said Hollie with a raised eyebrow.

Indi then had another thought. 'He's not taking his meds at the moment. He hates how spaced out they make him feel, but without them I'm a bit worried that he's done something stupid without thinking clearly.'

Hollie was silent for a few moments, thinking. 'I think you just need to trust him, Ind. Connor said he wouldn't call the police for a few days, right? Maybe leave it a bit longer before calling Kyle again. Maybe he will get the money back. And right now he clearly doesn't want to speak.'

Indi nodded slowly. She knew her friend was being rational and logical, but she was still fraught with worry at what her brother might have got himself into. Just then her phone rang and she jumped, hoping it would be Kyle. Instead, Miles's name flashed up on the screen.

'Hey Miles, what's up?'

'I've got some good news.' He sounded pleased with himself.

'God knows I need some right now,' Indi replied wearily.

'Ever heard of a publicist called Ashley Deacon? She works for that big publicist, Felicia Fitzpatrick'

Indi sighed and said that she hadn't.

'We've been tipped off that she's the one Elliot Blake is shagging. They've been having an affair for months. Gilly tracked down one of her mates, who gave up a load of pictures of the both of them at her birthday party. They're all over each other. And, get this, Ashley has admitted it and given Gilly a big interview. She claims she's completely in love with him and Elliot has promised to leave his wife. It's all going online over the next few days.'

'Wow. I can't believe Ashley's friend would sell her out like that by tipping off the press.'

'No, someone else tipped us off. It was Gilly's source and she hasn't revealed it. But, Ashley's mate wasn't hard to break when we confronted her, and Ashley doesn't even seem to mind. In fact, she seems to be loving all the attention. No doubt she'll be flooded with chat-show offers now. But the important thing is, the heat is off you and your family.'

'That's fantastic,' said Indi unconvincingly. It was great news, but even that couldn't lift the misery she was feeling over Connor and worry for Kyle.

'Oh. You don't seem very pleased.'

'No, I am, thank you, Miles. Sorry, I've just got a lot on my mind. This really is brilliant, thank you.'

Hollie was making impatient signals at Indi to tell her what had happened. 'Hold on,' Indi mouthed back.

'Cool. Well, I thought you'd like to know. I'll let you get back to Connor now. I'm sure you're having a good weekend.'

'Oh, er, Connor isn't here. I'm with Hollie, actually, we're just on our way back from Brighton. Connor and I broke up.'

Indi fully expected Miles to scoff and say he told her so, but instead he was completely sympathetic and said how sorry he was. 'I was never his biggest fan, as you know, but I know he made you happy.'

'Yeah, well. Apparently you were right. Once a player, always a player.'

'Why don't you let me take you out? Just as friends. You've been going through such a bad time. Come for a drink with me and I bet I'll cheer you up.'

Miles was relentless and Indi was about to object as she always did. But then she wondered what the harm would be in going for a drink with him. After all, Miles had been nothing but supportive these past few weeks. He was an old friend. And now that News Hub were finally off her back, things were certainly looking up. Anything sounded better than staying at home feeling depressed about Connor. 'OK, Miles, you've got it. But I'm getting the first round. I owe you. And, Miles? Thank you. You're a really good friend.'

It wasn't anything like the dates with Connor, of course. Getting ready, Indi wasn't excited, had no heart flutters and there were zero rushed texts to Hollie asking for fashion advice. It was five days after Brighton and there was still no word from Connor or Kyle. Tom told Hollie that Connor had gone to Miami for a few days for a business meeting. Indi was so depressed and consumed with thoughts of what he was up to (probably shagging Anja senseless as soon as he landed back on British soil), and what trouble Kyle had got himself into, that she had entirely forgotten she was due to meet Miles that evening. He'd suggested a pub in Finsbury Park – hardly the glamorous restaurants she'd become accustomed to while dating Connor, but Indi told herself to stop being such a diva and to get over herself. It wasn't Miles's fault that she was bitter and heartbroken. She turned up in skinny black jeans, a blue denim shirt and black ankle boots, her hair refreshed with some dry shampoo because she hadn't been bothered to wash it.

'Hi, babe.' Miles got up at once and kissed her cheek. 'Drink?' He was also wearing black skinny jeans, which didn't look too bad on him as he was tall and slim himself, a faded red t-shirt and a brown leather jacket. His stubble was beginning to grow into a beard. He looked cool, like he'd fallen straight out of an indie band, but he did nothing for Indi. She couldn't help but compare him to Connor, so strong and masculine and always impeccably dressed. No, she had to stop thinking about Connor.

'Gin and tonic, please,' Indi replied glumly. 'Double.'

'That's my girl.' He winked. Back from the bar, Miles asked after her family. Indi replied that they were great now that News Hub had lost interest, but refrained from telling Miles about Kyle's latest drama. She'd been waiting for two days to get the dreaded call that he'd been arrested, but so far, nothing. She wondered what Connor was waiting for and why he hadn't gone to the police yet. Kyle, meanwhile, was still avoiding her, and not answering any questions about what had happened to the money, or why he'd stolen it in the first place. And Alan was completely oblivious to any of it.

'Well, with Christmas coming up at least you can relax now,' said Miles, sipping from a bottle of Beck's.

Christmas. Indi normally adored Christmas, but with everything that was happening she felt flat – and missed her mum more than ever. 'Yeah,' was all she could manage.

Over the next two hours, Indi relaxed slightly as she and Miles reminisced about their old uni days and discussed what their fellow student friends were up to now. He didn't ask her many more questions, and dominated the conversation, which normally Indi would have hated, but she couldn't be bothered to talk much tonight so was happy to let Miles go on. He talked at length about his own job, telling her he was in line for a promotion to be Features Editor.

'It will mean much more money. And more holiday. They'll probably want to fly me out to LA to cover the Oscars' red carpet in January. Everyone wants to go, but my boss says I'm the only one he trusts to get anything done properly. They're talking about opening a New Hub office in Australia so I imagine they'll want me to go over and help set things up. They'll probably promote me again. That place would fall apart without me.'

'That's great,' Indi replied, thinking how totally arrogant Miles sounded.

'And I should be able to afford to move out on my own this time next year. Which will beat living in a house share with four other people. But I reckon I can rent a nice little studio flat, get a big flat-screen plasma TV and an Xbox. And a car. I'll probably be able to run petrol through as a work expense. They let me get away with anything!'

An Xbox? Seriously, how old was he?

As Miles kept talking about himself, Indi said nothing, just took a gulp of her gin and tonic, hoping the alcohol would numb her pain.

Connor threw his phone angrily on to the hotel bed. He knew he shouldn't have looked at Hollie's Instagram feed.

Indi's personal one had been closed down, nothing new had been posted on Glamour To Go's page, and her Facebook account was still deactivated after the News Hub exposé on her family. Connor felt pathetic at the way he was trying to find out what Indi had been up to by stalking her and her friends on social media. His phone's screen saver was still the picture of him and Indi jumping off the boat in Saint Lucia, and he couldn't bring himself to take it down. God, he was like a lovesick teenager! It hadn't helped that Hollie had posted a series of pictures of her and Indi having a wild night in Brighton town with two blokes. Had Indi forgotten about him so quickly? The last few months had flown by in a loved-up, lustful haze, and Connor had truly fallen in love. He'd thought she felt the same. But since finding out his own version of the truth, he didn't know what to believe.

Connor went to the gym to let off steam, spending half an hour on the treadmill, then an hour in the weights room at his five-star hotel in Miami. He finished the workout with a swim on the rooftop pool. He wasn't a highly strung person. He generally maintained a laid-back attitude and always managed to think about things rationally and logically, essential traits in his line of work. However, he did have a temper. And on the rare occasions it came out, it came out big and didn't go away easily. The epic row with Indi had left him furious and he still hadn't got over it. A heavy workout normally cleared his head and relieved any tension. Not at the moment. He just couldn't make sense of the past two weeks' events. One minute he had been lying on a beach with Indigo, sublimely happy and in love, convinced that she was the woman of his dreams. But one stupid drunken night out he'd copped off with Anja Kovac, of all people, and the worst thing was, Indi thought they'd had full-on sex. Like he'd have been able to get it up in that state even if he'd wanted to!

The Miami business trip with a group of new investors who were expanding there couldn't have come at a better time. He was able to avoid Anja entirely, nervous that their drunken, messy night would give her the wrong idea. Mercifully she had texted him to say she had a modelling job in Milan and couldn't come in for the next couple of weeks. At least now he had some space and time to think about what the next step should be. He hated how things had been left with Indi.

As if he wasn't feeling wretched enough about his romantic life, he was also extremely bothered about the business with Kyle. Connor was a superb businessman, fair but firm, and would never let anyone get away with stealing from his club. Equally, he also couldn't bring himself to report Kyle to the police. He'd bonded with the kid over the past few months and genuinely liked him. Having to sack Kyle pained him, but Kyle had taken it surprisingly well and didn't even try to argue.

'Mate, just tell me why you did it,' Connor had pleaded, after calling Kyle into his office at 360.

Kyle had said nothing, just looked at the floor.

'Eddie told one of the waitresses he's shagging what you did. She blabbed to everyone else, so they all know and now I have to let you go, otherwise they're going to think I tolerate people stealing from me,' Connor said. 'You know this is hard for me but I have no choice.'

'I understand, Connor, really,' Kyle replied. 'I don't blame you at all. I'll never be able to repay you for what you've done for me. And I know how happy you make my sister.'

Connor shifted in his seat. Clearly Indi hadn't told her family about their break-up. 'Tell me why you did it. Why did you take the money?'

Kyle shook his head. 'I can't break my promise. I'm sorry, Connor.'

Out of the gym, Connor checked his phone again. One message from Tom asking him to meet for a beer when he was back in London. Connor replied: *Yes*. He hadn't spoken to his best friend, or anyone else for that matter, even though Hollie would of course have told Tom everything. Connor had better get his side of the story across before he was made out to be the bad guy. There was still no reply from Indi to his text about sacking Kyle. They'd had no contact whatsoever since the break-up, and he'd be damned if he was going to apologise first.

Chapter Twenty-One

Stepping out of the taxi, Saskia straightened her blazer and checked her appearance in the reflection of the car mirror. Her electric-blue trouser suit was a new buy from Whistles and she'd had her hair blow-dried at her favourite salon on Clapham High Street. Today was important, and she didn't want to mess it up. Running into Felicia outside their kids' school gates had been the best thing to happen to Saskia in months. Their coffee had turned to wine, wine had turned to dinner, and dinner had ignited some light-bulb moments in Saskia's brain – and some very interesting career developments.

Felicia opened the door to her Chelsea town house wearing a long multicoloured kaftan and dozens of jangling silver bangles. Her curly red hair fell wildly over her shoulders. Her home also acted as her office. 'Come in, come in.' She kissed Saskia on both cheeks and led her into a huge airy front room. One end had big leather sofas and a glass coffee table piled neatly with magazines and a vase of flowers. The other end had been transformed into an office with three desks, but was so big that it could easily fit more. It led out to a garden. It was so friendly compared to Saskia's poky rented office. Felicia's assistant, Ashley, sat on one of the sofas. Felicia sat opposite her and motioned for Saskia to sit next to her.

'I think we should get straight to it, don't you?' she said. 'Now, Ashley, of course you've got your job here, but in light of recent revelations and your various . . . opportunities, Saskia and I propose to take over your personal publicity while you're so in demand.'

Ashley Deacon beamed. She was going to be famous!

'Saskia and I need to iron out the details but, as she and her team will be joining us, and that this was all her idea, I think she should take the reins with you. Don't you think, Sass?'

Saskia reached for her new iPad. 'The offers have already come flooding in since your News Hub interview. *This Morning* and *Loose Women* both want the first TV interview and I think we should do a magazine shoot.' As Saskia spoke, the other two nodded along, and soon Ashley was dismissed so Felicia and Saskia could get down to the finer details of their venture.

'Such a great idea to tip off the tabloids, sweetie,' said Felicia as she sat back on the sofa and crossed her legs. 'Ashley gets her fifteen minutes of fame and we control the whole thing.'

Saskia smiled. Tipping off News Hub had indeed been

her idea, one she'd thought up over dinner with Felicia, but furthering her own career wasn't her only motive. She also wanted to help Indigo Edwards.

'And you're sure about this, Felicia?' she asked.

'It is the most wonderful solution!' Everything Felicia said was loud and animated with hand gestures. 'I can't possibly handle all this work myself, and I'm simply being the most ghastly mother to Milo and Wolfie. I have to cut way back if I'm to spend any time with them. Partnering up with Sass PR is genius, absolute genius. You'll move your team in here and we'll become Fitz & Sass PR. Now let's sign these damn contracts and open the bubbly!'

Saskia returned home that evening weighed down with shopping bags from Marks & Spencer. She was going to make her daughter's favourite dinner, chicken fajitas followed by chocolate and caramel ice cream.

'Millie, I'm home!'

She laid out the ingredients on the big wooden table in her kitchen, popped open a chilled bottle of Pinot Grigio from the fridge and poured herself a generous glass. This was a time to celebrate, after all, and there was no one she'd rather do that with than her daughter. Their recent shopping trip had been a great success: Millie hadn't been glued to her phone and had even told Saskia about a boy at school she fancied. They had gone to Ed's Diner and giggled over milkshakes and burgers, just like they used to before Millie turned into a grumpy teenager. Millie skulked into the kitchen.

'Aha, there you are! I have your favourite supper and I thought we could go to the cinema later, or just stay in and watch a DVD? Whatever you fancy.'

'Um, Mum. I need to talk to you about something.' Millie was biting her nails and staring at the floor. For once, she didn't have her iPhone in her hand.

Saskia put her glass of wine down at once and rushed over to her daughter. 'You're pregnant! Oh, darling, don't you worry about a thing.' She gave her daughter a hug but Millie pulled away.

'No, Mum! You're always *so* dramatic.' Millie sat on one of the stools at the wooden table and began biting her nails again. 'I'm worried about you.'

'Me?'

'About the drinking, Mum. I think you have a problem.'

'Oh, darling, don't be silly.' Saskia went back to chopping red peppers. *Who's being dramatic now?* she thought.

'I know you've been off work lately, and all you do is sit around the house depressed, playing around on Twitter and Facebook and drinking wine. I went to your office after school last week and Jo said you weren't there. She thinks you drink too much, too.'

Saskia slammed the knife down. How dare Jo discuss Saskia's drinking habits with her teenage daughter?

'That was incredibly rude and inconsiderate of Jo to worry you like that,' she said. 'I'll be having a very stern word with her on Monday.'

'But she's worried about you!' Millie's voice rose. 'It hurts me that you can't see what you're doing to yourself.'

This made Saskia freeze. No mother ever wants her child to be hurt, let alone be the one that's causing the pain. Millie's big blue eyes filled with tears.

'One of the girls at school, her mum was an alcoholic and got liver cancer and now she's in hospital all the time. I've already lost Dad to that awful blonde bimbo and their stupid baby-to-be. I don't think I could handle losing you, Mum!'

She pulled her skinny legs on to the stool and sat hunched up and sobbing. Saskia ran to her daughter and held her as tight as she could, forcing back her own tears. How on earth could she have been so selfish? All these months she'd been consumed with herself, she hadn't stopped to think how her misery could have affected her daughter. As she squeezed Millie tightly and kissed her forehead, she made a mental note of how much booze she'd been knocking back lately. Maybe it was a lot? She thought back to the dreaded night at 360 when she'd verbally abused Indigo. She had certainly been drunk then, and even Nicolas had remarked on how much she'd been drinking. It was true, she enjoyed a glass of wine in the evening like any other forty-year-old career woman. But she knew all too well that it was more like a bottle these days. She didn't care what happened to her, but the thought of frightening her daughter was too much to bear.

'My darling girl. I am not going *anywhere*, do you understand? Your father and I may not love each other any more, but we both love you more than life itself. No, we didn't have the easiest divorce but that doesn't change his love for you. And, Millie, you are my world. I won't

212

take another sip of alcohol ever again if it bothers you that much.'

Millie looked and wiped her face with her sleeve. 'Really, Mum?'

'Absolutely. In fact . . .' Saskia marched over and poured her remaining glass of wine, and the entire contents of the bottle, down the sink.

Millie laughed. 'You didn't have to do that. I mean, I know what I said, but you can still have the occasional glass, obvs. I just don't want you turning into an alcoholic.'

'I am not an alcoholic,' said Saskia firmly. And she believed it. Yes, she'd been using alcohol as a crutch recently, but her daughter was the only crutch she needed.

'Thanks, Mum. I love you.'

'I love you, too, darling. Now how about some food? Why don't you pick out a DVD for later?'

'Can we watch *The Witch*? It's soooo good and so scary!'

Saskia grimaced. She hated scary movies. 'Do we have to? What about *Mamma Mia* like we used to, love?'

'That's boring! Come on, Mum, pleeeeease.'

'But I get scared!'

Millie gave her a hug. 'Don't worry, Mum, I'll look after you.'

Later, Millie fell asleep in Saskia's arms on the sofa. Saskia stroked her daughter's hair and gazed at her, smiling proudly. What an intelligent, grown-up young woman she'd raised. How lucky she was. She thought of Indigo, who had been Millie's age when her own mother had passed away. The thought seemed so terrible, and Saskia's guilt came flooding back like a tense, dark cloud. She knew what she had to do next.

Indi fingered the row of lipsticks at the MAC counter at House of Fraser on Oxford Street where Hollie worked. Hollie was expertly applying an eyebrow pencil to a woman in her late forties, who was perching on a stool.

'This is perfect for you,' she told the woman. 'See how it brings out your eyes and defines your brows so much better? It really shapes your face.'

Indi smiled and shook her head from behind the counter. Hollie could sell snow to an Eskimo! Waiting for her friend, she picked out a shimmery bubblegum-pink lipstick. She was so bored of her dark smoky eye and nude lip combination.

All done with her latest sale, Hollie approached Indi and pretended she was a new customer. 'Need any help, madam?'

Indi giggled. 'Yes, please, I'd love to try this colour. And don't skimp on the lip liner, either.'

Hollie frowned. 'It's a bit girly for you, isn't it, Indi?' The role play didn't last long.

'I want a new look. Miles has a thing for pink lips.' She had another date with him tonight and thought she'd better make an effort.

'Indi, what are you playing at? I know you don't fancy Miles. There's nothing remotely fanciable about him for starters, but he's especially not your type.'

Indi sat on Hollie's make-up stool and handed Hollie the lipstick.

'I need a distraction. Connor isn't coming back, is he?' The two still hadn't spoken since their row. So many times Indi had typed a message to him and then deleted it, or hovered her finger over the call button. She missed him with every fibre in her soul, but hated him for cheating on her.

'Tom's seeing Connor later this week,' said Hollie, as she buffed Indi's lips with primer. 'I'll get all the gossip. He got back from Miami days ago, but I've still seen no sign of him.'

'I know where he's been.' Indi reached for her phone. 'I know you told me not to look on social media and that it would only make me feel worse, but you know how easy it is.'

Hollie gasped. 'Has Connor posted something?'

Indi shook her head. 'But Anja has. He took her on a minibreak to Milan, look.' She showed Hollie Anja's Instagram feed. There was an arty picture of two champagne glasses clinking by a sunset, captioned: *Reunited and it feels sooooo good.* Another was a picture of Anja naked in bed, her modesty covered by a thin sheet and her hands over her face, though you could make out her grin underneath. *Someone thinking it's fun to take a picture of me first thing!!!* read the caption. Connor didn't feature in the photos but he was tagged in them both, as was her Milan location. And they were just the sort of photos he'd allow to be posted on Instagram. He hated being in pictures himself.

Ben had alerted Indi to the photos that morning, saying he wasn't sure whether or not to tell her but hated keeping secrets from her. Indi felt as if she'd been punched in the stomach when she saw them, proof that Connor and Anja were back together, but reasoned that perhaps it was the jolt of reality she needed. Connor wasn't hers any more. And he'd cheated on her, so why should she care anyway?

'And, there's more,' Indi added, showing Hollie the picture of them together with Matt and James she'd posted to Instagram when they were in Brighton. 'More comments, look.' Hollie read through. Sure enough, comments from anonymous accounts were written underneath. This time there weren't just a couple, there were fifteen:

She looks cheap and tacky dressed like that.

Vile woman from a toxic family.

Rough face, rough clothes.

What a really pathetic existence, everyday just poncing and posing about taking pictures of yourself. Must be so insecure.

Hahaha why does she love herself so much?

'Oh, Indi . . .' Hollie didn't know what to say. The trolling was sickening and she didn't want to believe for a second that Connor was back with Anja or that he wasn't madly in love with Indi. But it was hard to deny the evidence. 'Block them all. Now.'

'What's the point? It takes minutes to start a new account. I'm going to make all my accounts private now so no one can write anything. I hope the business doesn't suffer, though.'

'Course it won't. And it's only temporary.'

Indi fought back tears.

'Please let's not talk about it. I'm so bored of thinking about him and the damn trolls and getting upset. Connor is a cheating scumbag. End of. And I know you don't think I like Miles, but I do.'

Hollie raised an eyebrow.

'Well, he likes me, Holl, and he treats me well. That's more than I can say for Connor. Miles might be a bit cringe and clingy sometimes, but isn't it better to have a guy that's more into you than you are into him? That way you won't ever get hurt. Anyway, enough about me. How are things going with you and Tom?'

Hollie played down her feelings for Tom as she didn't want to seem insensitive. Indi knew her friend well, though, and pressed her for more information. No matter what heartache she was experiencing, seeing her best friend this loved-up made her genuinely happy.

Hollie bit her lip. 'I think he might ask me to move in.'

'That's amazing! It makes sense, though. You two spend most nights together anyway. It'll get you off my sofa half the week, too!'

'Cheeky cow! We'd have to find somewhere new, though. Have you been to Tom's flat? It's always cold and his bedroom is tiny. It wouldn't even fit my make-up kit, let alone my shoe collection!'

They laughed but were interrupted by Indi's phone ringing from a private number. 'One second, Holl, this might be work.' She answered.

'Indigo? It's Saskia Taylor.'

'Oh, er, hello, Saskia. What can I do for you?'

'Indigo, I'd like to talk to you. I owe you an apology. A big apology. I understand if you don't want to, but perhaps I could buy you coffee? I'll work around your schedule.

I know you must be busy.' If only, thought Indi. Not only had she lost that bareMinerals contract, but Ben had found out that Connor had decided to arrange Print Room's New Year's Eve party in-house, plainly wanting to avoid spending any more time with Indi than necessary. She was still contracted to arrange 360's Christmas party and would soon be working closely with Connor again. Not only was she dreading it, but there was no other work to distract her.

'I'm actually pretty free. Tell me where and when.'

Chapter Twenty-Two

It was a chilly autumnal day in November. Indi detested winter as she hated snow and loved being warm, but autumn was still bearable, she thought. The ground was littered with leaves in shades of brown, copper and amber, and the weather wasn't too fierce.

'The best thing about autumn is boots and coats,' Hollie always said cheerfully. That girl really did see the upside to everything! Indi sprayed herself generously with her favourite Tom Ford perfume and zipped up her prize LK Bennett leather boots and long camel coat. She looked smart and professional, even if she felt anything but. She'd been dreading the day all week. Not only was she meeting Connor to catch up on 360's imminent Christmas party, Saskia was coming to meet her afterwards, and Indi had no idea what her agenda was. The only contact she'd had with Connor since his text to tell her he'd fired Kyle was a curt email asking her to go to Print Room for their meeting. Indi shuddered at the memory of the last time she had been there, when Anja had given her the news that had made Indi's world crash down. She replied to Connor, equally formally, saying she had meetings in central London that day and please could they meet at the Sanderson Hotel. Neutral territory, Indi concluded. The only hopeful aspect about her meeting with him, however, was that she'd thought of a way to save Kyle. It had been days since Connor had threatened to call the police. Indi had no idea why he hadn't, but she hoped her idea would prevent him from ever doing so. She just prayed it wasn't too late.

The thought of seeing Connor made her feel so anxious that she'd barely slept the night before and had not managed to eat a thing. She really was experiencing the heartbreak diet and looked skinnier than ever – and Indi had never needed to lose weight. Her normally perfectly fitted trousers were looser around her tiny hips and her face was so pale she needed to apply an extra layer of foundation.

Her heart raced as she made the short walk from Tottenham Court Road Station to the Sanderson. Connor was already waiting at a table, a black espresso in front of him. He looked so unnervingly handsome that Indi was at once overcome with desire and disgust. She wanted more than anything to throw her arms around him as if nothing had happened, and at the same time she struggled to look at him. She had to let her feelings go. She had never allowed a man to walk all over her, and Connor Scott would be no exception. She took a deep breath, put on her steely poker face and approached him. He shot up from his chair the moment he saw her.

'Hi.' He stared at her, his face flushed. *Is that a note of guilt and shame in his expression?* thought Indi. *Good.*

'Hi,' she replied coolly.

There was an awkward silence, then they both spoke at the same time, asking how the other one was.

'Sorry,' said Connor. 'I'm fine.'

'Me too, fine.' Another awkward silence. *Why isn't he apologising?* She knew he was with Anja now, the woman he really loved, but out of respect didn't she deserve some sort of apology? Had she meant so little to him that he could have sex with Anja and not feel even the slightest bit of remorse? She took in Connor's demeanour. Yes, he looked gorgeous, but he seemed cold, rude and uninterested. So different from the Connor she had known and fallen in love with; the man who had kissed her hand when he held it, the man who'd laughed at her jokes and rubbed his foot against hers affectionately under every table they had dinner at.

They were both avoiding each other's eyes. Then Connor broke the next awkward silence. 'Let's just get on with this, shall we? I've got to be somewhere after this.'

With Anja? Indi wanted to scream. 'Fine,' she said instead, hoping he didn't see how hurt she was. 'The priority is invitations. I've emailed you the guest list Nicolas has approved. It just needs your sign-off.'

'Just go with it, I trust you.'

Could he be any less interested? 'And here's my sketch of the ski lifts I'm having installed. They'll double up as photo booths so guests can take pictures inside. We'll cover the furniture with fake fur; there will be buckets of champagne by every table, of course, and Swiss-inspired cocktails and canapés.'

'Looks good. What about security?'

'Same team as before. All over the red carpet and by the lifts, and also inside.'

They spent a few more minutes agreeing details, and then Connor looked at his phone.

'I've gotta go. I'll pay the bill on my way out. Keep me posted.' He got up to leave but Indi held out a hand to stop him.

'Connor, before you go. I just wanted to say thanks for not calling the police on Kyle. I thought you would have by now. We both did. And I don't know if you're planning to, but I just wanted to say, please don't. *Please*, please don't. It would hurt my dad so much to see Kyle in trouble.'

Connor started to speak but Indi talked over him.

'I'll pay you back the money myself. I can't believe I didn't think of that earlier, to be honest. I mean, it's the most obvious solution when you think about it.' She was rambling now. 'Anyway, I'll take it from my savings account and transfer it over to you today.'

Connor sat down again. 'I'm not going to call the police. I thought about it after we . . . Well, I was angry with you. But, I couldn't do that to Kyle. Or your dad.'

'Angry with *me*? And I still have no idea why—' Indi stared at Connor, her face contorted in shock and fury.

Connor got up again. 'I'm not doing this here, Indigo. I don't want another fight with you. The police won't know anything, let's leave it at that.'

Indi dropped her shoulders. What was the point? 'OK,

write down your bank details and I'll send you the money now.'

'I'll text them to you,' Connor said briskly. And with that he was gone. Indi was dumbfounded. Angry with her, what had he meant? *He* was the one who'd cheated on *her*. This needed serious analysis with Hollie, but right now she had work to do – and didn't have the time or energy to dissect Connor's bizarre behaviour. One good thing had come out of their meeting, though. She texted Kyle: *I'd phone you but there's no point seeing as you never pick up to me any more. I've spoken to Connor. Don't worry about the police or the money. I've dealt with it. x*

A few seconds she sent another: *Love you and miss you. xx*

She did miss her brother. They had always been so close, but recently he'd become distant, and since stealing the money had pretty much ignored her entirely. She didn't know what was going on with Kyle but just hoped he'd confide in her soon and things would go back to normal. She was so deep in thought that she jumped when her phone rang.

'Hi, Miles.'

'Hey! You OK, babe? I rang you twice earlier and you didn't answer.' Indi didn't like it when Miles called her 'babe'. She hadn't minded Connor using the phrase, and when she and Hollie used the term it was affectionate, but coming from Miles it made her squirm. In fact, lots of the things Miles said made her squirm. Like his ever-increasing arrogance. Indi hated people gloating about how much money they had, or boasting about their achievements, as Miles frequently did. He was also annoyingly clingy and insecure, getting worried if she didn't answer his call immediately and phoning her incessantly if she went out with Hollie instead of him.

They'd been on five dates in total. The first had been the drink at the pub, followed by a second date at the same pub, for dinner this time. Their third date was a DVD and dinner at Indi's, where they'd kissed for the first time before Indi said that she was tired and could they call it a night? For their fourth date Miles took her to the opening of a restaurant in Covent Garden, a freebie from his job, where he complained about the food and service all night. Their fifth was at the cinema – her idea, as she figured she wouldn't have to talk to him. Or rather, listen as he talked at her. She couldn't avoid kissing him again, but doing so made her feel sick; not because he was a bad kisser, but because he wasn't Connor. But she figured the best way to move on from the love of her life was to date someone else. And at least Miles would never hurt her. Indi was sure she'd grow to care for him, it would just take a bit of time.

'I've been working, Miles. I was in the office with Ben and I've just had a meeting with Connor at the Sanderson.'

'Connor?'

'Yes. He is the co-owner of 360, remember? And I do have a contract with them.'

'Oh. Of course, yeah. Sorry, babe, I just missed you, that's all. I hate not being with you.'

Indi shifted uncomfortably in her seat. 'I'm sorry but I do need to go. My two o'clock meeting will be here any minute. Call you later?'

'Sure! I'm at work but I'll have my mobile by me all day. Or if not just call the office. You have that number, right?'

'Yes, I have it. Bye, Miles.'

'Bye!'

Saskia had been having a great morning. Millie had accepted her offer of a lift to school and didn't even shy away when Saskia kissed her at the gates. Usually she'd walk with her friend Sadie and scold Saskia for embarrassing her if she so much as smiled her way. On top of that, Fitz & Sass PR was now an official company, and a press release announcing their union had just gone out. Saskia was also having such fun organising a drinks party to officially welcome their company to the industry. Finally things seemed to be looking up for her, but reconciling with Indigo was a priority.

Saskia tipped the taxi driver as he pulled up outside the Sanderson and lightly stepped out of the car and through the glass doors of the hotel. She spotted Indi at once, and was taken aback at how thin she looked. Gorgeous, still, her dark brown hair flowing in tousled waves over her shoulders, but pale and withdrawn. Her laptop was open in front of her, but she was staring into space. Saskia walked over gingerly.

'Indi?'

'Saskia. Hi.' She got up and they shook hands before sitting opposite one another, both nervous. 'I saw the press release about Fitz & Sass, that's great, Saskia. Congratulations.'

'Thank you.' Saskia blushed. Even after the awful things

she'd said, Indi was still so polite. Coffees ordered and a few more pleasantries over with, Saskia's speech came blurting out.

'Indi, I owe you a huge apology. I acted so hideously towards you from the second we met at The Square. I know you were just being friendly and helpful. And the things I said to you at 360 . . . Well, they were unforgivable.'

'Thank you, Saskia.'

'The last few months have been incredibly stressful,' Saskia went on, feeling there should be more explanation. 'My husband, my ex-husband, is about to have a baby. Work has been almost non-existent and I thought my daughter hated me. I've known Nicolas for years, and when he picked you over me for that 360 contract, I just saw red. I know none of this is an excuse but I want you to know how truly sorry I am for the way I acted towards you and the things I said. It was out of line. That's all I came to say.'

'I'm sorry to hear things have been so tough for you,' Indi replied quietly. 'Nicolas actually told me how highly he thought of you, but that he was a little concerned.'

'Really? He said that?'

'Oh, yes. He said you were the best in the business and that he'd been meaning to call you. I think he's a bit nervous.'

Saskia smirked. 'Typical man. Ruthless when it comes to business but useless when it comes to talking to women!'

They both laughed.

'I really appreciate you coming down here to say that,' said Indi. 'I never wanted to take anything from you.'

Saskia held out her hand as a peace offering, but Indi batted it away and went in for a hug instead. Saskia felt her bony figure.

'Now that's all sorted, I don't know about you but I need a drink,' said Indi. 'Fancy sharing a bottle of prosecco?'

Saskia shook her head. 'No thanks, I'm trying to cut back on the booze.'

'Good for you. I'm ordering a large glass of wine anyway. Screw it. Another cappuccino?'

Saskia's maternal instinct was coming out now, she couldn't help it. Ordering wine alone on a Wednesday afternoon was a little too familiar to her. 'Indi, I hope you don't mind me asking,' she said as the waiter disappeared with their order, 'but are you OK?'

'I'm fine, why?' Indi snapped back.

'I just noticed that you're much thinner than I've seen you before and you look a little peaky. I'm not rude by saying that, am I?'

Indi did think it was a tad rude. She and Saskia might have reconciled, but they were hardly best mates. 'I think your phone is ringing,' she replied, somewhat defensively.

Saskia disappeared to take the call and Indi took a gulp of white wine. Normally she loved a chilled glass of Sauvignon, but this tasted acidic in her empty stomach.

'Sorry about that,' said Saskia when she returned to the table. 'That was my daughter. Her useless father was supposed to take her for pizza after school and buy her some new trainers, but he's bailed. Again.'

'That sucks. How old is your daughter?'

'Millie is fifteen. That sweet age!' Saskia gave an ironic laugh.

Indi smiled. She remembered her teenage years all too well. Mainly because they were clouded in grief over losing her beloved mother.

'I see. Has she decided the whole world is against her yet?'

Saskia grinned and nodded. 'Oh yes. And that everything is generally my fault.'

'Standard,' said Indi, even though she really didn't know what that felt like at all.

Saskia clocked this at once. 'Why don't you come over later for dinner? I mean, if you're not doing anything. I'm sure you've got tons of better plans. Millie would no doubt think you're the coolest young woman in the world and that would get me extra brownie points! I'm not the best cook, mind you, but you can't go wrong with a load of spaghetti Bolognese, right?'

Indi considered this. She certainly didn't want to spend another boring evening listening to Miles bang on about how successful he was, but she also felt guilty cancelling on him again.

'That's really kind of you. And a home-cooked meal does sound utterly delicious, but there's something I have to do tonight. Maybe another time, though?'

'Why don't I email you some dates when I'm back in the office? Millie would so love to meet you. I know this is forward, Indigo, but if you need someone to talk to – about anything – I would be happy to listen.'

There was so much on Indi's mind. She found herself

warming to Saskia, who suddenly seemed so familiar. She barely knew her but felt as though she could talk to her. But then her independent side took over and she told herself she didn't need anyone else.

'Thank you, Saskia. But, I'm fine, really.'

Chapter Twenty-Three

Connor hurried out of the Sanderson and away from Indi. He told her that he had another appointment, but his meeting with a new investor wasn't for another hour. Seeing Indi was more difficult than he'd anticipated it would be. He felt utterly conflicted. It was torture sitting in front of her, looking at her tiny frame and pained, pale face and not taking her in his arms. He was riddled with guilt over what he'd done with Anja, and wanted to tell Indi this so badly, but at the same time she'd hurt him too. For as long as Connor could remember he'd built a wall to protect himself. He didn't need a shrink to tell him he had abandonment issues from his father leaving him and his family when he was so young. He had shown more vulnerability with Indi than he had ever done with a girlfriend, but that had changed now. He didn't know if he could trust her. He didn't know if he could forgive himself. How could he feel so much anger towards her, as well as guilt and desire? The wall was up again, taller and stronger than ever.

Later he walked through the doors of the Old King's Head where Tom was already waiting with two full pints of lager. It was a dingy, dark, old man's pub with a darts board and sofas that still smelt of smoke ten years after London's smoking ban, but Connor and Tom had been going since they were teenagers. It was still their favourite pub. The boys greeted each other with a hug.

'Good to see you, mate,' said Tom. 'It's been a while.'

Connor sat down and took off his black wool coat. 'Yeah. I've been taking some time out.'

'As you always do when things go tits up,' Tom replied. 'Want to tell me what's been going on? I thought you and Indigo were the perfect couple. God knows you've been banging on about her enough for the last few months!'

'How much did Hollie tell you?'

'That you slept with Anja and that Indi has taken it pretty badly. She says she can't believe that you'd do something like that, though. And neither do I. I told her that couldn't be true.' Tom took a sip of beer. 'I mean, Anja is fit as fuck. I get that. But she's mental!' Tom had known about the incessant texting and begging Connor to come back since way before Indi.

Connor rubbed his forehead wearily. 'I don't know what happened with Anja. I was drunker that night than I have been in years.'

'Drunker than when we went to Magaluf and you

231

took your trousers off and passed out in the kebab shop?' teased Tom.

Connor groaned. 'We were eighteen! And you swore never to mention that again. And yes, if you can believe it, even drunker than that. It's a total mess, mate.' He told Tom about Kyle and the CCTV footage, then gave him a full account of his subsequent row with Indi.

'She stormed out, telling me to go fuck myself, basically.' Connor took a few gulps of beer. 'Later that day I got an email – I didn't know who it was from, an anonymous email address. They sent me pictures. Pictures of Indigo and that actor Elliot bloody Blake, cosied up in some café. She's looking like she's about to cry, he's got his arms round her.'

'Who on earth would bother sending you that?' asked Tom.

'I don't know. But the point isn't who sent me them, it's what the hell is Indi doing with him, letting him be all over her, after claiming she doesn't even know him?' Connor spoke with feeling now. 'I was pissed off anyway after our fight, and seeing those pictures just sent me over the edge, so I made Eddie take the afternoon off and get shit-faced with me at Print Room. A couple of the waitresses joined us and by the evening I was hammered. Anja came over to join the group and we ordered more booze. Then, you know what she told me? That her mate had told her Elliot and Indi had been at The Square a couple of weeks ago, all over each other.'

'And you believed her?'

'It makes sense, doesn't it?'

232

Tom sighed. 'Then what happened?'

'Anja came back to mine. The next thing I knew, I'd woken up in my boxers to the sound of Indi banging my door down and screaming what a prick I am.'

'You are a prick. It's much more likely Anja was telling you lies. You know she's crazy in love with you. Like, *literally* crazy in love with you.'

Connor did know this. But would she go so far as to make up these lies? And what about the anonymous pictures of Indi and Elliot looking so close?

'She certainly isn't the innocent party in all this,' he grumbled.

'Are you sure you don't *want* to believe that something was going on with her and the actor so it makes you feel less guilty about sleeping with Anja?' asked Tom.

Connor looked up sheepishly. It was true: so much of the anger he felt towards Indi was anger at himself. The thought of hurting her burned a hole in his heart.

Tom continued, knowing that it was difficult for his friend to hear, but if he wasn't frank with him, no one else would be.

'Do you really believe she cheated on you? Those pictures could have been anything. Has she been upset over anything else lately? Like, before you two broke up?'

'Yes. There were all those stories in the press about how she was having an affair with Elliot, and that News Hub exposé on her family. But she should have talked to me, not him! She told me she didn't even know the guy! It looks like they got to know each other pretty well.'

'I get that.' Tom nodded. 'But, mate, you should've just

talked to her. Indi isn't a cheater. I could see the way she looked at you. Hollie saw it too. She said Indi has never been like this around any bloke.'

'She said that?'

'Yep. And I would put money on the fact that Anja made up that bollocks about her mate seeing those two all over each other, knowing you were hammered and angry anyway, so she could seduce you and tell Indi all about it.'

'Yeah. I know. But the pictures—'

'Are rubbish. The only person you need to speak to about them is Indigo. Which you should have done in the first place and avoided this sorry mess. Go and talk to her now.'

But Connor didn't think he could. Things had been left for so long it somehow seemed easier just to believe it. 'What would I say?'

'That you're sorry and that you love her?'

'I hear she's seeing someone else anyway. That fucking journalist who looks about twelve and always hangs around Print Room with Anja. I knew he had a crush on Indi, but I gave her more credit.'

'Rebound,' Tom snorted.

There was a pause while the two men silently finished their beers and Connor then slipped off to get another round. He returned and placed the pints and two bags of dry roasted peanuts on the table.

'She won't want anything to do with me after I sacked her brother.'

'I'm sure she'd understand if you explained.' Tom gobbled down some peanuts and spoke with a mouthful.

'And you said she'd offered to pay back the money. Doesn't sound like she blames you for firing him, just that she's grateful you haven't grassed him up to the police.'

Connor shook his head. 'I've paid the money back myself. I couldn't take anything from her. I'm angry with her over those pictures, I was so angry I wanted to get the police involved, but I would never have been able to go through with it.'

'You need to tell her all of this, mate.'

'Promise me you won't say anything to Hollie? I know she'll tell Indi, and I just think if anything needs to be said it should come from me.'

Tom groaned. Hollie knew he was seeing Connor tonight and would be giving him an extensive grilling about what exactly had been said. 'Ah, mate. We're supposed to be looking at flats this weekend. I can't keep secrets from her, can I?'

'You'd better.' Connor was indignant. 'I'm your best mate, after all.'

'OK, OK. Just make sure you talk to Indigo. And soon. She'll understand.'

'Really?' Connor wasn't so sure.

Chapter Twenty-Four

Indi stepped out of Clapham North Underground Station with purpose. She had on a black skirt, which was much shorter and tighter than she normally felt comfortable in, but Miles had told her she looked so sexy in short skirts, she thought she should make an effort for him. She had on her frosted-pink, bubblegum lipstick and extra eyeshadow. Miles would probably have loved it if she'd worn a tight, low-cut top, but it felt too much for Indi, so instead she wore a fitted white shirt.

She felt sorry for Miles. He really had been so attentive recently (verging on clingy) but she had to make a go of it. Seeing Connor earlier that day had only reinforced the realisation that she was still in love with him; but he was back with Anja now and Indi was determined to put all her efforts into getting over him. Miles was kind of cute, she supposed, with his indie-boy haircut and dishevelled look. Hollie was right, it wasn't a look Indi usually went for in a bloke, and was certainly a far cry from Connor's polished image, but Indi kept telling herself to not be so narrow-minded and to look beyond all that.

Revolution bar was busy for a Wednesday night, but Miles had found a booth tucked away in the corner. It wasn't the location Indi would ideally have chosen for a quiet date, but at least most of the crowds were towards the front, hovering around the bar doing shots. It didn't take a genius to guess that Miles had purposely selected a bar close to his own house, to entice Indi to spend the night with him. She was dreading it, quite frankly.

'Hi, Miles,' she said, slipping on to the sofa next to him.

'Hello, gorgeous.' Miles went in for a long kiss on the mouth. Indi felt sick. It wasn't that he was a bad kisser, but she felt that she was somehow being unfaithful to Connor, which was ridiculous as he was so obviously over her.

'I got you a white wine.' Then with a wink he added, 'Large.'

Cringe! 'Thanks, Miles, that's really sweet.' She took a sip and felt her stomach churn. She'd still not eaten today and feared she'd pass out if she didn't get something to eat. 'I'm going to order some chips, do you want anything?'

'Yeah, I'll have a bowl of chips thanks, babe.' She sloped off to order the food and when she returned Miles gazed at her figure. 'You look amazing by the way, Indi. Very sexy outfit.'

'Really? Everyone's been telling me lately how ill I'm looking. I guess I've not had much of an appetite, what with everything that's been going on. But I think they're right. I don't want to waste away.'

'Oh no, being skinny really suits you!'

'Thanks . . .' Indi didn't quite know what he meant by that. 'So, how was work today?'

Miles happily talked about how great his job was and his latest scoop about an *X Factor* contestant whose ex-boyfriend had sold Miles a video of them having sex. Indi winced as Miles boasted about it. It didn't sound like a raunchy sex tape, more like a girl being intimate with her boyfriend, who then cruelly sold it to a tabloid website the minute she got famous. Indi understood that she needed a good relationship with the press to give her coverage of her celebrity-filled parties, and she was immensely grateful for all the support they and Miles had given her over the years. But there was a side to the tabloids she really hated. Not everyone asked to have their personal lives splashed around for the world to see. She thought of how hurt her dad had been when it happened to him. But Indi didn't feel like getting into a debate with Miles over morals and ethics, so when the food came she ate silently while he talked, downing her wine and immediately fetching another. By 10.30 p.m. she was tipsy but feeling far more relaxed, and even managed to have a laugh with Miles about some old university memories.

'It's getting pretty late, Ind, do you, er, fancy coming back mine? For a cup of tea or whatever.'

'Or whatever?' Indi teased, masking her tension.

'I'll just pop to the loo,' he replied. As Indi waited, she scrolled through her phone. She knew she should stay well clear of Connor's social media account, but she couldn't help herself. She had to see what he was up to. There were no new posts. He wasn't much of an Instagrammer anyway.

She cautiously checked Anja's feed. No new pictures here, but various comments underneath the one of her in bed, saying how beautiful she looked and how she and Connor were the 'best couple ever'. Indi felt sick again. Screw Connor, she thought, swigging the dregs of her wine. Miles was her new man. Anja and Connor deserved each other. At least Miles wouldn't hurt her.

'So, what do you want to do?' asked Miles when he returned to their booth. Indi pulled him towards her and kissed him. It was the hard, passionate sort of kiss she'd usually reserved for Connor. But Connor was history.

'Back to yours,' she said confidently. A huge grin spread over Miles's face and he led her by the hand out of the bar.

Miles lived in a huge house just off Clapham High Street with four others – a French girl who was studying medicine, a lad who was a picture researcher from News Hub, a girl who worked in TV production and an out-of-work actor. Three of them were slumped on the sofa watching TV when Indi came in. She felt extremely awkward in her short skirt, especially when the boys winked at Miles, not so subtly. They probably thought he'd just picked her up at the bar. *Cringe!* You could tell the house had once been beautiful, with cream carpets, white walls and nice sofas, but had been tainted by various house-share groups messing it up over the years. There were mud stains all over the carpet and washing-up piled high in the kitchen.

'Reminds me of your house on Mare Street!' teased Indi, referring to his grotty student house in Sussex.

'A few notches up from that, I should hope! Do you want

239

a cup of tea or anything?' But Indi felt uncomfortable in his bright, cold kitchen, so suggested they just go straight upstairs. Part of her was thinking, *Let's just get this over with*, while the other was totting up all the nice things about Miles that should make her fancy him. *Likes me, treats me well, sweet, attentive, makes an effort, nice jacket . . .*

Miles had a big bedroom on the top floor. The bed was all made up in the corner and his huge wooden desk with his laptop and work folders were arranged neatly.

'Did you tidy up just for me?' she teased again, looking around and kicking off her black high heels. It was so obvious he did.

'No! It's always this tidy, I swear.'

'Yeah, right! Well, that's sweet. If presumptuous . . .' She sat on the edge of his bed while he switched off the main light and turned on a dim side lamp, then came to sit next to her.

'You know I really like you, don't you, Indi? In fact, I've developed really strong feelings for you.'

'Aw, Miles.'

'I mean it. I know you felt strongly about Connor, but I just want the chance to make you happy.' At the mention of Connor, Indi tensed inside, then shook the memory away. She inched closer to Miles and whispered closely.

'Don't mention his name. I'm here with you.' And she kissed him, ignoring how wrong it felt, how much she wanted it to be Connor. She ran her hands over Miles's chest. Connor's chest was so firm and manly; Miles felt like a skinny boy who'd never even seen the gym. *No, stop! Stop comparing them!* She channelled the anger she felt for herself into passion and pulled herself on top of Miles so she was straddling him, her skirt up by her waist.

'Oh, Indi,' he murmured in between kisses, 'I want you so much.' Then they were tugging at each other's clothes. She lifted his t-shirt off and his cold hands fumbled underneath her shirt, reaching for her breasts but pinching her nipples.

'Ow!' she reacted.

'Sorry,' and his hands were on her breasts but squeezing instead of caressing. It wasn't sexy. She pushed his hands downwards – *maybe he's better down there*, she thought.

'Ohh, yeah, baby,' he muttered. Then he was squeezing her bum, slapping it gently then hard.

'Ow! Miles!'

'Sorry, babe.' God, she really just wanted to get this over with now. She lay back so he was on top of her, unzipping her skirt and pulling down her tights. His kisses were fast. Too fast. This felt more than unsexy, it felt wrong. As his fingers plunged hard inside her she recoiled and pushed him off her.

'What's wrong?' he asked breathlessly, kissing her neck sloppily and trying to push her back down on to the bed.

'No, Miles, stop.'

'Indi, what the fuck?' The insensitive reaction made her instinctively cover her exposed breasts with her arms.

'Miles, I'm sorry. I – I don't think I can do this,' she said quietly, doing up her shirt and pulling up her tights.

'*What?*' he fumed. His reaction just cemented the fact that she couldn't go through with it. She put her heels back on.

Miles, realising his angry approach wasn't working, tried a different one: begging.

'I'm sorry, please come back to bed.' She sat at the edge of his bed but shook her head as he tried to kiss her. 'What's wrong?'

'I just can't do this.'

'Indi. You know how much I like you. You know I've had a crush on you since pretty much the minute I met you, right?' Indi was too modest to say so, but of course she had known.

'The thing is,' Miles continued, 'I think I've fallen in love with you, Indigo.' And he was kissing her again, hands straight down to her crotch.

'No, Miles. I can't do this. It's not fair to you. I think I should call a cab and go home.'

'No!'

'I'm so flattered by what you just said, but it just proves why we shouldn't go any further. I can't pretend I feel the same way about you. I feel terrible. I never meant to lead you on.'

'But why? Just give me a chance. You're here now.'

'I've got so much going on at the moment with my family and with work that I just haven't got time for a new relationship.'

'But, Indi—'

'Please, let me say this. If those were the only reasons, then maybe there would be a chance with us, but we both know what the real reason is. I'm still in love with Connor. It's not even been a month since we broke up and I'm just not ready to date anyone. I know he's not in love with me but I need time to move on. And I need to be alone to do that. I'm sorry.'

A dark expression came over Miles's face. He didn't look hurt so much as incensed. He flew off the bed, zipped his jeans back up and put his t-shirt back on, frustrated.

'I'm sorry,' she said again. 'I'm going to order an Uber.' Suddenly she wanted to get the hell out of there as quickly as she could. Thankfully there was an Uber just five minutes away. 'I'll wait outside.'

Miles paced up and down his room a few times, then his face dropped into a smile again. 'Sure. Don't worry about it,' he said curtly.

'I never meant to lead you on or anything. I do care for you, Miles, but as a friend. I hope you understand.'

'I've told you, it's fine.'

'Really?' Indi was surprised that he was so calm. She gingery leant towards him for a hug, to show that there were no hard feelings. He reciprocated with a rather brisk hug, squeezing her tightly then letting her go abruptly.

'Thank you for understanding, Miles. I hope we can still be friends?'

'Sure. We can be friends. Whatever is meant to be will be, as they say. I'm sure you and Connor will both get what you deserve. You can see yourself out.' And with that Miles stormed into his bathroom and locked the door. She heard the shower start to run. It was a pretty cold response but Indi didn't really blame him for being dismissive. He probably thought she was a total prick-tease. She certainly felt like one. A dirty one. She took her bag and coat and slipped out as quickly and quietly as she could so that his housemates wouldn't hear.

She waited outside his house for her Uber, shivering in the cold. This skirt was going straight to Oxfam. She felt like a hooker! She thought about Miles. It was such a strange response and a weird comment. *I'm sure you'll both get what you deserve.* But Indi reasoned that she'd probably hurt his ego and he was simply feeling a bit resentful. He had every right to be grumpy towards her. He'd get over it.

'Have you spoken to Kyle yet?' Hollie asked, peering down at Indi, who was carefully applying luminous orange nail varnish to Hollie's toes. It was Saturday evening and they were sharing a bottle of wine in Indi's living room. Hollie had brought Indi a bag of new MAC samples and Indi had ordered a Chinese takeaway feast of chicken noodles, vegetable dishes, duck and pancakes and spring rolls.

'Nope. He's still not answering any of my texts. Dad has cottoned on that there is some distance between us too, now. He keeps asking why I haven't been round to the house for a couple of weeks. Apparently every time he asks Kyle about me, Kyle goes silent.' It had been weeks since Indi had confronted her brother about stealing the money from 360's safe and Kyle had been doing an excellent job of avoiding her, despite her incessant texts and phone calls.

'I want to go and see my dad, but it would be so awkward if Kyle was there and we hadn't spoken. I just think he and I need to talk alone first, but he clearly doesn't want to.'

'It's so strange, not like Kyle at all,' Hollie mused with a mouthful of prawn cracker. After a pause she spoke again.

'Ind, I wanted to wait tell you this in person. But Tom saw Connor the other day.'

Indi looked up instantly. She'd been trying for days not to think about Connor but to no avail. Even though she hated herself for it, she was desperate to know what the boys had talked about. Unfortunately, she was in for a disappointment. Hollie threw her hands up in the air dramatically. 'But don't bother asking what was said, because Tom is completely useless at gossip. He just gives me one-word answers whenever I ask him what Connor said, and then changes the subject.'

Indi rolled her eyes. 'Typical boys, babe. Connor would have made Tom swear not to tell you anything. He's so secretive anyway and he knows you're the biggest gossip in London.'

'Hey!' But Hollie laughed. 'Well, he did say that he highly doubts Connor ever slept with Anja and they are *definitely* not a couple.'

'Really? What about those pictures Anja posted from Milan?'

Hollie shrugged. 'I asked for a word-for-word account of their evening, but all he said was that. I told him Connor *must* have said more than that, but he claimed they didn't even talk about girls, just football.' She shook her head. 'Useless!'

Indi laughed. 'To be fair, I can believe that. How those two can dissect a bloody football match for four hours is beyond me. Did he really say that he and Anja aren't together?'

That was some relief, but what good did it do? If it

wasn't Anja who Connor was shagging, it was some other girl. In any case, his lack of contact made it obvious that he was well and truly over Indi. She decided to change the subject.

'So, how did the flat-hunt go today?'

'Really good,' replied Hollie. 'We viewed a few places in our budget so it's looking hopeful, but we're still not one hundred per cent agreeing. I'm all about a shiny new-build flat like you've got, but Tom says older buildings have more character. At least he's happy to be in north London so I'll be close to you and my family.'

At that, Indi's doorbell buzzed. 'Wonder who that can be?' she said. She answered the entry phone.

'It's me. I'm sorry for just turning up. Can I come in?'

Chapter Twenty-Five

'Of course you can! I'll buzz you in now.' Indi turned to Hollie. 'Kyle's here.'

'Thanks for letting me in.' Kyle shuffled into Indi's open-plan kitchen and living room. He was wearing trainers and a grey Adidas tracksuit speckled with rain.

'Oh, babe, you're drenched!' exclaimed Hollie. 'Where have you been?'

'Just at the gym. It's nothing, just a few drops of rain.'

Half a bottle of wine had taken effect, and Hollie threw her arms around him. Indi would normally roll her eyes at Hollie's dramatics, but she was so pleased to see her brother that she was equally attentive, ushering him in and making him a plate of food, piling on chicken wings and anything else she could find that the girls hadn't eaten.

'Holl, I think Connor left some beer in the fridge. Grab one for Kyle, would you?'

'On it!' came the reply.

'Wow, I should come round more often if this is the

service I get,' teased Kyle, relaxing as the girls fussed over him.

'Here, have some more chicken,' Indi said after Kyle had finished off the mountain of food she'd put in front of him. But he rubbed his belly and insisted he was fine.

The three sat on the sofas sipping their drinks. Kyle didn't say anything so Indi and Hollie glanced at each other.

'We always order too much, so it's a good thing you came round,' Indi offered. 'So, how's Dad?'

Kyle nodded. 'He's OK. Keeps asking why you and I aren't speaking.'

'What did you tell him?' There was another awkward silence and then Hollie sensed that maybe Indi and her brother needed some alone time, so offered to load the dishwasher.

'No, it's OK, Holl, you should probably hear this too,' said Kyle. Hollie sat back down on the sofa next to Indi and the girls glanced at each other again.

'I know you've been wondering why I took the money from 360.' The girls stared at him blankly. He took a deep breath. 'The truth is, I didn't steal it. I mean, I took it, but I didn't steal it. It was for someone else. They gave me the passcode to the safe.'

'Who?' said the girls in unison.

Another deep breath. 'Anja.'

'*Anja?*'

'She told me Connor had told her it was OK to take the money. She said he'd approved the loan, that she'd pay him back every penny and that it was all fine.'

Indi shook her head in disbelief. 'I don't understand. Anja asked you to take £8,000 out of the safe at 360?'

'She doesn't work there so she couldn't do it herself. She had the passcode, said that he'd given it to her, so why wouldn't I believe her?'

'But . . . But why?'

'She's in trouble with a loan shark. She borrowed money off them ages ago for modelling headshots; it was some dodgy guy who a dodgy photographer had put her in touch with. She's been really struggling to pay him back, and he started threatening her and adding interest.'

Indi doubted Anja struggled for anything. Connor told Indi when they were going out that Anja's parents owned a house in Fulham, one in the Cotswolds, and had bought the apartment that Anja and her model friend lived in. She paid no rent, worked as a hostess at Print Room and modelled occasionally. How broke could she be? But Indi didn't say anything and let her brother continue.

'It didn't seem like a big deal. Like I say, she told me Connor knew all about it.'

'But why *you*?' This from Hollie.

'Has Dad told you that I've been sleeping over at my mate's house a lot recently?'

'Yeah,' replied Indi, still confused. Kyle fidgeted nervously.

'I've been sleeping with Anja since I started working at 360. It's been going on for months but she wanted to keep it a secret so it wouldn't interfere with work. She said because Print Room and 360 are run by the same people, she didn't want it to get complicated. When she told me about the loan shark I was so worried, so I said I'd do anything I could to help her, but I never would have taken the money if I'd known it was stealing. When I told her you'd come round with CCTV pictures, and told me what Connor had said about going to the police, she burst into tears and made me promise not to tell anyone and swore that she'd sort it out with Connor and return the money.'

Indi stood up now, furious. 'And you believed her!'

'Of course I did. I *love* her!'

Indi threw her hands in the air and Hollie pulled her gently back to the sofa.

Kyle looked at the ground, shuffling in the armchair. 'Then she disappeared to Milan for a modelling job and told me she needed space. When Connor fired me, she dumped me and said she couldn't be with someone as young and unstable as me. I begged her to rethink, but she blocked me on her phone so I can't ring or text her. I was so ashamed I didn't know how to tell you, so I just avoided you. I wanted to tell Connor but I didn't think he'd believe me. No one would believe me because I'm useless and mental. But I couldn't keep it to myself any more.' Kyle looked as if he was about to cry. 'Anja kept the money. Now I'm going to go to jail.'

Indi leaped over to the chair and flung her arms around Kyle, while Hollie wrapped her arms around both of them.

Hollie was the first to speak. 'That fucking bitch. She's not going to get away with it. Right, Indi?'

'Abso-fucking-lutely right she's not getting away with it,' Indi shouted. She took in her brother's forlorn expression and stroked his head. 'First things first, you are *not* going to jail. I told you that the other day. The money is sorted. Well, it will be.'

Kyle looked up at her. 'What do you mean?'

'Connor promised me he wouldn't call the police. He says even after everything between us, he couldn't do that to you. I've told him I'll pay the money back out of my savings.'

'No, Indi. I can't let you do that. And, what are you talking about "everything between you"?'

Indi realised that Kyle didn't even know that she and Connor had split up. 'We broke up. Almost a month ago.'

'And it's time you knew the truth about Anja,' put in Hollie. 'She's the reason they broke up. She's madly, fully, psychotically in love with Connor and has been for *months*!'

Kyle looked sceptically at the girls. 'Connor? Connor is just her boss. I don't think she has mentioned him once since I've known her. She asks about you, Indi, all the time, and how your love life is, but I just thought she was taking an interest because you're my sister.'

Indi sighed. If only it were that simple. 'She and Connor used to date. Not for long, before you and I came on the scene, but he told me he dumped her when she got too clingy. When he and I started going out she was texting him constantly, begging him back. He told me there was nothing going on and he wanted nothing to do with her. She even came to my office in tears, apologising for stalking him.'

'I didn't even know Connor and Anja used to date,' Kyle said. 'I swear she never once mentioned it.'

'She conveniently left that part out,' snorted Hollie. 'Why admit to you that she's crazy-obsessed with Connor when she's convincing you that she's into you? I'm sorry to say this, mate, but you have been well and truly played.'

'We all have,' said Indi.

Hollie continued the story. 'Then Connor and Indi had a huge fight about you and the money from 360, and the next thing she knows Anja comes to her in floods of tears saying she'd slept with Connor and they were back together!'

Indi nodded. 'I went round to his house, confronted him; he said he could barely remember anything but could remember them kissing and taking their clothes off clearly enough.'

'That wanker!' exclaimed Kyle, shooting up from his seat. 'I'll go round. Let's see if he'll remember anything after I break his jaw.'

Indi pulled him back down. 'Don't be silly, Kyle, that won't do any good.'

'I'll pay you back, Indi, every penny, I swear,' cried Kyle, and he hit his palm against his head sharply. 'I can't believe what an idiot I am. I'm so stupid. Stupid, stupid, stupid. Thinking for a second someone like her could love someone like me.'

'Stop that right now,' Indi ordered. 'She's a master manipulator.' She couldn't believe what she'd heard. If she hated Anja before, she despised her with a passion now. 'And there's nothing to pay back yet. I keep asking Connor for his bank details so I can make the transfer, but he ignores me.'

'He won't take back the money?' Hollie asked. Indi

shook her head. 'So, he's not reporting Kyle but he's also not taking the money back,' Hollie said slowly. 'That's . . . nice of him.'

But Indi wasn't thinking about Connor. She could deal with what Anja had done to her, sleeping with Connor and rubbing it in her face by pretending she was sorry. But this, how she'd treated Kyle, Indi was never going to let her get away with it.

'I'm going to see Anja first thing tomorrow,' she said defiantly.

'What for?' asked Kyle. 'She'll only deny it. I haven't got any proof, Indi.'

'He's right,' Hollie said. 'I don't see what good it can do.'

'She needs to admit what she's done and pay the money back herself!' shouted Indi. 'And she owes my brother one hell of an apology.'

Hollie shook her head. 'That's never going to happen. Connor is the one you need to speak to. He needs to know the truth about what a complete psycho bitch Anja really is. Then he can fire her and re-employ Kyle.'

Indi mulled this over. She didn't look forward to that difficult conversation with Connor, but Hollie was right. She fired off a text to Connor, telling him they needed to talk asap and that it was important, and braced herself for the response. If he responded at all, that is. Much to Indi's surprise, he hit back minutes later: *I'm dropping Tom at Hollie's tomorrow afternoon. I can pop by yours afterwards?*

Indi replied – *yes* – and poured herself more wine. This wasn't going to be easy.

*

253

Hollie slept in Indi's bed that night, and Kyle on her living-room sofa. Indi woke before anyone and went out for an early morning run. She needed to clear her head and prepare herself for seeing Connor later. She couldn't comprehend the lengths Anja had gone to in order to deceive her brother, but she was relieved that Kyle had finally told her the truth and that the distance between them had disappeared.

When she returned to the flat, Hollie and Kyle were both still asleep. She looked at Kyle, passed out on the sofa. He was so tall his feet went over the edge of the furniture, but to her he still looked young and innocent. Indi thought back to when Kyle was born. She had been six at the time. Alan had led her into the hospital room, holding a finger over his lips. They'd crept in to see Kyle fast asleep in Lou's arms. She was red-faced and exhausted, hair stuck in sweat to her forehead, but she still looked beautiful to Indi – and completely elated.

'This is your baby brother, Indigo,' Lou said, as Alan carefully lifted Indi on to the bed so she could stare in wonder at the tiny, scrunched-up face. Lou leant across, kissed her daughter's head and whispered, 'You're going to be the best big sister in the world.'

Nine years later, Lou was on another hospital bed, but this time no one was smiling. Kyle had been so distraught when she was dying, he'd had to be taken out of the room screaming by Cat and Tim. Alan kept excusing himself to go outside for air, he was so overcome with pain, but Indi never left her mother's side. She held her hand tightly. Lou was so weak her voice was nothing more than a whisper.

'You'll always be my special girl.' She smiled. 'Promise me you'll look after Kyle. And one day let someone look after you.'

The flashback was so vivid. 'I promise, Mum,' she'd said.

She'd not managed to let anyone take care of her (although Connor had come close), but Indi had fulfilled her vow to take care of Kyle as best she could, always looking out for him and putting his needs before her own. But she couldn't help feeling that she'd failed now. She'd been so caught up in her own drama lately, she couldn't see that Kyle had started a whole relationship and even fallen in love. Or at least, had thought he was in love. The thought of Anja toying with Kyle's tender heart made Indi quake with rage. He had certainly done a good job of keeping their liaison under wraps for so long, but Indi still felt guilty for not sensing something wasn't right.

She diverted attention away from her guilt by cleaning the kitchen and making a pot of fresh coffee. The other two were still sound asleep, so she flipped open her laptop to do some work on the 360 Christmas party. It was just four weeks away now. It had been a while since Indi had checked Twitter, Instagram or Facebook, but curiosity got the better of her now, and she logged into Glamour To Go's social media accounts. Thankfully, there were no tweets to her, except from Davidas, her florist, posting about his new website and thanking Indi for all their work together. She also had a bunch of new followers, which was good. There was nothing derogatory on Facebook, but one strange comment on Instagram. Ben had posted a picture of the 360 Christmas party VIP invitation, with the caption: *One month to go until our fabulous ski lodge extravaganza!*

The picture had 167 'likes', and comments underneath ranged from hands-clapping emojis to people begging to be added to the guest list. The final comment strangely just read: *Can't wait for the showdown.* Next to it were three emojis – the red devil face, the crying with laughter face, and a flame.

Chapter Twenty-Six

At midday Hollie offered to drop Kyle home as she had her mum's car, before getting ready to meet Tom who was having lunch with her family.

'Are you going to be all right?' Hollie asked Indi as she slipped on her gold Converse trainers. Indi wasn't embracing the prospect of a cold and uneasy conversation with her ex. He'd be arriving in an hour.

'I'll just get it over with.'

'Call me if you need me. And come over afterwards? Mum and Dad are complaining they haven't seen you in ages and I don't want you to feel that you're alone.'

Indi hugged her friend. 'I will, babe, thanks.' And to Kyle, 'Tell Dad we're friends again, won't you? He'll be delighted, I'm sure. And tell him I'll call him later.'

'OK. Thanks, Ind. I'm sorry again for dragging you into all this.'

Indi tidied the flat and took her time getting ready. A hefty meal last night and a run this morning had put colour in her cheeks for the first time in weeks. She used a deep-conditioning almond hair mask to give her hair a healthy boost and a mud face mask to give her skin a glow. Make-up was just a slick of black mascara, pink blusher and lip balm. She came across the outlandish bubblegum-pink lipstick in her dressing-table drawer, the one she'd bought to please Miles when she'd tried to make a go of it with him. Hollie was right; it was an awful colour and not Indi's style at all. Miles had loved it, of course, and suggested she wear even more make-up. He loved that fake, WAG image. Indi felt most comfortable with the natural look. She selected a pair of light blue skinny jeans and a snug purple cashmere jumper with three-quarter-length sleeves. Simple and elegant. The doorbell rang. She stared at herself in the mirror. *You got this.*

'Hiya,' Indi said breezily. She stood back and caught Connor's rich aftershave as he brushed past her, the smell that had intoxicated her so many times before. He looked sexy as ever in jeans and a V-neck black jumper, but Indi wasn't about to lose her cool. 'Come in.'

Generally, nothing unnerved Connor Scott, but today he felt anxious. Being in Indi's flat brought back happy memories. He was ashamed of how discourteously he'd acted towards her at their Sanderson meeting. Talking to Tom had made him see things so differently. He didn't know if Indi was calling to reconcile but, whatever the reason, it would give him a chance to apologise.

'Place looks tidier than usual,' he commented with a smile. They always used to banter with each other, and mocking her messy habits was Connor's favourite playful insult.

'Yeah, well, I've hardly been here these past few weeks I've been so busy,' Indi replied coolly, not wanting to let on that she'd been so nervous before he arrived that she'd plumped the cushions up six times.

'Ah. I thought your new boyfriend might be bringing out some good habits in you.' Connor pretended it was more banter but waited for Indi's answer expectantly.

'My what?'

'Your new boyfriend. Miles, isn't it? That journalist lad. Never had him down as your type, to be honest . . .'

Indi crossed her arms. 'Not that it's any of your business, Connor, but Miles is not my boyfriend.' Her mind flashed back to the awful night at Miles's house, his cold hands poking and squeezing. 'Look, do you want a drink or something?'

Connor shook his head, turning away so she couldn't see his smile of relief at the admission that Indi and Miles weren't a couple after all.

She motioned for him to sit on an armchair while she sat on the sofa opposite, a friendly distance apart. There were a couple more minutes of polite conversation – Indi asked after Marion, Mark, Lauren and the kids, and Connor told her they'd all been asking after her; he then asked whether Alan was still into his gardening. Indi replied that he was but that there wasn't much gardening he could do now the weather had turned.

'And Kyle? How's he doing?'

Indi curled her legs on to the sofa. 'Actually, that's what

I wanted to talk to you about. I need to tell you what really happened with the money.' She repeated everything Kyle had told her the previous night. 'So, you see, Anja was deceiving him the whole time. She told him you'd given her the passcode to the safe and that's why he took the money, for her. He thought you were loaning it to her and that he was simply collecting it on her behalf. And she knew Kyle would never grass her up. He totally fell for her and, even though he knows now how manipulative she is, he didn't know how to tell you. It took him this long even to tell me. He feels terrible, Connor. He can't face you.'

Connor stared at the ceiling. 'Jesus Christ,' was all he said.

'How do you think she got the passcode in the first place?' Indi wanted to know. 'Did you give it to her?'

'Me? Never. If she's as devious as this, though, she probably leafed through my drawers at work. God knows she's been in there enough times.'

Indi flinched, not wanting to know what Anja was doing in Connor's office so many times.

'No, not that,' he replied quickly, reading her thoughts. 'I mean, she was an employee. All the senior staff have been down to speak with me or Eddie at some point. I keep all my files for 360 and Print Room organised but not locked away.'

Indi nodded. She and Connor had dozens of questions for each other, but neither of them knew what to say next. Connor broke the silence. He couldn't bear the awkwardness any longer and needed to hear her say, once and for all, that the rumours about her and Elliot Blake were rubbish.

'Indi. There's something I need to ask you. About the actor.'

'Elliot?'

'Yes.' He took a breath. 'Did you cheat on me with him?'

Indi looked truly offended. 'How could you ask me that? After what you did.'

'I need to know, Indi. I need to hear you say it. The whole reason I even let Anja come back to mine that night was because she told me that her friend had seen the two of you all over each other at The Square.'

Indi snorted. 'Of course she would say that. And you believed her?' Her blue eyes were fixed on him, but he was too ashamed to meet them.

'I – I was angry. And hurt. And I didn't know what to believe. Earlier that day, after we had a fight about Kyle and you stormed out of 360, someone emailed me pictures from an anonymous account. They were pictures of you and Elliot in a café. You were crying and he was hugging you. It looked intimate.'

Indi clocked. The meeting in Primrose Hill. 'That's what you meant when you said I'd started it all?' she asked. Connor nodded.

'Well, it's all bollocks.' Indi scowled, furious at Anja for saying such a thing, furious at Connor for believing it. 'Is that what you need to hear, Connor? Nothing ever happened between me and Elliot. I met up with him to ask him to tell the press that we weren't having an affair so they'd get off my back. I was tired and emotional and for a split second he hugged me. Someone had obviously known about it and set up those photos.'

Miles! she thought suddenly. He set the whole meeting up. Would he really have stooped so low, though? Surely not? But no one else knew, did they, apart from Elliot himself, and surely he wouldn't have stitched her up like that? Something wasn't adding up.

'Why didn't you just talk to me?' she said after a long pause.

'I wish I had,' he replied softly. 'I know how ridiculous all this must sound, especially now after we know how unhinged Anja really is. At the time it just made sense. I was angry, drunk, upset and stupid. Eddie and I got wasted all afternoon. Anja was just . . . there.'

'And that's why you went home with her.' Indi turned away. It hurt too much to think of them together.

Connor moved from the armchair to the sofa next to her. 'Indigo, listen to me. Anja means *nothing* to me. I will never, ever forgive myself for being so stupid. Even being in the same room as her was an idiotic mistake, let alone getting hammered, letting her come back to mine and, well, you know. If I could take it back I would. I can't even remember doing it, I was so hammered.'

Indi exhaled impatiently. 'You don't remember sleeping with her? Please.'

He shook his head. 'Indi, I would never have done that to you. Yes, I vaguely remember kissing her. I was so drunk my head was spinning and I'm pretty sure that's when I passed out. I mean, even if I'd wanted to, I wouldn't have been able to have sex. The next thing I knew, I was waking up to you breaking my door down with your fists. Most of the previous night was a blackout.'

Indi thought back to Connor's dazed and confused state. 'I remember you seemed completely out of it. I thought you were just hung-over.'

'I guess I was. But I never get hangovers that badly. And I've never blacked out from drink in my life. You know me, I can take my booze.' It was true. A decade of working on London's nightlife scene had given Connor a pretty good tolerance to booze, even though he was far from a party animal and preferred being in control than being completely wasted. Even on the rare occasion he got very drunk, he'd never be so inebriated that he couldn't remember anything the next day.

A thought came to Indi, so far-fetched she almost didn't say it. 'You don't think . . . ? No.' She shook her head.

'What?' Connor asked.

'It's silly. I mean, it's ridiculous. But, you don't think Anja put something in your drink, do you?'

'*Spiked* me?' The notion made Connor laugh.

'Look at her behaviour over the past few months, Connor. How extreme it is; how obsessed she is with you. This could all have been one great plan to seduce you. She could see how drunk you were. Maybe you still resisted her and she decided to go one step further? I know it sounds crazy, but hasn't all of Anja's behaviour been crazy?'

Connor reflected for a few moments in silence.

'It would certainly explain the blackout,' Indi went on. 'Why you were so unusually groggy and spaced out the next day.'

'Jesus!' Connor sprang up from the sofa. 'You're telling me I've been fucking date-raped?'

263

Indi grimaced. 'Fortunately for you it doesn't sound like you'd have been able to get it up in that state. More likely she just wanted you to *think* that you'd done it so that you and I would break up and she could be your shoulder to cry on.'

'She was calling me incessantly afterwards, but I was so mortified I ignored her.'

'And I suppose you didn't check your Instagram account?'

'No, I haven't been on there for weeks, why?'

Indi described the pictures Anja had taken in Milan. Connor took out his phone, checked his Instagram account and, sure enough, saw that he'd been tagged with her in Milan – in bed, on a balcony, all over the city, in fact.

'She's fucking insane,' Connor muttered.

'So . . . You really didn't have sex with her?' Indi asked hopefully.

'No way! I really think I'd know if I'd had sex.' He knelt on the floor by Indi and took her hands. 'You're the one I want, Indigo. You're the one I've wanted all this time. I couldn't live with myself after that night. It was easier to blame you for cheating with Elliot but I knew deep down it wasn't true. I love you. I would do anything to have you back. Please say you love me too.' At that, Connor took Indi's head in his hands and kissed her passionately.

Chapter Twenty-Seven

Her body was like a magnet to his and she kissed him back, pulling him towards her, on top of her. Being in his arms again felt so good, so familiar, and hadn't he just said everything she'd wanted to hear? What, then, was holding her back? Suddenly Indi pushed him away.

'Indi, I love you,' he said again, looking into her eyes. Then they were kissing again. It felt so right and so very wrong at the same time. She pulled away.

'No, Connor.'

'What's the matter? Don't you love me too?'

Indi did love him too. But she couldn't bring herself to say it. Everything was happening so quickly. She took her hands from his and stood up. 'I need time to process all this.'

'I understand. If it's time you need, I'll give it to you, but please tell me I still have a chance?'

Indi didn't know how to answer him. Questions raced through her mind. Could they recover from the past few weeks? She believed he was sorry, but Connor being semi-naked with Anja, kissing her in his bed, was not an image she could erase from her mind easily. Could she fully trust him? Did she even want a relationship at the moment? Kyle needed her now more than ever; she had to get him focused and into college soon. That meant throwing herself into work wholeheartedly. The £8,000 from her savings was a setback. Which reminded her ... 'Why didn't you return my messages asking for your bank details so I could pay you back the money that Kyle took?'

Connor looked uncomfortable and walked into the kitchen to get a glass of water. Indi followed him in and repeated the question.

'It's covered, don't worry.'

'Covered by who?'

Connor poured another glass from the tap and handed it to Indi. 'I've taken it from my account. It's no big deal. I know how hard you've been working to save to put Kyle through college and to help your dad out.'

It certainly was a big deal. Indi didn't like to take charity from anyone, let alone an ex-boyfriend.

'That's very generous, but I can't let you do that,' she said sternly.

Connor shrugged. 'It's done. It's not that much money.' Connor co-owned two of the most successful bars in London, plus his own zone 1 flat outright, but that made no difference to Indi, who was fiercely self-sufficient.

'Perhaps £8,000 isn't that much money to you, but I don't take handouts and I'm not about to let Anja get

266

away with this. I'm paying you back every penny and then she's paying me back. It's not your problem to fix.'

'We can talk about that later. What are we going to do about Anja?'

Indi slammed her glass down. 'We're going to tell the police. But not before I get my hands on her.'

'You know if you hit her you're just doing what she wants,' said Connor. 'She'll have you done for assault.'

Indi sniffed. The thought of wrapping her hands around Anja Kovac's scrawny little neck was certainly appealing, but a fantasy she would never fulfil. Indi was smart, not reckless. Connor didn't have to know that, though.

'She deserves everything she gets.'

Connor laughed, approaching Indi and snaking his arms around her waist. 'You forget how well I know you,' he said quietly, his eyes boring into her own and making her legs weak with desire. 'Fighting isn't your style.'

'Then you should know me well enough to know that no one messes with my family.' Connor bent forward to kiss her but Indi moved to the door and held it open for him. 'I need some space to figure out my next move,' she told him. 'I'm going to talk to Anja and see what she has to say for herself. Then I'm going to have her arrested. I can't think about anything else right now.'

Connor nodded, but as he walked past Indi to leave, he clutched her waist with one strong arm and kissed her on the mouth, a hard and lingering kiss that said he wanted her. Then he whispered once again that he loved her, and left. Indi badly wanted to pull him back in and drag him to her bed to make up for lost time. But she couldn't let him back into her life so easily. She closed the door firmly.

It was one month until Christmas, but just two weeks until 360's Swiss Alpine-themed party. Indi was chasing celebrity and press RSVPs and keeping her huge master spreadsheet updated with who was coming, making sure she had their addresses to book cars and see if any of them wanted hair or make-up beforehand, hoping she could throw more work Hollie's way. She'd invited journalists from all the leading tabloids as well as the BBC and Sky News. Indi had swiped Miles off the guest list. Having thought long and hard about it, she knew it must've been him who set up the Elliot Blake pictures, but she didn't have a plan for dealing with him yet. The thought of him made her feel entirely uncomfortable.

Even though Indi hated the winter cold, she adored Christmas, and loved dressing the small tree in her flat – and her dad's house – in decorations, despite Alan's grumbling about it being 'far too over the top'. It had always been Alan's job to collect the tree from the local garden centre and Indi's job to decorate it in glittery baubles, pine cones, tinsel and other colourful trinkets, while Kyle made hot chocolate with brandy for them all. No matter what was going on with her and Kyle, Indi never would have bailed on the annual tree-decorating ceremony at her dad's house but, luckily, since he'd confessed his troubles with Anja, the siblings had been closer than ever. They wrote and sent off Kyle's college application to study Sports Therapy at City College in north London. If accepted, he'd start the following March.

Indi spent every night in, working on the upcoming party, updating her own website with new pictures and news and arranging meetings with prospective new clients. Kyle came round most nights and cooked them dinner while Indi worked, then they'd watch a DVD. He was doing a good job of getting over Anja, and was disgusted not only by how much she'd deceived him, but also by how she had broken up Connor and Indi. He was as protective of his sister as she was of him, and Anja certainly wasn't going to come in the way of that.

Hollie and Tom often popped round for dinner as well, and Indi tried to ignore her longing for Connor to be there too. But she still wasn't ready to forgive and forget. She had been so broken by their love, wasn't it better to be alone and feel strong and successful? She missed him with every bone in her body, but figured she could get over that eventually.

'Connor would love to be here,' Tom often commented. 'You know he's still not over you, Ind?' Indi would busy herself in the kitchen and try not to cry. It was all too much. She needed space.

Over at her dad's house, she topped the Christmas tree with a big red star and stepped back to admire her handiwork. There were white lights wrapped from top to bottom, and this year Indi had gone for a colour scheme of red, silver and gold. She prided herself on picking specific colour schemes every year. Last year it was purple and gold. It was just another way that she liked to be organised and in control.

'Very nice, sweetheart.' Alan patted Indi on the back. 'And, Kyle, good job with the lights.'

'Yeah, I noticed that you swerved that job, Dad,' teased Kyle.

'I was busy making mince pies, thank you very much!'

Indi frowned. 'Dad, I saw the Waitrose boxes in the bin.'

Alan cleared his throat. 'Yes, well, I've definitely been busy making the Christmas pudding. It's my speciality and I'm bloody well doing it right. I'm having a brandy. Anyone care to join me?' As was tradition, Alan made the Christmas pudding weeks in advance of Christmas, even though he was the only one who'd eat it, as Indi and Kyle both disliked it immensely. They would always go round to Cat and Tim's on Boxing Day, however, where it would be promptly finished off.

'Sugary fruit, gross,' muttered Kyle, eyes glued to his laptop screen, where he was reading the sports pages. 'Beer for me, please.'

'Got any wine, Dad?' Indi asked, following her father into the kitchen. She started looking through cupboards until she found some nuts to snack on, then stirred the steaming pot of beef stew on the stove.

'Smells delicious,' said Alan. Then, after a pause, 'Connor hasn't been around for a while. You two haven't kissed and made up, I presume?'

Indi went red. *They certainly had kissed – not so much made up, though.*

'Shame,' Alan went on. 'I liked the lad. Then again, can't trust a West Ham fan, so if you did get rid of him it wouldn't be the end of the world.' Indi appreciated the joke, but she knew her dad was fond of Connor. 'I just want to know you're all right, love,' he said. 'Thank goodness you seem to have got your appetite back, anyway. A couple of weeks ago it looked like you were wasting away.'

'Yeah, the break-up was pretty tough, to be honest, Dad.'

'You don't have to talk about it if you don't want.'

Indi added salt to the stew and kept stirring. 'He wants to get back together. I'm just not sure if I'm a relationship sort of person.'

'Funny, that's exactly what your mum used to say before she met me.'

Indi shot him a look. 'Mum said that?'

She had always had her mum down as a very commitment-friendly woman. She had been married to Alan for fifteen years and had had one long-term boyfriend, Anthony, before that, for seven years. They'd gone backpacking around Thailand together, as Lou loved more than anything to travel. 'I thought there was Anthony and then you?'

'After Anthony she didn't date for years. All the men were after her, of course, you know how gorgeous your mum was. But she was busy travelling the world, having her adventures.'

Indi remembered all the stories Lou had told her about her travels around Europe, Asia and America. 'I assumed they were all with Anthony.'

Alan shook his head. 'No, after they broke up she went off alone for months. Then came back and met little old me at a party. I was after her for ages, but she said that she

271

wasn't meant to be tied down.' He grinned. 'Then we fell in love. I took her on holiday to Italy with a ring in my pocket, all ready to propose, and she popped the question herself. You know your mum, always in control.'

Indi nodded, remembering Lou telling her about their Italy proposal. 'A couple of years later she got pregnant with you and the rest is history.' Alan gave Indi a sad smile, and Indi hugged him.

'So, you see, Indigo, people change. Lou said that the best times of her life were with us, her family. Sometimes you don't think you're meant to be in a relationship until the right person comes along and makes you realise it's what you wanted all along. You take such good care of us. There's nothing wrong with letting someone take care of you for a change.'

Indi went back to stirring her stew. 'Let's call Kyle in. Dinner is ready.'

Chapter Twenty-Eight

Indi pulled her Fiat 500 up outside Anja's flat on the King's Road in Fulham. She checked the address Connor had texted her. This was it. Indi rang the shrill doorbell. She didn't know whether Anja was in but, judging by her Instagram profile, she'd landed back in London days ago after another holiday – this time a trip to Dubai – and Connor had informed her that Anja was due to work at Print Room that night, so Indi assumed she'd be home now getting ready, which no doubt she took hours to do. A size zero blonde opened the door with a yawn.

'Yez?'

'Is Anja here?'

The blonde cocked her head to the stairs. 'Arnyaa! Arnyaaaaaaaa!' She turned back to Indi, entirely expressionless. 'She in the bath, I zink. Come.'

The girl led Indi up the stairs and into a very grown-up apartment. It was split level, Indi noticed, with a kitchen, dining and living room on the first floor, and no doubt the bedrooms and bathroom on the second. Everything inside was white, cream or mint green. There was no sign of life: no books, DVDs or magazines lying about. The blonde pointed to a cream sofa and disappeared upstairs, calling Anja's name again. Indi wasn't staying long and didn't see the point in getting too comfortable, so she perched on one arm of the sofa, holding her coat to her chest, legs crossed over in her black pencil dress.

A few minutes later Anja padded down the stairs. 'Indi? Hi! Whatever are you doing here?' Her black hair, just washed and wet, was thrown into a topknot. She wore nothing except an oversized grey t-shirt, showing off her skinny long legs. Indi recognised the t-shirt instantly and laughed. Two days ago, seeing Anja wearing one of Connor's t-shirts would have broken her, now it only made Anja look more bat-shit crazy. The overly sweet and friendly tone in her voice pissed Indi off, too. Who did this girl think she was?

'If you're looking for Connor, he's not here, but I can get a message to him.' Anja smiled wickedly.

Indi threw her head back and laughed again. 'Wow! You really are delusional, aren't you? Connor wants nothing to do with you, as you well know. He loves me. He knows you're crazy. Crazy enough to drug him, steal his t-shirt and pretend that you guys slept together. Crazy enough to pretend he went to Milan with you, and make up a bunch of crap from thin air about me and Elliot kissing. Crazy enough to dupe my little brother into falling in love with you and stealing £8,000, which you had no intention of ever returning. And damn well crazy enough

274

to actually believe for a second that Connor would ever be interested in you.'

Anja's smile dropped and she glared at Indi. She was rooted to the spot in rage; her hands had clenched into fists. Indi hadn't finished. 'You know, if you weren't such a manipulative, destructive, deranged bitch, I'd actually feel sorry for you. I did feel sorry for you at one point. Oh, you were so good, turning up at my office with your big teary eyes, pretending you were sorry.' Indi clapped her hands. 'Congratulations, Anja, you had me fooled. You had us all fooled. But, you know what? The game is over. You're going to pay back every penny of that money and get the hell out of our lives. Quit Print Room if you'd like to keep at least a shred of dignity. Connor is going to fire you tonight anyway, and I'm pretty sure he'll do it in front of a crowd, he's that fuming. You've seriously fucked yourself, Anja, and you need help.'

Indi hadn't planned the speech. In fact, she hadn't known what to say to Anja at all, even though she'd tried to think of the best way to express herself during the whole course of her journey there. She'd definitely planned on staying cool and calm, but seeing Anja standing there in Connor's t-shirt, still feeding Indi those delusional lies, Indi just couldn't help herself. She prepared for Anja to come back with a cutting retort, or burst into fake tears and try to play the sympathy card again. Like that would work. Instead, Anja stood still and silent for a few moments, staring Indi in the eye. Then she reached for a red dressing gown on the banister and wrapped it over herself. She looked guilty, and rightly so. She stepped past Indi, into the

275

kitchen (a kitchen that had never been used, certainly not for cooking food, Indi was certain) and poured herself a large glass of vodka. She held it up to Indi as if to say, 'Want one?'

'I don't want a fucking drink,' Indi snapped. 'What have you got to say for yourself?' With no words and shaking hands, Anja downed the vodka and poured another. Finally, she spoke gravely.

'It's all true. I don't know what to say.' She looked up at Indi. There was no sadness or regret in her eyes, just a blank gaze.

'You can start by saying that you're going to dip into the bank of Mummy and Daddy and return that £8,000.'

Anja took another sip of vodka. 'Fine.'

'And then there's the small matter of attempted date rape. I wonder what the police will say about that?'

Anja turned to Indi, looking panicked. 'You can't call the police.'

'So, you admit that you drugged my boyfriend and pretended he'd slept with you?'

Anja downed her second vodka and lit a Marlboro Light cigarette.

'It wasn't like Rohypnol or anything.' She took another deep drag. 'I take Valium sometimes, you know, to relax me.'

Indi rolled her eyes. 'Why? Because life is so hard on you? You've got a prescription drug habit as well as a coke one. God, Anja, you're a mess.' Indi was still seething. If she hadn't had to drive back to Manor House, she would have polished off that bottle of vodka herself.

'I didn't plan it, Indigo, OK?' Anja snapped back. 'For

fuck's sake. Everything is so easy for you, isn't it? With your perfect family, perfect life, perfect career and perfect boyfriend.'

'It's not easy at all! You don't know a thing about me. You have no idea what I've been through in my life. How hard I've worked for my career. You just get everything handed to you because of your looks and how rich your parents are.'

Anja rubbed her temples. 'I can't go to prison, Indigo. My parents are close to disowning me as it is. They've entirely cut me off, that's why I needed the money, so I could pay the extortionate rent here as well as paying off all my debts.' Indi snorted. Another lie – she'd told Kyle she owed a loan shark the money. This girl was unbelievable.

'I don't give a shit. You will come clean to your parents, or your sugar daddy, or whoever else will fund you. Tell them whatever you like, in fact, as long as the money is back with Connor tonight.'

'And, if I do, you won't call the police?'

Indi put her coat back on. 'We'll see. You need to get the hell out of all our lives and never show your face again, that's for sure.'

Anja scowled again, taking a long drag of her cigarette before nodding. Indi turned on her Louboutin heels to leave, before remembering one other key thread in Anja's web of deceit. 'Oh, and another thing. The tweets, the Instagram comments, I kept screen-shots of all of them. Now I know you're behind them all, I'm sure the police would be very interested in that too. Trolling is a criminal offence now, after all.' Indi didn't know if the police would really take any notice, they certainly hadn't the last time, but her one-upmanship on Anja was precious, and she wanted to scare her.

'Huh?' Anja scrunched up her cold, beautiful face in bewilderment.

Indi rolled her eyes. 'Don't play dumb, Anja. The trolling, the abusive tweets and the bitchy comments everywhere. It's pathetic.'

'I really don't know what you're talking about. I'm not on Twitter. I'll admit that the Instagram pics in Milan were . . . far-fetched, perhaps. God, you all really need to lighten up. It was just a joke. But trolling? Please, Indigo, I'm not fifteen years old.'

'You expect me to believe they are nothing to do with you?'

Anja shrugged. 'Believe what you want. I've admitted to everything else, I don't know why you'd think I'd lie about this. Now kindly get out so I can make some calls and get you your damn money. I need longer, though. I can't come up with that sort of cash in an hour.'

'Fine. You've got until first thing Monday.'

'That's less than two days away! How am I going to get that money by then?'

'Figure it out. I wouldn't bother going into work tonight. You've got more important things to do and there isn't a job for you there anyway. Check with Eddie if you don't believe me. I'll let myself out.'

Chapter Twenty-Nine

Since cutting out booze, Saskia had never felt better. She'd joined a gym in Richmond and went running or swimming for thirty minutes every morning before work. It wasn't the most strenuous exercising, but it vastly improved her mood and sleeping, and made her feel energised for the day ahead. Her skin had a fresh, dewy glow she hadn't seen since her early thirties and, with the money she'd saved from not drinking wine every night, she had treated herself to a much-needed head of fresh blonde highlights at the Daniel Hersheson salon off Regent's Street. There, she'd run into Tasha Phelps, who was desperately in need of a new publicist after firing her own for selling a story on her. Saskia gave Tasha one of her shiny new pink Sass & Fitz PR business cards, and suggested Tasha come in for a meeting. Since teaming up with Felicia and getting her confidence and sparkle back, Saskia had landed a contract with a top jewellery brand, to do their PR and organise their new earring launch at the top of The Shard. Things were better than ever.

That night, Indigo was coming round for dinner. It had been weeks since their reconciliation at the Sanderson and both their schedules had been so busy, but Saskia had insisted they kept their date. She still felt she had some making up to do with Indi. They'd also had some further contact over email. Saskia had invited Indi to any and every event that she was organising, even though Indi didn't always reply. Something in Saskia made her feel protective towards Indi. There was definitely still residual guilt from the way she'd spoken and acted towards her.

Millie was at her friend Sadie's house, so Saskia took the opportunity to make sea bass – her daughter hated fish – with couscous and roasted vegetable salad. At seven p.m. on the dot, her doorbell rang.

'Indigo, darling, come on in.'

'I know you're not drinking much at the moment, but I brought you a bottle of white wine anyway. I figured it's always nice to have one chilling in your fridge. And here are some flowers.' She handed Saskia a colourful bunch. 'Something smells delicious.'

'Thank you! That's so sweet.' Saskia showed Indi into her kitchen, where nibbles of olives, nuts, and smoked salmon blinis were laid out on her wooden table. She poured two glasses of sparkling water. 'Would you like a glass of wine?'

Indi was desperate for one, but didn't want to be the only one drinking, so shook her head. 'I'm trying to keep a clear head at the moment. I've not been sleeping too well, so maybe it's a good idea to lay off the wine.'

Saskia looked up from the stove where some asparagus

spears were gently frying. 'Anything I can help with? Is work OK?'

Indi shrugged. 'The Christmas party is going well, I think. I'll hopefully get the club some good press as the guest list is shaping up nicely. There isn't much more work around, though. I'm struggling to secure my next big project for 2018.'

'It's always slow this time of year, try not to worry. Things will pick up when everyone is back in January and starting to plan their year ahead. In the meantime, it's a good time for you to relax and take some time for yourself.' Saskia raised an eyebrow. 'I bet you're not very good at taking holidays, are you?'

'I went on holiday not long ago with my ex – the guy I'm working with for the Christmas party at 360. I was actually supposed to manage Print Room's New Year's Eve bash, too, but with everything that's happened with Connor, I suppose I shouldn't be surprised that he decided to plan it in-house.'

'Connor Scott? Ah, yes, I'd heard that you two were an item. What a genetically blessed couple!'

Indi gulped some water. The temptation of wine was getting stronger. 'You know Connor?'

'By reputation alone. Co-owner of Print Room and 360, he used to run the Skylon bar and the Mayfair Hotel's bar and restaurant.'

'You certainly know your stuff.'

'Everyone in the game knows Connor Scott! He's one of the city's most sought-after bachelors.'

Indi sighed. 'I'm sure he is.' She looked away, feeling the

tears rising up. God, what was *wrong* with her at the moment? Any mention of Connor these days made her feel so hopeless. Saskia stared at her, quizzically, and reached out an arm, touching Indi's gently.

'Indi?'

The physical interaction did it. A couple of tears ran down Indi's face and she wiped them away quickly, hoping that Saskia wouldn't notice, but even looking down at her plate Indi could feel Saskia's concern.

'We were together,' she said. 'We were in love. At least, I thought we were in love. He says he still loves me, but I don't know what I'm thinking or feeling. Part of me wants to scream to the world how much I love him, and the other part wants to never see him again and never let my guard down to anyone else.'

Saskia took a seat beside Indi. 'That's not the way to go through life, my dear. Especially when you're so young. You can't write off love just because someone hurt you. Believe me, being bitter gets you nowhere.'

'What if I can forgive but I can't forget?'

'Well . . . That's difficult. What exactly did he do to you?'

Indi took a deep breath and proceeded to tell Saskia all about Anja and the drama that had been going on in her and Connor's relationship, and the whole money-framing debacle.

'So, you see, I believe that it was all Anja's doing, and I know he was drunk. Really drunk. But he still kissed her, and I just can't seem to shake that image of them doing that on his bed. I was so heartbroken when I thought that he really did sleep with her, I don't know if I can come back from it. I'm so used to being alone, you know? If someone hurts me, I usually never think about them in the same way again. But, with him, I can't get over it. I don't know what to do.'

'Everybody makes mistakes, Indi. He really does sound as if he's sorry. What has the contact been since that last time you saw him at your flat?'

'A few texts here and there. He gave me Anja's address, I told him I confronted her and that she'd stolen his t-shirt and pretended they were still together. He's giving me space, which I asked for.'

'That's supportive of him.'

'Yeah. And he's sent me a couple of messages just saying again how sorry he is.'

'In my experience, men like Connor don't go out of their way to make such an effort with someone unless it's for real,' said Saskia, serving Indi a plate of lemon-infused steamed sea bass and salad.

'Wow, this tastes delicious,' Indi said with her mouth full, before checking her manners and blushing. 'Sorry, it's not often these days I get properly cooked meals, and this is the best I've had in ages!'

'Don't you cook at home?'

'I don't really have the time. Connor loved to cook so was in charge of all the meals. I can make a decent roast dinner or stew, things like that, but there never seems much point when it's just for me, so I only ever tend to cook properly when I'm at my dad's. My younger brother,

Kyle, still lives with him and I go round there every week or so.'

'And your dad, does he like to cook?'

'Yeah, he's great now. He really enjoys it. My mum used to do most of the cooking but she taught him a few great recipes when she got sick, and he carried on practising after she . . .' Indi swallowed another mouthful. She didn't mind opening up to Saskia. 'She died about twelve years ago.'

Saskia contemplated feigning surprise, then contemplated telling Indi that, yes, she found that out recently. Instead she said nothing, getting the impression that Indi had more to say. She was right.

'It was just me doing all the cooking and cleaning and stuff. You know, right after she died. My dad was in a really bad way. Kyle was only nine. I took some time off school to look after them but did all my reading and coursework at night so I wouldn't fall that far behind. I still passed all my GCSEs. Mum would've gone ballistic if I hadn't.' At that, she and Saskia smiled at each other.

'Then, a couple of years after that, Kyle's behaviour got even worse. He's ADHD and it peaked when he was ten. Dad fell into a depression and couldn't work so I had to do all the accounts for his business. It was fine, though, taught me a lot, and then he started getting counselling and it helped him so much.' Indi shook her head. She'd never been this open with anyone she barely knew. 'Sorry, I've been waffling.'

Saskia placed her hand over Indi's. 'I think your mum would be so proud of you. You've got your own business, car, flat. In London, I might add. You're an amazingly accomplished young woman.'

Indi smiled warmly. 'Thank you, Saskia.' At that, the front door was flung open and Millie trooped in.

'Muuuum! Anything for dinner? I'm starving.'

Saskia rolled her eyes at Indi. 'I thought you were having dinner at Sadie's?' Saskia shouted back.

Millie walked into the kitchen and threw her silver backpack on the floor. She wore black leggings and heavy black boots with a black t-shirt underneath a plaid red shirt. It was a tough look, but her long, almost white-blonde hair and blue eyes were ultra-feminine. She looked like a typically cool teenager. Indi thought she resembled Lottie Moss, the half-sister of supermodel Kate. Millie flung open the fridge and peered inside for something quick and easy to eat.

'Nah, Sadie's mum is on some vegan health kick and was going to cook vegetarian sausages. Gross. I had them last time. They taste like cardboard!'

'There's plenty of fish if you'd like,' offered Saskia, but Millie turned her nose up at that and got to work on making a cheese, ham and tomato toastie.

'Have you forgotten your manners, young lady?' Saskia said, nodding her head towards Indi.

'Hi, I'm Indigo, but everyone calls me Indi.' She stretched out her hand.

'Soz. Hi, I'm Millie. Everyone calls me, um, Millie.'

Saskia tutted. 'Don't be cheeky! Are you going to sit down and tell us about your day or skulk off to your room?'

'Can I have a glass of wine?' Millie asked hopefully, eyes wide.

'Pah!' replied Saskia, turning to Indi. 'She must like you, she's showing off.'

'Am not!' Millie protested.

Indi smiled. 'I like your shirt, Millie. Is it Jack Wills?'

'Yeah! Mum chose it, actually. During our last shopping trip. Couldn't believe she'd pick out something I'd actually like.' Saskia tutted again, but shared a smile with Millie.

'Believe it or not, I do take notice of my daughter's fashion sense, you know. I was once something of a fashionista myself.'

'You still are,' put in Indi. 'I've seen you rock some Aquascutum suits. You always look fab.'

Saskia beamed. She did like to make an effort, especially since she'd lost a few pounds through exercising and not drinking. Getting praise from Indi was praise indeed! As Indi and Millie talked about high-street trends, Saskia noticed how much Millie was in awe of her, and barely took her eyes off her. It must be hard, Saskia reflected, for Millie not to have any siblings (apart from the imminent Real Housewife of Radlett's baby). Suddenly Saskia felt guilty that she'd not been able to give Millie a sister.

'I'd better go and finish my homework,' Millie finally said after a great deal of animated chat with Indi about clothes, make-up and celebrities. 'I can't really be bothered, but my essay is due tomorrow and my sociology teacher, Mrs Gill, will give me triple detention if I don't do it.'

'I like this Mrs Gill,' said Saskia, clearing away plates.

Indi laughed. 'What's the essay on?'

'The rise of social media and whether it's having a good or bad effect on society.'

Indi had no intention of contributing to a conversation about social media after all the trolling she'd had.

'Anyway, see you later!' said Millie, disappearing up the stairs as Indi waved.

'What a great kid,' she said, helping Saskia load the dishwasher.

'I think she took a shine to you,' Saskia replied.

'Writing an essay on social media, though, urgh. I'm glad I'm not in school any more. There was nothing like that when I was growing up, and being a teenager still sucked. I feel so sorry for girls these days who are forced to compare themselves to filtered, Photoshopped images that bombard them all the time. And there's so much bullying and trolling online.'

'Trolling?'

'Yeah, you know, trolls? People who post nasty comments on social media about other people. It's called trolling. And apparently it's not exclusive to teenage girls.' Indi took a cloth to the wooden table and started wiping away food debris. It was her instinct to clear up, even at other people's homes, and Saskia motioned for her to sit down instead and relax as she made a pot of coffee. 'What do you mean by that?' she asked.

Indi shrugged. 'Oh, just some tweets I was getting. Nasty comments tweeted to my business account and my personal one, bitchy comments written underneath pictures that Ben posted on 360's page. They started off spiteful, but I thought it was just kids messing about. Then more came, from different accounts, all anonymous of course, so I couldn't see who they were from. Then it got really bad when someone threatened my life.' Indi shuddered at the memory. 'Anyway, they seem to have quietened down for now, so I'm hoping that's the end of it. Are you OK? You've gone a bit pale.'

Saskia's face had indeed gone white. It was stupid to think she could have made it through this evening without the truth coming out. And the truth always came out eventually.

'Indi, there's something I need to tell you.'

Chapter Thirty

After Saskia finished, Indi sat back, stunned. 'You mean, all this time, it was you? You publicly wrote that I was a whore? That I should be *dead*, Saskia? Those awful things about my brother and . . . and *my mum*?'

Saskia put her wine glass down firmly. Before her confession, she'd cracked open the bottle Indi had brought round and poured them both two large glasses. Screw it. If this wasn't an emergency, she didn't know what was. 'No. Those terrible comments were not by me. I would never dream of writing anything like that to anyone. I didn't know what your poor brother had gone through. I didn't even know about your mum until a few weeks ago when Felicia told me.'

'Felicia?' Indi stood up.

'Felicia Fitzpatrick. My business partner. The only reason she is my business partner is because I ran into her outside Millie's school, as I do from time to time. Her twin boys go there, you see. Between you and me, bloody awful nightmare boys. Spoilt rotten, if you ask me. And the way she keeps feeding them, they are both heading towards child obesity.'

'Saskia!'

'Sorry, I digress. Anyway, she told me about those stories News Hub had written about you and your family. I had no idea, you see, because I hadn't seen them. But it was her assistant Ashley having an affair with Elliot Blake the whole time.' Indi remembered Miles telling her that.

'It was me who tipped off the journalist at News Hub,' Saskia continued. 'To get them off your back.'

'You tipped off the press?'

'Yes! Because I felt so guilty.'

'Because you'd been trolling me for the previous four months!'

'No!' Saskia took a swig of white wine. 'No more than two comments, I promise. I was drunk, obviously, and it was after I found out that you'd got the 360 contract. Millie had just taught me how to use Twitter. I didn't know what I was doing, for God's sake. I was drunk. I am *mortified*, Indigo.'

Indi thought back to all the comments. Each and every one was etched in her mind. 'You're userxx0177 or whatever it was?' she guessed. '"*Bitch, stop pretending you're something you're not?*" "*Fucking stupid whore*"!'

Saskia nodded solemnly. She had never felt more ashamed and mortified in her entire life.

'The month and year I was born. Predictable, right? I'm just an old, useless fart, or at least I definitely was a few months ago. Bitter and resentful and desperate.'

Indi was speechless. She had every right to be furious. A few months ago she would have stormed out of Saskia's house and never looked back. But she was fed up with having enemies, and frankly too damn tired to argue any more. It felt as if that was all she was doing these days.

Saskia broke the silence. 'And as soon as Felicia told me about the horrible News Hub feature and all the nasty things they'd said about you and your family, I made it my mission to make it up to you. Please believe me. I am utterly ashamed. But I swear on my life, on Millie's life, it was just those two comments. Nothing after that. Nothing about your family and certainly nothing about you being dead.'

Indi saw the desperation in her eyes. To swear on one's daughter's life wasn't something to be taken lightly. And she *had* been instrumental in getting News Hub off Indi's back.

'I appreciate that, Saskia. And I suppose I can see how something like that could happen when you're drunk and upset near a computer.'

'Thank you, thank you so much. I mean it, Indi, I really want us to be friends.' Saskia went to hug Indi but Indi stepped back. Forgiving was one thing, forgetting was quite another.

'I need a bit of time to process all this, Saskia. I don't think we can be best friends all of a sudden.'

Saskia nodded solemnly, knowing not to push her luck any further.

'I'd better go,' Indi said, reaching for her bag. 'I'll . . . I'll talk to you soon. Say bye to Millie for me.'

*

Saskia offered to pay for a taxi but, as Indi had only drunk half her glass of wine, she concluded that she was safe to drive. She couldn't wait to get home now. Driving through London at night had its usual calming effect on her. She needed some relaxation after the evening's revelations. Many of the streets were quiet and, winding her way through them, passing lit-up shops and iconic buildings, her head cleared. As she sped over Vauxhall Bridge and into central London to cross over to the north of the city, she felt oddly comforted by what Saskia had told her. She was still angry, of course, but at least now she knew where two of the comments had come from. But who on earth was responsible for the rest?

Indi called Hollie on her hands-free on the way home and told her everything over speakerphone. Hollie was convinced Anja was still responsible. Indi mulled this over. True, Anja sure had enough hatred for Indi. If she was capable of drugging a man and pretending they'd slept together, she was certainly well able to send some nasty social media comments. But why not admit to it? She had admitted to all her other crimes. Anja told Indi adamantly that she never used Twitter, only Instagram. Was she lying? Who else hated Indi so much? Then it came to her like a lightning bolt. Helen Blake, Elliot's disgruntled wife, who had tried to attack Indi at the make-up launch.

Indi thought of the scornful look in Helen's eyes as she had gripped Indi's arm, digging her long acrylic nails into her skin like a mad woman. *Of course!* She had every reason to despise Indi and was no doubt unhinged. And she could have easily found out about Kyle and Lou from the News

Hub feature. It made sense now. Indi was pleased with herself for figuring it out, but there was nothing she could do about it. As Mark had said, there had been no specific threats made to her, so it was pointless informing the police. And there hadn't been any fresh comments for a while, so Helen had clearly moved on from her campaign of hatred towards Indi. She hoped Ashley Deacon wasn't suffering the same treatment, though from the TV appearances and magazine interviews, she was clearly revelling in her new-found fame. Elliot was yet to announce his version of events, but Indi stayed as far away from that scandalous story as possible. They could crack on with their drama, but as far as she was concerned she was ready to see the year off with a bang and leave all that behind her.

Chapter Thirty-One

It was the night of the Christmas party at 360. Anja had missed her deadline for paying back the money by now, and had never even gone back to Print Room to collect her last pay slip. Indi was fully prepared to pay Anja another visit soon, or even go straight to the police, though she didn't want to implicate Kyle. Anyway, it would have to wait until after the party. She and Connor had been so busy in the days up to it. Indi had been finalising everything from cars, names and interior design – she'd barely had any time to sleep. The faux-fur blankets to go over the chairs and sofas had been lost in Christmas transit and never arrived, so Indi had to find replacements at the last minute. Fortunately a contact supplied her with fake cow-skin rugs, which actually looked much nicer. Waiters and waitresses were dressed the part too – the boys in lederhosen (which would have looked ridiculous anywhere else, but Indi had employed waiters who were also male models and they were so good-looking they made even shorts and braces look cool). The waitresses wore their hair in pigtails and had on cute, sexy red and white dresses with white stockings. They carried trays of drinks and food. Canapés were mini mushroom burgers, smoked bacon croquettes, smoked-salmon blinis and wild boar sausages.

The bitterly cold mid-December temperature thankfully didn't stop the glitterati coming out in full, sequined force. Michelle Keegan and her husband Mark Wright got the eager photographers in a frenzy when they took to the red carpet, followed by Harry Styles and his latest model girlfriend, plus dozens of other celebrities. Tasha Phelps looked typically sensational in a long gold dress, with her party squad of singers, models and TV presenters. Premiership footballers and their glamorous wives also made up the star numbers. Everything was going according to plan.

Indi was wearing a beautiful, ultra-feminine pink tulle skirt with a slinky black camisole and silver sparkling Louboutins. She was relieved that her best friends were at the party this time. Hollie, Tom, Hollie's younger sister Tina, and Tina's boyfriend Hugh were some of the first to arrive, as Hollie was desperate to catch some celebrity sightings. She looked stunning in a white jumpsuit with a plunging neckline, her Afro hair tied in an elegant topknot, while her make-up was bright pink lipstick and purple eyeshadow. Hollie looked so cool, and everyone stopped to compliment her on her expertly applied trend-setting make-up. Tina was dressed in a cute black skater dress and Hollie had insisted on giving her a bold pink lip as well. Tina and Hugh rarely went out as they were generally so tied up with their jobs. Hugh was a teacher, Tina was a teacher's assistant at a different school, and was in the process of getting her full qualifications. They certainly never went to clubs as glamorous as this, and now they stared wide-eyed at everyone and everything in the room. Kyle had come with the group, too. Indi had insisted he enjoy 360 as a guest for once. He deserved a night out.

Indi was busy on the red carpet with Ben, greeting guests and thanking them all for coming, while complimenting the women on how stunning they looked. She stiffened when Saskia gingerly approached her. She wore elegant, high-waisted black trousers with a long green crushed-velvet coat.

'How are you, Indi? Thank you for letting me come.' She kissed the side of Indi's cheek but Indi just stood still. She couldn't yet bring herself to be completely relaxed around Saskia.

'No worries. I'm fine. Busy, you know. I'll see you in there.' And with a curt smile she turned to face Ben. She had nothing else to say to Saskia right now.

'Are you OK down here if I slip upstairs and check that we're all good?' she asked him, a few handshakes and air-kisses later. Ben gave her a thumbs up.

Indi stepped out of the lift and was about to find her friends when she felt a light touch on her arm. She froze. 'I'm calling for security.'

'Please don't,' said Helen Blake. She took her hand off Indi's arm and looked sheepishly at the ground. She'd lost weight since the news had broken about Ashley and

Elliot's affair, Indi noticed. Helen's strapless green dress was pretty and her make-up looked less fierce than when she'd stormed into 360 to assault Indi.

'How did you get in?'

'Elliot gave me his ticket. He's gone back to LA with Ashley for a few days. They've moved in together. It's only a matter of time before that story comes out.'

Indi folded her arms over her chest.

'We're getting a divorce. It's all pretty amicable, actually. Elliot's given me the house and a lump sum to keep it civil.'

'That's nice of him,' Indi snorted sarcastically.

'I'm sorry for what happened here.'

'You mean assaulting me?'

Helen glanced away. 'Yes. I, um, overreacted. A lot. But you have to understand, he's the love of my life. *Was* the love of my life. I saw red.' She took a deep breath. 'I threw him out and didn't give him a chance to explain, but when we finally talked he came clean about Ashley and told me you weren't involved at all. He said great things about you, actually; that you'd been treated so unfairly by the press.'

'And by you.' Indi wasn't forgiving this easily.

'And by me.' Helen nodded solemnly. 'I don't expect you to forgive me, but I hope you do. And, to show how sorry I am, I was wondering if you'd consider doing the PR for my new company. It's a fashion range I'm starting with the money Elliot has given me. Alimony. Least he can do after humiliating me. But I'm a trained fashion cutter, and have always wanted to do this instead of just being "Elliot Blake's wife". I'd love to show you my designs. What do you say?'

Indi still had Helen as a prime suspect for trolling her. 'I don't think so,' she replied.

Helen held up her hands. 'I understand. No pressure. Perhaps I could email you some more information on Monday and we can set up a meeting?'

'I'll think about it.'

Helen handed her a white business card. 'Here's my card anyway. I'll leave it with you. I really am sorry, Indi. My friends are over there with some Arsenal players. I'll leave if you want me to.'

Indi batted her hand away. 'Just stay, it's fine. Enjoy yourself.'

'Thank you. And I really am sorry for what happened. I hope we can work together.'

Indi watched Helen leave. She certainly didn't look menacing now, but she decided to forget about her for the meantime. She wanted to have some fun.

Indi avoided Connor as best she could. He looked gorgeous, of course, in a perfectly tailored midnight-blue suit and white shirt, a pink handkerchief peeking out of the breast pocket of the suit.

'Don't look at him, just enjoy yourself,' whispered Hollie, when she saw Connor and Indi's eyes meet.

Tina grabbed three full glasses from a waitress. 'Here, have a glass of champagne. Tom and Hugh have gone over to talk to him.'

Indi gratefully accepted the drink. 'Thanks, girls. I'm so glad you're both here. Do you think everyone is having a good time?'

'Yes, stop worrying!' Hollie said. Then she let out a dramatic gasp and grabbed Indi's arm. 'Fuck!' She turned to Indi. 'Don't panic, but you'll *never* guess who's turned up!'

Indi turned around to see Anja, dressed in a floor-length black dress with an extremely long slit up the right leg. Who did she think she was, Angelina Jolie at the Oscars? To her side was the blonde flatmate who'd answered the door at Anja's flat. Judging by her equally lithe frame, she was probably a fellow model. Scrolling through a diamanté-encrusted phone, she looked just as bored as when Indi had last seen her. And, standing with them, in a scruffy suit, was Miles. Anja threw her head back in laughter. Miles was lapping up the attention. Since when were they mates?

'What the fuck is she doing here?' snapped Indi. 'Is she shagging Miles now? Jesus, she gets about. And Miles isn't even supposed to be here. Where's Kyle?'

'He went to the loo,' put in Tina.

'We need to keep him away from her,' said Indi, as usual thinking about her brother. 'I don't want anything upsetting him tonight.'

'He's got all of us here,' said Tina reassuringly.

Hollie knocked back some champagne. 'It's OK, she's leaving anyway. Let me deal with her.'

'No, Holl, don't make a scene,' said Indi. 'I'll go over and tell them all to leave.'

Anja stopped laughing as soon as Indi marched over.

'Before you say anything, we're here as guests of Miles's editor who couldn't make it and asked Miles to stand in.' She pouted. 'And Eddie said it was fine.' She jutted her hip out, resting a bony hand on it defensively.

Indi looked at Miles. 'Really?'

Miles shrugged. 'Yeah, I noticed how you struck me off the guest list. Pathetic.'

Indi stared at him. The arrogance of that boy was unbelievable! 'How dare you? All of you?' She was about to call for security when Nicolas bounded over and draped his arm around her, not noticing who she was talking to.

'Indigo, darling, I must introduce you to Tasha's family, they're all here. Come, come, they are dying to meet you.'

Indi was about to object, but the last thing she wanted was for Nicolas to think the party was anything but perfect, so she smiled and said cheerfully, 'Right behind you, Nicolas!' She turned back to Anja. 'I'm watching you,' she hissed quietly as Nicolas strode off towards Tasha's family. 'If you cause any trouble, or even try to go near my brother, I'll throw you out personally, do you understand? And don't think for one second that you're going to get away with what you did to Connor and Kyle. I'm reporting you tomorrow morning. Got that?' Then to Miles, 'I'll deal with *you* later.'

Anja shot Indi a scornful look, then smiled at her patronisingly. 'Whatever.' Miles downed his beer while Tamzina, the vacant blonde, was still on her phone without the slightest idea what was going on.

After politely chatting to Nicolas and Tasha's family, Indi went to find her friends, grabbing a large Cosmopolitan cocktail from the bar on her way. She ran straight into Connor, almost spilling her red drink all over her pink skirt.

'Sorry!' he said. 'I saw you talking to Anja before and I wanted to check you were OK. I don't know who let her in. I didn't ruin your skirt, did I?'

'I'm fine. The skirt's fine too.'

'I can get security over here right away.'

Indi shrugged. 'She's only going to make a scene. I could do without the drama.'

'You and me both.'

'I've told her to behave herself anyway. I just want to enjoy tonight, you know?'

'I do. Congratulations, by the way. You've outdone yourself again tonight. I think Nicolas is planning a very generous bonus for you this Christmas.'

They clinked glasses. 'And you look more beautiful than ever,' Connor said, his green eyes fixed on her.

Indi couldn't resist meeting his gaze. As soon as she did, her legs felt weak. 'Thank you.'

Connor opened his mouth to say something else, but Indi spoke first. 'Anyway, I'd better find Hollie. See you later, Connor.' And she slipped into the crowds.

'Are you OK?' Hollie enquired, once Indi found her and Tina.

Indi wanted to relax and have fun. 'Let's get some pictures in the photo booth,' she suggested.

As the three made their way excitedly across the room, Ben halted them in their tracks.

'Sorry to interrupt, girls. Ind, Felix is missing some adaptor, he said you had a spare one?' 360's resident DJ was on the decks tonight, but Indi had also booked Felix Fox, the hot new Radio 1 DJ, for a special two-hour slot.

'Oh shit, yeah. He said his one was a bit dodgy. I have another lead in the office.'

'Want me to go down and get it?' asked Ben.

'No, it's cool, I'll go. You can take my place here and get some photos with the sisters!'

Hollie linked her arm through Ben's. 'Come on, Benji. Chillax and have some fun with us!' Ben looked terrified as Hollie led him away. Indi waved them off with a laugh. She did a quick scan of the room to make sure everything looked good. Satisfied that it did, she made her way to Connor's office.

There was a long corridor that came off the main club, with mirrors all along the right side. To the left were men's, women's and disabled toilets, and a fourth door, locked by a passcode. Behind that were stairs that connected and led to the main hotel – the nineteenth floor – and another corridor where the office was. Since the stolen-money catastrophe, Connor had changed the passcodes to get through this door and the door into the office. Only he, and for tonight's purposes Indi, knew what the new codes were. Indi checked her reflection quickly in the mirrors and turned to tap the code in. Suddenly, someone squeezed her lower back, giving her goose bumps all over her body. She didn't need to turn around to know who it was. 'Connor, please . . .'

Connor wrapped both his hands around her waist and pulled her around so their faces were almost touching. His familiar smell made her feel exhilarated.

'I can't do this any more,' he said. 'I can't keep away

from you. I need you.' And before she could protest, they were kissing. Indi couldn't tear herself away, kissing him back harder, her hands gripping his head. His hair felt so good in her fingers, his body so strong. A gaggle of drunk girls emerged from the toilets and 'whooped' at the couple, making Indi and Connor start and pull away, remembering where they were. But Connor immediately pulled her back into him.

After more kissing he spoke softly, looking Indi straight in her eyes. 'I know I hurt you, Indi. I never will again, as long as I live, I swear. It's driving me mad not being with you. I love you. Tell me you love me too.'

'I love you too. I just don't want to get hurt again, Connor.'

'You won't,' he said firmly. 'Just take me back.' Then they were kissing again. There was no use denying it. Indi had tried to get over Connor, but he was ingrained in her heart. She didn't want to keep people away for ever, never experiencing love because she was scared of getting hurt. Suddenly being back with Connor seemed like the most normal thing in the world.

'There's something else I need to tell you,' he said, a serious expression on his face. 'You know that business I was doing in Miami?'

Indi nodded.

'There were various meetings with a big investor out there. They've been working with Nicolas for a while. They're opening a Degree Hotel in Miami. The deal is done. He's offering me part-ownership – and a huge stake in it.'

'Connor, that's amazing!'

'He wants me to move there to set it up and run it. And, Indi, I want you to come with me.'

'Oh wow, Connor. I – I don't know what to say.'

'Just say you'll think about it. Please. I don't want you to come and just be my girlfriend; I think you can set up over there, too. I've thought long and hard and it's what I want.'

Before she could answer, they were startled again, this time by someone clearing their throat loudly and deliberately. Indi jumped. 'Miles.'

'Didn't take you two long to get back on track, did it? Or were you screwing while you were pretending to be into me?' Miles leant in to Indi, making her feel uncomfortable. He had a look of fury in his eyes that Indi had never seen before. His forehead was beaded with sweat and his breath smelt strongly of beer.

Connor stepped between them and gently placed a hand on Miles's shoulder. 'Come on, mate, let's go back to the party.'

Miles shook Connor's hand away, staring at Indi in disgust. 'Don't worry, I'm going,' he snarled.

Connor turned back to Indi as Miles headed unsteadily down the corridor. 'He's clearly as obsessed with you as Anja is with me,' he said quietly, his eyes full of concern.

Indi stared at Miles as he stumbled into the men's toilets. 'I've never seen him like that before.' Then she smacked her hand against her forehead. 'Shit! The adaptor. I've got to run down to the office to get stuff for the DJ.'

'I'll come with you.'

'No, it's fine, I'll only be a minute. Actually, can you go and check on Ben? He's probably wondering what's taken me so long. And I've left him in the clutches of Hollie, the poor thing.'

'Sure,' Connor said. He kissed Indi again. 'You know you've made me the happiest guy in the world by forgiving me, right?'

Indi couldn't help but beam. They were meant to be together, and now they were going to be. Everything made sense. 'Go!' she laughed. Connor gave her one more kiss on her head and went off into the party. Indi breathed a sigh of relief and turned to the door, tapping in the passcode and scurrying to the office. The quicker she could get in and out of the office, the sooner she would be back with Connor, Kyle and her friends. Everything was perfect, she thought, as she headed for the office, assuming the heavy door had slammed shut behind her.

Chapter Thirty-Two

The office was a grey, windowless room. It was much
smaller and more cramped than Connor's light and
modern office at Print Room. He'd previously told her
that he wanted to refurbish it in the New Year. There
was no art on the wall, simply the safe and a few shelves
with upright filing cabinets. There was one steel desk
propped against the wall, and boxes, still not unpacked, lay
about everywhere. Clearly Connor didn't do much business
here; it would be far too unpleasant to work in and felt
more like a storage cupboard. The only sign of him was an
expensive, unopened bottle of whisky on the desk with a
blue bow on it and a tag that read: 'Connor, here's to a
bright future ahead. Cheers, Nicolas.' Indi ran her fingers
over the bottle. Maybe she'd get Connor to open it after
the party so they could celebrate their reunion. Upstairs,
she heard the thumping of feet and the muffled sound
of music from the party. Felix was kicking off his set with
a dance remix of 'Let Me Love You' by DJ Snake

featuring Justin Bieber. Indi scrambled through the box of equipment placed on one of the desks, which was exactly where Indi had asked her intern to put it when Felix's own personal sound equipment had arrived earlier that day. The box was filled with wires, cables and leads. Indi found the correct adaptor and made a move to leave when a figure appeared in the doorway, blocking Indi's exit. Indi tutted.

'Anja! How did you get down here? Whatever, I don't care. Just get out of my way, please.'

Indi pushed past Anja, only to be forcefully thrown back into the room. For such a scrawny girl, Anja was strong. She pushed Indi again, harder this time, so she fell sharply against the desk.

'You just couldn't keep your hands off him, could you, bitch?'

Indi tried to push past Anja again, but she was shoved back again, so hard this time that it made her gasp. Anja stood over her, pushing Indi into the desk so that the cold metal dug into her lower back. She held Indi in place by clutching each of her arms tightly.

Indi took a deep breath in. *Don't panic. Trying to fight back will only antagonise her. Try to reason with her.* Indi looked Anja straight in the eye and spoke firmly, slowly.

'Anja. We don't need to do this.'

Anja's eyes burned intensely, with fury, insanity and a glint of pure evil. Her shaking hands gripped Indi's arms even tighter. She was using all her strength to hold Indi in place. 'It doesn't need to be like this,' Indi repeated. 'Let go of me, and we can talk about it.'

Anja spat in her face. 'Fuck you!' She hurled Indi across the room with all her might.

Indi crashed into the wall and felt a stab of pain in the left side of her head so intense that her vision was blurred for a few seconds. Trembling, she reached to her wound and felt blood trickle down. She leant against the wall to compose herself.

Anja towered over her menacingly. 'You think you're so perfect, don't you? You have everyone thinking that you're this angel but you're just a whore. You knew he loved me but you just had to steal him away. He would be with me now if it weren't for you!'

Indi stood up, her head throbbing. 'Anja—'

'Shut up! Shut the fuck up!' Anja was screaming now and started rambling. She'd completely lost it. She paced up and down the small office in front of Indi, sniffing and wiping her red nose. She was coked up to the eyeballs. Indi regained her balance but her head was still throbbing. She rose up and was about to push Anja out of her way when she heard a voice coming from the doorway.

'Anja, what are you doing down here? Indi?'

'Oh, Miles, thank God!' She rushed over to the doorway where Miles was standing, and held on to his arm for comfort. She never thought she'd be so pleased to see him.

'Indi, your head, it's bleeding,' he said, confused. 'Anja what the—?'

'Just please get me the fuck out of here and away from *her*.' They both moved to leave when Miles stopped dead in his tracks.

'Hmm,' he said thoughtfully. 'Actually, no, I don't think

I will.' Now it was him gripping Indi's arms and guiding her to the back of the office.

'Miles, what are you doing?' Indi was panicking now, trying desperately to get out of Miles's clutches, but he was too strong for her. He pinned Indi against the wall. He was so close she could feel his hot sickly breath on her cheek.

'I followed her down here,' said Anja, wiping her nose again, her eyes burning with fury. 'It was too good an opportunity to miss, Miles. She needs a slap back to reality.'

Miles simply nodded, fixing his stare on Indi. 'Such a shame, Indi. We could have been so good together, you and me. From the moment I saw you, I knew I could make you happy, but you just had to play hard to get, didn't you? Then you had to go with *him*. So disappointing. I thought you were such a good girl, but you really are just a slut like your mother, aren't you?'

Anja stood with her arms folded, trembling slightly with rage and her drug-high, but clearly enjoying how scared Indi was.

Indi cried in pain and terror as Miles pinned her harder against the wall and kicked her hard in the legs. 'It was you,' she realised out loud. 'All the trolling.'

Miles laughed. 'Interns really will do whatever you tell them to. I don't get my hands dirty, Indigo, you should know that. Even when I gave Gilly all those sordid details about your family for the feature, I made sure she didn't name me. And that I got a hefty tip-off fee.'

Indi was really scared now. There was no use her crying for help – it was impossible for anyone to hear her from the club.

'You know, when Anja and I got talking, we realised we had so much in common,' continued Miles. 'We've both been wronged and treated like shit by the people we loved.' He sighed. 'This was all so easy, though. Setting up the meeting between you and the actor, sending pictures to Connor of you and him kissing. I tried to sell them to my editor, of course, but you were old news by that point and he was only interested in the new girl Elliot was shagging. Fickle business, isn't it? Still, it was worth it. Oh, I bet you hadn't even worked out that it was Anja who started the fire in your retard brother's school, did you? She has brains as well as beauty, it turns out.' Then, with a laugh, 'She's good at playing with fire.'

Indi stared at Anja, gobsmacked. Anja rolled her eyes from the doorway and anxiously looked back to see if anyone was coming. 'Come on, Miles, let's go, now. This wasn't part of the plan.'

Plan?

'Tell her!' roared Miles.

Anja shouted back. 'I would have sent that idiot down except his damn alibis came through, but then another little runt from the school was only too happy to take the blame. Amazing what £8,000 can get you. After a few months in juvenile detention, he'll be the richest teenager in his school.'

Indi was utterly horrified. '*That's* what you needed the money for?'

'The best way to get to you was to get to your brother. Which was more fun than I thought it would be. He'd do anything I wanted once I trained him up.' Anja let out a small cackle then shot Indi a look of disgust. 'And, believe me, Indigo, I do want to get to you after you stole Connor from me.'

Indi looked to Miles, who was still holding her firmly against the wall, staring at her with disdain, then back at Anja.

'I didn't steal him from you,' she protested, but there was no point in trying to reason with either of them. They were both demented. Indi realised quickly that they could very well kill her right now.

She started crying and Miles squeezed his hand around her neck.

'Please, Miles . . .' she sobbed, but his grip only tightened.

'Mmm, I like you like this,' he whispered. 'Begging me. If only you'd played nice from the beginning.'

With one hand around her neck, his other glided over Indi's body. She was terrified and scrambled up, only for Anja to walk over. 'Let me,' she hissed, kicking Indi in the stomach so hard that she dropped to the floor again, unable to breathe.

Anja turned to Miles. 'She'll be fine,' she said, 'let's get out of here.'

Struggling for breath and with her vision swimming, Indi watched as Miles and Anja turned their backs on her and ran out of the office. Feebly standing upright, Indi fell back down in agony, hitting her head on the side of the desk. She'd blacked out entirely by the time the fire alarm went off.

Chapter Thirty-Three

'Everyone stay calm and please slowly make your way to the exit,' Connor shouted to the party revellers, half of them disappointed that their fun night was interrupted, the other half excited to be witnessing the potential drama of a fire. 'I repeat, *slowly* make your way to the exit where you'll be safely escorted down the stairs. No pushing or shoving, please. The fire brigade are on their way and everyone will get out safely.'

'*Twenty flights of stairs?*' a man shouted, disbelief in his voice.

'I'm sure you'll be able to use the lift at some point, sir, but as per our health and safety procedure, you have to head to the stairs for now. It's probably a false alarm anyway.' Connor, Eddie and the security team did their best to shepherd everyone out in an orderly fashion, but the smell of smoke was rising and drunk revellers were charging out and over each other. 'Jesus fucking Christ,' hissed Connor to Eddie. 'This is going to cost us. I think the smoke is coming from the women's toilets.'

Eddie simply shook his head. 'If we can get everyone downstairs we can investigate properly. I'll go back to check the club floor and make sure no one is still inside.'

'Good idea,' replied Connor, trying Indi's phone once again, but it was switched off.

He stood in the corridor for a few minutes, ushering people down the stairs and reassuring them everything would be all right. He knew he should wait until everyone was out, but he desperately wanted to find Indi. He noticed a familiar head of hair piled up so high it went over everyone else's heads. 'Hollie?' he shouted.

She turned. 'Oh hey! Can you *believe* this?'

'Where's Indi?'

Hollie shrugged. 'She's not with you and the boys?'

'No she's not, I haven't seen her since the alarm started,' he called, but Hollie and Tina were being pushed further away by the crowds and she strained to hear him, pointing a finger to the outside of her ear. 'She must be with Kyle,' called back Hollie. 'I'll meet you outside!'

Connor anxiously looked around to see if Indi was among the crowd. She was nowhere to be seen.

Flames and smoke were beginning to billow from the women's toilet. The fire alarm was still ringing loudly. Just a corridor away, Indi was lying unconscious in the office. The fire brigade were on their way and security guards were getting everyone out of the building as quickly as possible. Nicolas had Tasha on one arm, Tasha's mother on the other, and Saskia was directly behind as they made their way down the stairs. The women gossiped about what was going on and Nicolas fumed that this would cost him a fortune. Saskia was proud of herself for not drinking the whole night and spending the evening catching up with Nicolas, schmoozing with Tasha and networking with prospective new clients.

'All the bloody press will write about now is the fire,' grumbled Nicolas.

'Bad press is better than no press,' said Saskia. 'It's all rather sudden, though, isn't it? What do you think could have happened?'

'I can hear the sirens coming in the distance,' said Tasha. 'Listen.'

They were being pushed from behind by throngs of people trying to get out, despite the security guards repeatedly asking everyone to act calmly. 'Everyone's hammered, no wonder they're pushing and shoving,' said Tasha again, not seeming to mind the chaos. Saskia certainly did, and was left lagging behind as a group of drunk girls pushed in front of her.

'Saskia?' called Nicolas.

'I'm right behind! Just go on,' Saskia called back. It really was mayhem. A couple were talking softly behind her while everyone else was drunkenly chanting the words to 'London's Burning'. *Charming*, thought Saskia. Then the couple were squashed up so close behind her, she could make out every word they were saying.

'Why the hell did you tell her about the school? Now she'll know it was us,' said the female voice.

'Hey, you were the one that staged an attack in the office without telling me,' came the male's voice in reply. 'That wasn't part of the plan, Anja.'

'Well, you certainly seemed to enjoy it. Do you think she got out OK? Maybe we should go back.'

'Don't be ridiculous, we can't go back now. She'll be fine; she's probably outside already. Anyway she can't prove it was you and me. We've just destroyed the club, the thing that matters most to them. That's the important thing. And once I run an exclusive about how the fire started, pretending the fireman tipped me off, I'll get a fat bonus and will be rich.'

'We both will, sweetie. Remember? Fifty-fifty.'

Appalled by what she'd just heard, Saskia tried to twist around to clock who the voices belonged to, but there were so many people it was impossible. It wasn't until they'd made it down the stairs and on to the nineteenth floor, where hotel staff and security were ushering people in different directions, that Saskia got a glimpse of the couple behind her. She recognised that name, Anja, and the tall and stunning woman – with jet-black hair and a very dramatic black dress – matched the image in her head from what Indi had told her. The man was in a dull grey suit and was sweating. She had a feeling she'd seen him somewhere before, but couldn't place where. She had to tell someone. Connor. He'd been outside the toilets, making sure everyone got out safely. Saskia hoped he was still there as she headed back towards the club. It took several minutes, as everyone was coming at her in the opposite direction.

'Ms, I'm sorry but you have to go this way.' A burly security man had spotted her.

'No, I have to get back up there, thank you.' Saskia tried to force her way past the security man, but he put an arm across the stairway and blocked her. It was no use. She did as he said initially, but when his back was turned she sneaked past him up the stairs, pushing through the crowds as best she could and eventually saw Connor.

'Connor! Connor, thank God.'

He looked puzzled. 'Who are you?'

'Saskia Taylor. It doesn't matter now. Listen, have you seen Indigo?'

'I'm looking for her now. Miles told me she'd gone outside already.'

'Miles?'

'That journalist from News Hub. Bad suit, greasy hair?'

That fitted the description of the man Saskia had just overheard talking. 'I think Indigo is in trouble, Connor.' Saskia gave Connor a quick rundown of what she'd heard. 'They mentioned an office, could she be in there?' Around them the crowds thinned from the stairs – everyone was on the nineteenth floor or below by now – but the smell of smoke was growing closer and more intense.

'Tell the police what you heard, Saskia. Tell them it's Miles Horner and Anja Kovac. And when the fire brigade arrive, tell them there is a girl possibly unconscious in the club and I've gone to get her.'

Without another word, Connor turned and raced up the stairs.

'Connor,' called Saskia.

'I have to save her!' Connor called back.

Indi had told Saskia all about Anja Kovac. The drugging, the money. The smoke was billowing out now.

'It's dangerous!' she called back to Connor. But he'd disappeared.

The loud ringing from the fire alarm was still going when Indi slowly opened her eyes, blinking into consciousness. She was lying on the floor in the foetal position, clutching her stomach, and it took a few moments for her to remember where she was. As she lifted her head, she cried out in pain. The left side was throbbing and warm blood stuck to her tangled hair. As her senses returned she recognised the potent smell of smoke coming from outside. 'You are not going to die here,' Indi said out loud. She ignored the pain from her head, legs and stomach and reached for a heavy metal chair by one of the desks. Screaming in agony, she stood up weakly, hunched over, but managed to stumble towards the door, out of the office and into the smoke.

The fire that Anja had started in the women's toilets had spread down the corridor. Smoke was thickening and the flames were growing more ferocious as Connor headed towards the office. His exposed skin was heating up rapidly too. It wouldn't be much longer before they were both burned to a crisp.

'Indi!' he called.

'Connor?' came the reply through the smoke.

Connor squinted, trying hard to focus. His head was dizzy. He tried to ignore the pain and through the smoke suddenly saw the crumpled figure of Indi trying to find her way out.

'Indi!' he called again, stumbling towards her. Both of them were coughing. Connor's heart raced with relief that he'd found her, and fear that they might not get out of the building alive. He hoisted her up into his arms and ran back down the corridor as fast as he could manage and down the stairs. Flames rose around him and he was coughing severely.

'Put me down, I can walk,' Indi said, but he refused to let her go.

Somehow, Connor made it to the stairs, still holding Indi in his arms, where a team of fireman met them. One of them took Indi and two more hoisted up Connor. He tried to protest – he didn't want to be an inch away from her – but by now he couldn't speak for coughing so much. The last thing he saw was Indi being carried away, her arms stretched back, reaching for him. Then, he collapsed.

Chapter Thirty-Four

Crowds gathered outside the Degree Hotel, looking up at the flames at the top of the building. Reporters and TV crew spread around getting footage of the fire and interviewing witnesses. Ambulance crew and policemen told everyone to step back. Saskia marched straight up to a policewoman.

'I need to speak to your supervisor now.'

'Ms, if you could just wait over there, please. We have a lot to get through here, so please be patient.' The policewoman was young, only twenty-three or so, and was only trying to do her job, but she hadn't reckoned on the willpower of Saskia Taylor.

'No, I want to speak to your supervisor *now*. I have a crime to report. I know who started this fire and who may have killed a woman who may or may not still be trapped up there. Unless you'd like me to tell a reporter instead and mention that I was ignored by the Metropolitan Police?'

The junior officer went pale. 'Just wait here, I'll go and get her.'

Detective Inspector Williams was a serious-looking woman in her fifties, who took notes as Saskia plainly described exactly what Connor had told her to say and what she'd overheard Miles and Anja saying. She added that Anja had stolen £8,000 from 360 and had tried to frame an innocent boy.

'Could you describe the suspects, please?' asked DI Williams, not looking up from her pad.

Saskia gave her their full descriptions. 'But the fireman need to save Indigo and Connor, they may still be in there!'

'The firemen have been in there for some time; if anyone was in the building, they would have rescued them.'

Saskia threw her hands up in the air, then saw a team of fireman running away from the building. Indi was in one of their arms and an ambulance crew ran towards her with a thick foil blanket. Her face was badly bruised and the left side of her head was covered in blood. Saskia ran towards her. 'Indi! Darling girl. Thank God, you're alive.'

'Ms, please keep away and let us treat the young woman,' said one of the paramedics.

'But I'm a friend!'

'I'm OK,' Indi whispered through coughs, as Saskia stroked her face and paramedics saw to her wounds. 'Where's – where's Connor?'

Saskia glanced around. Two firemen called for help as they hoisted a limp figure on to a stretcher. The eyes were closed, the face was red and stained with black charcoal, and the suit was torn, but it was definitely Connor.

'Connor?' She rushed over but a paramedic blocked her.

'Ms, please stand back and give us room to work. The man needs to be taken to hospital immediately.'

'What's wrong with him?'

But the team ignored her. In seconds they'd placed Connor on a stretcher in the back of the ambulance and were fixing machines and drips all around him. It sped off, siren wailing. Thick clouds of black smoke rose from the top of the hotel and into the sky. Firemen from cranes were extinguishing the remaining flames.

'Indi!' came a panicked male voice. A young man with a shaved head and piercing blue eyes raced over. Two other men and two young women, one of whom Saskia recognised as Indi's friend Hollie, followed behind, shouting Indi's name.

'Sir, please stand back and give her some space,' said the paramedic.

'She's my sister! Indi, are you OK? What happened?' Turning to the paramedic, 'Is she going to be OK?'

'She's got a broken rib and some deep cuts around her head but she'll be OK. I'm checking for anything more serious and then we'll get her to hospital.'

Indi clasped Kyle's hand. 'Miles and Anja,' she whispered. 'They – they did this to me. They beat me up and they started the fire.' Kyle had to lean in closer to hear as Indi's voice was raspy and barely audible. 'They *what?*'

Saskia placed a hand on Kyle's arm. 'It's true. I overheard them talking.'

'Who are you?'

'Saskia Taylor, I'm a friend of Indi's.' Kyle looked to

Indi, who nodded slowly. She was so dizzy and exhausted it was difficult to make any movement.

'Indi told me how Anja set you up so she could pocket the money,' said Saskia. 'I've told the police everything.'

Kyle looked at Indi again. 'Miles and Anja did this to you?' A thunderous expression fell over his face and he clenched his fists. 'Where are they?'

Then Hollie spoke. 'I saw Miles! Just now! He was on his phone, and describing the fire as if he was telling a story. He must have been talking to his editor! That bastard was trying to get his story in first.'

'*Where?*' demanded Kyle. Hollie pointed to the cluster of reporters and camera crew. Miles was at the back of the huddle, holding his phone with one hand, the other over his opposite ear so he could hear. He must have just appeared, as the police were now on the hunt for him. Kyle ran over, with Tom and Hugh behind him in hot pursuit.

Saskia turned to Hollie. 'Find a police officer now! I'll look for the inspector.'

Miles was still talking on his phone when Kyle came up behind him. He yanked the phone away, dashed it to the floor and punched Miles hard in the face, causing him to drop to the ground. Police arrived on the scene, flanked by Tom, Hugh, Saskia, Hollie and Tina. An officer pulled Miles up and placed him in handcuffs. His lip was cut open and his eyes bleary.

'You are under arrest for arson and grievous bodily harm. You do not have to say anything, but it may harm your defence if you do not mention when questioned something which you later rely on in court . . .'

A third officer placed handcuffs on Kyle. 'No!' screamed Hollie, but Tom took her hand.

'They've just seen him punch Miles to the ground, Holl, they have to arrest him. Don't worry, I'm sure he'll be out soon.'

Hugh grabbed Miles's phone from the ground and handed it to the policeman. 'Miles's phone – there might be evidence on there.' The policeman nodded.

'What about Anja?' shouted Kyle as he was put in a separate police car to Miles. Saskia turned to DI Williams.

'We've circulated her as wanted,' she said. 'A description of her and all the charges have gone out on all the radios and we have officers on their way to her house, her parents' house and anywhere else connected to her. Don't worry, Ms Taylor, we'll find her. But we need you to come down to the station and give your statement.'

'The girl, Indigo, I need to go to hospital with her. Please. You've just arrested her brother. Please, let me be with her.'

DI Williams nodded. 'You will need to come to the station later and give a statement about all this, though. As soon as possible, please.'

Saskia thanked her and ran back to the ambulance where Indi was.

'Is she your daughter?' asked the paramedic.

Saskia shook her head, then Hollie appeared. 'We're all close friends of hers,' she said.

'Well, your friend has sustained some serious injuries and we need to check for internal bleeding. We're going to take her to hospital now.'

'I'm coming,' put in Hollie. She turned and gave Saskia a quick hug. 'Meet us at the hospital. Indi will want to see you. And thank you, Saskia.'

Saskia blushed and her eyes welled up with relief. Tina, Hugh and Tom all looked exhausted and worried about their friend and Saskia snapped back into mum mode. 'I've got my car parked a couple of streets away. Do you guys want a lift to the hospital? I'll get us some coffees and sandwiches on the way. It might be a long night.'

Indi woke from a deep sleep, her eyes squinting. She was in a bright room with white walls. There were empty beds around her. A hospital ward. She looked around and jerked when she spotted a machine to the right of her. All sorts of drips were attached to her arm. She sat up, but a throbbing pain made her lie back.

'She's awake,' said a familiar voice. 'Fetch the nurse, would you, Kyle?'

'Dad?' Indi spoke in a croak. Her mouth was dry.

Alan stroked her head. 'It's OK, sweetheart.' She looked at the drip, terrified. 'That's just to help you keep hydrated, love,' Alan said. 'You're OK.'

'Thirsty,' was all Indi could manage. Alan held a cup of water up to her lips and she glugged gratefully. Kyle came in followed by a nurse, who took Indi's pulse before making notes on a clipboard and adjusting the drip. Alan fed her another cup of water. Indi closed her eyes and sat up again, slowly, helped by Alan and the nurse. She looked at her body under a white blanket. A bandage covered her torso.

'Is it serious?'

The nurse shook her head. 'The worst is two broken ribs, which will heal nicely in time. You took a nasty blow to the head, but thankfully apart from some concussion you're fine. We do need to do a brain scan now you're awake, though, just to check everything is normal. There are a lot of cuts and bruises, mind, but they look far worse than they are. We'll need to run a few more tests but hopefully Dad can take you home tomorrow to rest up.'

Indi tried to sit further up now but found it difficult to breathe and agonising to cough. The nurse checked her heartbeat and blood pressure. 'Shortness of breath is normal because of your ribs,' she said. 'You must take it easy. No sudden movements for now.'

'Do you remember what happened, love?' asked Alan gently.

Indi nodded. 'Miles and Anja beat me up. From what they said, it wasn't planned, but they saw an opportunity. They left me to crawl out of the office while they started a fire. But I hit my head and blacked out. Connor – he was there.' An image flashed back in Indi's mind of being carried away by a fireman, arms outstretched to Connor. 'Where is he?' Alan and Kyle glanced at each other. Their nervousness worried her.

'Is Connor OK? Where is he? What happened?'

Alan cleared his throat and took Indi's hand in his own. 'Connor is here, sweetheart. In this hospital, I mean. He's . . . well, he's in intensive care.'

'*What?*' Indi's eyes immediately filled with tears.

'He inhaled a lot of smoke and collapsed after rescuing you. It's a miracle that his burns aren't bad, but he was deprived of oxygen so they had to intubate him in the ambulance. The paramedic said his last words before falling unconscious were asking after you – wanting to know if you were OK. They've put him in an induced coma until his respiratory system has healed and he is stable again.'

'How long?'

'About ten hours. You've been asleep for most of it.'

Indi stretched a battered and bruised leg out of the bed. 'I have to go to him.'

'You need to rest,' said Alan.

'I need to see him, Dad, please!' Alan looked up at the nurse.

'It's OK,' she said. 'We can take her to him. I'll get a wheelchair to be on the safe side. Wait here, love.' Alan and the nurse left, deep in conversation about Indi's welfare, and Kyle took a seat next to the bed.

'How are you feeling, sis?'

'I need to see Connor!' she cried, but Kyle shushed her.

'It's OK, sis, we're getting you to him. You need to calm down, all right?'

Indi listened to her brother and nodded, but shot him a look when she noticed his hand was bandaged up. 'What happened to you?'

'This? Oh nothing, just sprained my wrist punching Miles,' Kyle grinned. He explained what had happened the previous night, talking her through the fight.

'They never even charged me.' He shrugged. 'I got lucky, I guess. The detective even winked at me. She hates News Hub because they always slag off the police'

'Thank God. Did Dad hit the roof?'

'He said I was right to hit him! But he was more concerned about you, obviously. Anyway, the police are focused on nailing Miles and Anja. They found her at home that night and arrested her. I don't know the latest, but I assume they're going down for a very long time after what they did. I had to give the police a statement and so did Saskia. Thank fuck for her, by the way.'

Indi nodded. 'I have to thank her. Where is she now?'

'Down at the station, but she drove Tom, Tina and Hugh here first. Hollie came in the ambulance with you. They went home to sleep. I'll text Holl to let her know you've woken up. Tom is with Connor and his family, I think.'

Indi looked earnestly at her brother. 'He's going to be OK, isn't he?'

Kyle didn't know what answer to give, so instead wrapped his arms around Indi and held her gently. She cried into his chest.

Chapter Thirty-Five

The next afternoon, almost twenty-four hours after the fire, Connor was still unconscious. Marion and Indi refused to leave Connor's side. His bed was surrounded by machines, and wires, cables and tubes were attached all around his body. Doctors and nurses came in to do regular check-ups on him, shaking their heads often to signal that there was no improvement. He still wasn't stable enough to breathe on his own.

Mark – having called his police contacts – divulged that Miles and Anja had both been charged with arson and GBH. Miles had an added charge of harassment and Anja of fraud and double arson for Kyle's school. Not only were Saskia and Kyle witnesses, Miles had records of their text conversations on his phone, and Miles's terrified interns were only too happy to come forward and reveal that he had made them send Indi and Glamour To Go the nasty messages on social media, claiming it was research for a story. Anja was so terrified about going to prison that she broke down tearfully and admitted everything. She'd started a fire by lighting a match in the toilets of 360, and planned to burn the place to the ground in order to destroy the thing that mattered most to Indi and Connor. Beating Indi up wasn't part of the plan, but in her drug-fuelled rage, she had seen an opportunity. Miles had been in on the fire plan for months. It seemed that if he couldn't have Indi, no one else could. Despite claiming all that time that he loved her, he really despised her for rejecting him and choosing Connor. He tried to woo her to date him just so he could sleep with her and then dump her, but she'd messed up that plan. Anja told the police everything.

Meanwhile, the majority of the Degree Hotel was fine, aside from damage to the nineteenth floor, but 360 had been destroyed. Insurance would pay out, of course, but that wouldn't compensate for the months of business they would lose.

Alan and Kyle begged Indi to come home and rest, saying there was nothing she could do for Connor now, but she couldn't bear the thought of him waking up and her not being there. Marion had barely slept, she was so distraught, and Mark and Indi tried to comfort her as best they could while Lauren was home with the girls.

As the evening drew on, Indi slipped outside the hospital for some fresh air. She was wearing grey tracksuit bottoms and a blue t-shirt that Hollie had brought her. It was too uncomfortable wearing jeans as the tight denim rubbed against the wounds on her legs from where Miles had kicked her. Her ribs were still bandaged up, but her bruises were dying down. She popped her dose of painkillers with a gulp of water. Her entire body ached and she was exhausted. It was a freezing December day. Silver and gold decorations hung around the hospital, reminding Indi that Christmas was just a couple of weeks away. What a sad, sorry Christmas it would be if Connor never woke up.

Indi folded her arms and inhaled deeply. All these weeks she could have been with Connor, wrapped in his arms every night, but her own stupid pride had stopped her. What had she been thinking? So what if he'd kissed Anja? It was a stupid drunken mistake and it wasn't his fault she'd spiked his drink with Valium. He'd apologised, replaced the stolen money himself, gone out of his way to help Kyle – and even risked his own life to save hers! And now he wanted to be with her, in Miami of all places. Indi felt so wretchedly guilty. He was in intensive care because of her. She closed her eyes, taking comfort in the memory of their last beautiful kiss, the memory of his soft lips and his firm chest against hers, how his voice had sounded when he'd told her he loved her, how her heart ached for him every second that she wasn't with him. She imagined lying in his arms on a beach, the sun setting in front of them. Her lips quivered.

'Cold out here, isn't it?'

'Marion.' Indi quickly wiped tears from her face with her sleeve. Marion was in leggings, Ugg boots and a huge fleece duffle coat. Her eyes were red and swollen from crying. Indi's heart broke for her. Her own pain wasn't even a fraction of what Marion would be feeling, seeing her son lying unconscious in a hospital bed. Marion sat beside Indi and lit a Silk Cut cigarette and offered one to Indi. She shook her head. 'I didn't know you smoked,' she commented.

'For years. We all did in those days, but I gave up when I got pregnant with Mark and haven't touched one since. I need one now, let me tell you. Can you believe I got this pack from a doctor? Said he smokes a pack a day.'

'Wow, I thought all doctors were health freaks.' Indi tried to smile. There was a pause. Marion inhaled deeply on her cigarette. She was always so cheery; now it seemed as if her smile would never return.

'This is all my fault, Marion, I'm so sorry.'

'Don't be silly. I'm glad he met you, Indigo. He'd experienced every kind of professional success, but I was always waiting for him to meet the right girl. I don't think he'd ever been in love before with anything apart from me and his job.'

'And West Ham,' corrected Indi. The women smiled, and Indi hugged Marion.

'Mrs Scott?' came a voice behind them. It was Connor's doctor. 'I think you'd better come in immediately.'

Chapter Thirty-Six

Indi and Marion couldn't get in fast enough. Fear gripped both of them. In Connor's room, Dr Stein was listening to Connor's chest with a stethoscope. A nurse was fiddling with his drip.

Mark spoke. 'He moved his fingers. I was reading out the January signing predictions from *Match of the Day*'s website.' He laughed in disbelief. 'He wriggled his fingers!'

Connor's eyes started blinking and then were fully open, looking around the room and trying to place where he was. A nurse carefully removed his oxygen mask. Indi slipped out of the room to let Mark and Marion have a private moment.

After texting Tom, Hollie and her dad, she cupped her face in her hands, trying to catch her breath. She caught her reflection in a window and almost jumped. No sleep, no make-up and a baggy tracksuit. Great.

'Indi?' came Marion's soft voice.
    'How is he?'

'Very croaky. He's asking for you.'

Indi rushed into the room where Connor was sitting up in bed. She ran into his arms and held him tighter than she'd ever done before. 'I thought I was going to lose you,' she said into his chest.

He kissed her head. 'I'm not going anywhere,' he whispered.

Two weeks later . . .

'Rise and shine, sleepyhead. It's Christmas!'

Indi nudged Connor, who lay naked, sprawled on her bed. She took in the glorious sight. That boy's body never ceased to amaze her. He groaned as she nudged him again. 'For someone who recently slept for over twenty-four hours, it's amazing that you're still tired!'

Connor drew her into bed, his eyes still closed. 'Yeah, well you knackered me out last night.' He grinned.

Connor had been released from hospital three days after waking up. They'd kept him on an oxygen mask and he'd had X-rays, brain scans, and tests to check his lung function. His burns were astonishingly mild and had already healed up. Dr Stein said he was lucky not to have sustained bad burns or, worse, brain damage. A physiotherapist carried out mobility tests too, but everything was looking healthy.

'Ow, careful, broken ribs still healing, remember,' Indi complained, but Connor was already spooning her softly.

Indi melted into him. 'We need to be at your mum's in an hour,' she said feebly, not wanting to move in the slightest.

'Then we'd better be quick,' he replied, reaching his hand between her legs and kissing her neck. 'Oh, and Merry Christmas.'

Half an hour later, Indi was perfecting her make-up in the mirror as Connor emerged from the shower, looking every inch as gorgeous as ever.

'Your mum's going to kill us. Our first Christmas together and I turn up late. At least Dad and Kyle are already there, helping out with dinner. She won't hate me, will she?'

'Indi, you know my mum thinks you're an angel,' replied Connor, planting a kiss on Indi's cheek as he got dressed. 'I'll drive quickly. And, anyway, it was worth it.' They certainly had made up for lost time in the past week. Indi had driven Connor home once to collect a bag of his clothes, then taken him back to her flat where they'd spent every minute together, mainly in her bedroom, though disappointingly there was more cuddling and not nearly enough sex. Connor was under strict instruction from Dr Stein not to exhaust himself. They'd broken that rule a few times, though Connor got short of breath pretty quickly, and Indi joked that she was dating an old man. 'You'd better get used to dating an old-timer because I'm not going anywhere!' he'd said, kissing her. Indi smiled to herself. Her phone beeped.

'Oh, it's Saskia, She sends love and wishes us both a Happy Christmas and says she and Millie can't wait to see us next week. Aw, that's sweet.'

'Did she get everything sorted with her statement?'

'Yeah, she only had to go back in once after the detective spoke to us, just to answer a few more questions. We'll all have to testify in court, but there's no way they aren't going down. Anja has admitted everything and there's so much evidence against Miles. Thank God.'

'Good,' said Connor, snaking his arms around Indi and nuzzling her neck. 'And then you and I will be on a beach in Barbados for New Year, starting the year as we mean to go on.'

'Mmm, with lots of sun and sex, you mean?' she asked, grinning. They'd booked the holiday online last night.

'Yeah, in America, I hope. Don't think I'd forgotten you still owe me an answer about Miami. I'm due to leave in February, remember, so I can get things set up for summer.'

Indi smiled. 'I thought we'd agreed not to talk about it until Barbados? It's a big deal for me, leaving my friends and family, you know.'

Connor's phone rang. 'It's Mum,' he said. 'This conversation is to be continued!'

'I'll pack the car and meet you outside,' Indi replied.

Connor took the call and Indi started bundling presents into the car boot. She'd gone a little overboard, but was so pleased with her gifts for everyone, which included a Clinique gift box for Marion, a Peppa Pig picnic set for Lola, a pink onesie and nail varnishes for Izzy, perfume for Lauren and an expensive bottle of brandy for Mark, while Kyle and Alan were going to get football tickets. She'd spent the longest time selecting Connor's present, though, a beautiful Armani watch that he adored. They'd got so excited about their first Christmas together that they'd opened each other's presents the night before. Connor's gift to Indi had been the most beautiful delicate white gold necklace she'd ever seen, with a gorgeous diamond pendant. He'd bought it before the 360 party and had planned on giving it to her whether she took him back as her boyfriend or not. She ran her hand over it, thinking again about Connor's proposition.

Marion's house was filled with people: Mark, Lauren and the kids, plus the Edwards family and Hollie and Tom, who were having lunch there before going to Cat and Tim's in the evening and driving to Tom's family the next day. Everyone chipped in to help with the cooking and play with the girls. When it came to actually eating, Marion's table was so full of bowls of vegetables, trays of meat and glasses of prosecco, there was barely room for people's plates.

'I think a toast is in order!' called Alan over the noise. 'Quiet everyone, quiet! Let's all raise a glass to Marion, please. Thank you for being a wonderful host and welcoming us all into your home. You'll regret it when it's time to do the washing-up.'

The adults laughed and Alan continued. 'I'm so grateful for our new lifelong friends, the Scotts. Connor, I couldn't think of a better bloke for my daughter. Merry Christmas everyone!' The table clinked glasses and shouted in unison, 'Merry Christmas!'

Indi snaked her arm around Connor, who was sitting next to her. 'I'm going to miss this, you know.'

'Miss what, sweetheart?'

'Our families being together like this. It's going to be harder to pop round to your mum's while we're in Miami.'

Connor turned to her now, unable to repress a grin. 'While *we're* in Miami?'

'I made up my mind the day you asked me, Connor. I just quite enjoyed keeping you waiting. I know how much you hate not having things go your own way.' She giggled.

'That was very mean, Miss Edwards! But, are you sure about this?'

Indi leant in and spoke in a whisper. 'I've never been more certain about anything else, Mr Scott.'

Connor reached for his glass again. 'Everyone,' he announced, 'we need another toast.'

THE END

Acknowledgements

Many people have helped me with this book – I can't thank you all enough! Special thanks to Scarlett Russell, who really helped me bring the story to life; and my publishing team, Viola Hayden, Selina Walker, Charlotte Bush at Century and my publicist Diana Colbert. And of course my amazing family and friends who have been my support along the way: my darling Kieran and gorgeous children Harvey, Junior, Princess, Jett and Bunny – you are my rocks.

ALSO AVAILABLE BY KATIE PRICE

In the Name of Love

On a sun drenched beach in Barbados, feisty sports presenter Charlie meets the irresistibly gorgeous Felipe Castillo. Instantly attracted to each other, they have a passionate affair, until he walks out, leaving her heartbroken.

It is only then that she discovers that Felipe is related to the Spanish royal family, is a brilliant rider and the lynchpin of the Spanish Eventing team.But just when Charlie thinks she's managed to put her heartbreak behind her, Felipe returns, and she falls in love all over again. Soon they are the golden couple of sport, followed by the press wherever they go.

But as the pressure on the couple mounts, a dark shadow from Charlie's past comes back to haunt her.

CENTURY

CENTURY

ALSO AVAILABLE BY KATIE PRICE

He's The One

Can you ever forget your first love?

Liberty Evans hasn't. She has a beautiful daughter, a successful career as an actress, and she's married to one of Hollywood's most powerful directors.

But behind the glamour, things are not what they seem. Her daughter Brooke is turning into a spoiled teenager, her husband controls everything she does, and Liberty longs for Cory, the man she loved before she became famous.

Unable to live a lie any longer, Liberty returns to England with a reluctant Brooke to start a new life. While her daughter has to cope with a massive lifestyle change, Liberty finds that she cannot get Cory out of her head.

CENTURY

ALSO AVAILABLE BY KATIE PRICE

Make My Wish Come True

When Storm Saunders lands a job as a showbiz reporter on a national newspaper, she can't believe her luck. It's the only job she's ever wanted, and apart from having to work with her creepy ex, life couldn't be better. Until she's asked to go undercover to find out if sexy TV chef Nico Alvise is cheating on his girlfriend. Storm is horrified, but she agrees because she's determined to protect him.

She didn't bank on falling in love. But Nico has secrets to hide, and he hates journalists. So when he finds out Storm works for a tabloid, the fallout is brutal.

Suddenly jobless, friendless and heartbroken, Storm knows that no matter how hard she wishes, Nico will never forgive her . . .

CENTURY